DRAGON TAMER

RAY WILLIAMS

*To ÅSA
All the best*

National Library of Canada Cataloguing in Publication

Williams, Ray
    Dragon tamer / Ray Williams.

ISBN 1-55395-276-6

    I. Title.

PR6102.A77D72 2002   823'.92   C2002-905261-0

 *PRINTED IN CANADA*

This book was published *on-demand* in cooperation with Trafford Publishing. On-demand publishing is a unique process and service of making a book available for retail sale to the public taking advantage of on-demand manufacturing and Internet marketing.**On-demand publishing** includes promotions, retail sales, manufacturing, order fulfilment, accounting and collecting royalties on behalf of the author.

Suite 6E, 2333 Government St., Victoria, B.C. V8T 4P4, CANADA
Phone   250-383-6864   Toll-free   1-888-232-4444 (Canada & US)
Fax   250-383-6804   E-mail   sales@trafford.com
Website   www.trafford.com
TRAFFORD PUBLISHING IS A DIVISION OF TRAFFORD HOLDINGS LTD.
Trafford Catalogue #02-0990   www.trafford.com/robots/02-0990.html

10   9   8   7   6   5   4

With deepest appreciation to Maureen Medved, Richard Ladds, my sons, Travis, Bryn and Rhett, and most of all, to my wife, Diane, for her loving support and inspiration.

Prologue

Hong Kong sits at the mouth of the Pearl River, on the south coast of China, at the same latitude as Hawaii or Cuba. In Cantonese, the dominant language, Hong Kong means "Fragrant Harbor," a name that was inspired either by the incense factories that once dotted the island, or by the profusion of scented pink bauhinias, the national flower. Rounded granite hilltops and steep slopes, once covered in forest, are now carpeted with grass and sparse pine trees. But mostly Hong Kong is a city, a boiling cauldron of life enmeshed in a crazy latticework of roads and tunnels, exploding skyward into a forest of skyscrapers. Double-decker busses, clanging tramcars, exhaust-spewing cars and motorcycles battle rickety bicycles for every square foot of road space. Every inch of sidewalk flows with people. Old Buddhist and Taoist temples filled with the smell and smoke of joss-sticks and miniature pagodas are wedged in among the gleaming buildings and dirty factories. Along the shorelines, clinging to the ravines, and winding through narrow mountainous passes, the shanty towns of sticks, canvas and corrugated metal surround the homes of the wealthy.

Huge red banners and posters strung across streets, wooden poles draped with laundry, balconies littered with potted plants, instant plastic canopied street stalls selling herbs, kitchenware, pirated CDS and tapes, fruit, rows of shining ducks, sticky cakes and flickering television screens in shop windows and the fronts of buildings garishly decorated with red painted or gold-gilded dragons all assault the senses.

Just thirty-two miles square, Hong Kong is home to a mosaic of cultures. The official languages are English and Cantonese, but Mandarin, Hakka, Tanka, Shanghainese and Chinglish are spoken. Hong Kong has evolved very differently than China, with a variety of religious traditions in Buddhism, Taoism and Confusim. The Chinese in Hong Kong identify themselves not as Chinese, but as Hongkonese, perceiving them to be more advanced than the Chinese on the mainland. Most of the elite class came from humble origins and is open and non-exclusive. Elite status is based not on cultural accomplishments, moral excellence or politics, but on wealth, and few care about the origins of that wealth. The Hong Kong Chinese, entrepreneurs to a fault, never ask or give quarter. They are as petulant in vice as they are in business. Anything is possible in Hong Kong, anything is forgiven. It's a place where each person can make a fortune or die without a tear, escape into anonymity or exact personal vengeance without the raise of an eyebrow.

Three hundred years ago in China, a secret society named *Tin Tei Wu* (The Society of Heaven and Earth) divided into five lodges with the express aim of driving out foreigners and restoring the former Ming emperor to the throne of China. These lodges become known as Triads. While the Society failed to achieve its political aims, it has grown into multi-national criminal organizations. More than fifty triads flourish in Hong Kong, with more in mainland China, Taiwan, North America and Europe. They recruit street people, the poor, the middle-class and even the wealthy do business with the triads.

Hong Kong, city of the youth, of unrestrained vitality, painted grays and browns, blurring in an opaque light. And beneath that light, a darkness.

1

Hard rain pounded down from a black sky. The southeast wind pummeled Hong Kong harbor, sending small boats to shelter and scattering people from the bustling streets. A dark blue Rolls Royce rolled slowly along the Wan Chai docks and stopped in front of a deserted warehouse, its wipers straining to clear the waves of water from the windshield.

Inside the Rolls, Wang Chan, a small, thin man in his late seventies, dressed in English wool and brogues, peered through tiny round wire-framed glasses at the newspaper's headlines "Triad War Heats Up—Police Promise Crackdown."

A black limousine pulled up beside the Rolls. For a long minute both cars sat there, only their windshield wipers piercing the quiet.

Chan climbed out of the Rolls, walked over to the limousine and stood beside the rear door. It opened and an arm reached out of the dark interior to help him. Chan sank into a seat, a dim interior light casting an orange hue on his weathered face. His hand on an ivory-handled cane shook. He threw the newspaper into the lap of the man in the shadows.

"I'm giving you one last chance."

The shadows obscured everything but the hands of man who sat across from him. A tattoo of a red dragon emblazoned the back of one hand. The nicotine-stained middle finger of his other hand rubbed the tattoo.

"What's the panic, old friend?" the man in shadows asked.

"I don't like publicity and I don't like the police snooping around."

For several long moments, only the sounds of the windshield wipers and the rain pounding on the roof of the car could be heard.

"I have the right to defend my business. Surely you understand that," the voice from the shadows said.

Wang Chan shook his head. "Our business arrangement has been profitable for both of us but you've become too risky."

The tattooed man rubbed the window with his finger as though the raindrops were on the inside. "There was a time when you never worried about risk."

"Times have changed."

"So you've come with an ultimatum?"

"If you don't stop the war, I'll be forced to do business with one of your competitors, someone who takes a lower profile."

The tattooed man lit a cigarette, the flame reflecting in his deep-set, black eyes. He blew a curl of smoke which hung in the muted light. "What does your son think about this?"

Wang Chan's hand shook the cane. "Raymond knows nothing of our business arrangement and that's the way it's going to stay."

"Take it easy, old friend, I wouldn't want you to die of a heart attack. I'll think about what you've said."

"You've got until tomorrow at the same time."

"I need time to consider this."

"You've got all the time I'm going to give you."

Wang Chan slowly got out of the car and climbed back into his Rolls Royce. He sank back into the seat, and tapped the privacy glass with his cane. The Rolls turned around and headed back down the docks.

Inside the other car, only the light of the tattooed man's cigarette burned bright. He rubbed the tattoo on his hand with his fingers for several long moments and then he waved his hand to the driver. The limousine sped off into the night.

2

The day after the Pearl Harbor attack in December, 1941, massive Japanese forces had attacked Hong Kong, and within days, wiped out armed resistance. Thousands of European prisoners were marched into internment camps where they were starved, tortured and killed by the Japanese. One of those camps stood on the site of an abandoned prison, near the village of Stanley, overlooking the South China Sea. After the war, a memorial had been built for the prisoners. A short distance from the memorial, two graveyards sit, one with its rows upon rows of plain white stones, the other, with traditional stone markers.

A crisp linen shirt loosely tucked into beige cotton pants hung comfortably on Blake Morgan's lean and athletic six-foot frame. Curly, reddish-blond hair topped a freckled, angular face and brilliant blue eyes. Looking up at the bright sun, he cocked his characteristic crooked smile which pushed up one dimple on his cheek.

Blake handed a bauhinia, an orchid-like flower, to his sister-in-law, Sabrina Chan, a curvaceous, woman with long auburn hair. Her jade-green silk suit reflected deeply in her sea-green eyes. She unconsciously bit the corner of her bottom lip, a nervous habit she'd acquired as a child.

Blake gently took Sabrina's arm and together they walked along the rows of gravestones, then stopped and knelt before three stones. Blake placed a flower on his mother's and father's markers, while Sabrina placed one on her father's. They bowed their heads in silence for a few minutes, arose and slowly walked back toward the graveyard entrance.

Sabrina took Blake's hand and squeezed it. "I'm happy we could be here together."

Blake squeezed her hand back.

"You still feel the pain?" she asked.

Blake stopped and pointed at the memorial in the near distance. "Not just for our parents . . . but for all of them."

She looked up into his eyes. "Sometimes I think those left behind suffer more."

He looked out at the sea far below for a moment, then back into her eyes. "Perhaps. I just wish . . ."

"What?"

"If only I could have saved them."

Sabrina rubbed his arm gently. "Blake, you were just eight years old. Your mother was very sick from disease and malnutrition and weakened by your escape. Your father died a soldier's death, sacrificing his life for yours."

"I promised my father that I'd take care of her . . ."

"There's nothing more that you could have done . . . Oh, Blake, I hate seeing you still blame yourself."

Blake sighed, and then straightened up. "I stopped wishing that I'd died with her, but the nightmares still come."

"They'll pass eventually. Nothing lasts forever."

A silence fell between them for a few moments.

Blake cleared this throat. "How are things between you and Raymond?"

Sabrina shrugged. "He's filed for divorce."

"I didn't realize it had come to that."

"It's never been easy for me from the beginning, being accepted into a Chinese family."

While Sabrina was speaking, Blake's mind flashed back to a time ten years ago, when Sabrina and Raymond had announced their marriage plans. He'd been happy for them and yet he'd felt that small tight coil of jealousy in his chest. Over the years the feeling had disappeared, but now and again he still wondered if he and Sabrina could have been a couple.

"What about Wang Chan?" Blake asked.

Sabrina's eyes narrowed. "He never accepted me. He gave his blessing only on the condition of a prenuptial agreement that he personally drew up."

"Raymond never mentioned that . . . Listen, I don't need to know anymore."

Sabrina crossed her arms as though she was cold. "There's no one else I can talk to about this. You've been like a brother to me," she said softly, "and more."

"Do you want to stay with Raymond?" Blake asked, feeling some discomfort with her last words.

"Of course. But Raymond doesn't want me to pursue my own business and personal interests, which are quite different than his. He, or should I say, my father-in-law, would prefer that I stay at home and be one of Raymond's beautiful possessions."

Blake suddenly felt protective of Raymond. "Didn't you know these things when you decided to marry him?"

Sabrina flashed Blake an angry look. "You should know better than anyone that Raymond has a hard time being direct. He's not like you. I suggested we get marriage counseling, but he refused. Now he won't even discuss reconciliation."

Blake felt compassion for Sabrina, but he wanted to hear Raymond's side of the story. "Is there anything I can do? Talk to him?"

Sabrina smiled. "Thanks, but it's probably better if you don't get in the middle."

"I promise not to do any marriage counseling."

"Do what you think best, then."

They'd reached the graveyard gate where Blake's car was parked, just as a limousine pulled up.

A middle-aged, medium height, slimly built man with smooth skin and black hair, dressed in a white linen suit stepped out of the limousine.

"It's Raymond," Sabrina said.

"That's odd, he told me he doesn't like coming here."

Raymond walked over to them, shaking and wobbling. He embraced Blake. "Father's dead!"

"Oh, my God!" Sabrina cried out, covering her mouth with her hand.

Blake grabbed Raymond's shoulders. "What? How?"

Raymond sobbed. "Inspector Lai of the Hong Kong Police called me. He wants us to come down to police headquarters."

Blake put his hand on Raymond's shoulder. "I know Inspector Lai. I'll make sure he gets to the bottom of this. Tang, take Mr. and Mrs. Chan to the police station. I'll follow in my car."

Raymond reached out and embraced Blake. "Oh, Blake, father's dead!"

Blake held Raymond quietly for several moments, touched more by Raymond's unusual display of emotion than by any of his own feelings.

Sabrina put her arms around both of them. "I'm sorry for both of you."

Raymond and Sabrina climbed into the limousine and Tang drove them away. As Blake walked toward his car, he stopped, noticing for the first time a stone grave marker carved in the shape of a dragon and painted red, near the entrance to the graveyard.

3

Hong Kong Police headquarters, known as May House, a nine-story concrete building surrounded by a stone wall, stood on Arsenal Street in Wan Chai.

Blake, Sabrina and Raymond walked through the door marked, "Narcotics and Homicide Division," and sat in the waiting room.

Moments later, Inspector Peter Lai, age thirty-eight, a uniformed officer of slender build, shortly cropped hair and even white teeth, walked into the reception area and bowed. "Please accept my deepest sympathies, Mr. and Mrs. Chan, and Blake."

"Thank you, Inspector," Raymond replied sadly.

"What happened, Peter?" Blake asked.

"We can talk in my office," Lai replied.

Lai led them down a corridor to a simply furnished office. He walked past the bookcase lined with binders and some photographs of a cricket team and sat down at his desk. "Please sit down. May I offer you some tea?"

"Tell me what happened to my father!" Raymond snapped.

Blake placed his hand on Raymond's shoulder and squeezed gently.

Lai fidgeted with the buttons on his jacket. "We recovered a body from Aberden Harbor this morning which had Wang Chan's identification. We'd like you to confirm his identity."

"How did he die?" Blake asked.

Lai reached for the folder on his desk and read through the contents. "He was shot in the back of the head. He was dead before he was thrown into the water."

"Shot? Who? Why?" Raymond asked hysterically.

"His arms were tied behind him with plastic fasteners. Bruises and contusions on his face. He was probably beaten first."

"Execution-style," Blake said flatly.

"Certainly meant to look that way," Lai replied.

"Why would anyone want to kill him?" Raymond asked.

"I was going to ask you the same question," Lai replied.

Raymond frowned. "I don't know. That's your job isn't it, Inspector?"

"Wang Chan was a prominent businessman, with many competitors, but we weren't aware of anyone who'd want him dead," Sabrina said calmly.

Raymond nodded vigorously.

Lai cleared his throat. "Of course, I'm just trying to determine who'd have the motivation to kill Wang Chan . . . I know this is difficult, but I'll need you to identify the body, Mr. Chan."

Raymond shook his head.

Sabrina put her hand on Raymond's shoulder. "We'll be with you."

Blake nodded and put his hand on Sabrina's.

"Before we go down to the Morgue you might want a few minutes alone. There's an empty room next door," Lai said.

Raymond nodded.

"And rest assured, the Hong Kong Police will do everything in its power to find Wang Chan's killer," Lai said. He turned to Blake. "Could I have a word with you?"

"Sure," Blake replied. He looked at Raymond and Sabrina. "I'll join you in a few minutes."

Lai escorted Raymond and Sabrina to the waiting room, returned to his office and closed the door.

"How would you describe your relationship with Wang Chan and Raymond?"

"Am I a suspect, Peter?"

"You know the routine, Blake. I'm just doing my job."

Blake eyed Lai carefully. "Wang Chan was a generous man, but if you mean did we have a close father-son relationship, the answer is no. As for Raymond, I've been as close as an adopted brother can be."

"Wang Chan was a rich and powerful man. Rumor has it he made his fortune on the black market during the war."

"Like many others in Hong Kong."

Blake watched Lai carefully while he spoke. Lai's rapid rise in the ranks and appointment to Inspector at a young age had raised a few eyebrows in the establishment. And rumor had it that Lai had bigger, political ambitions.

"We've had suspicions that Wang Chan was involved with the triads. His death may be tied in."

"What kind of activities?"

"Laundering drug money."

"You've spent too long chasing dopers, Peter."

"You don't think we'd find a skeleton in the closets of many of Hong Kong's wealthiest?"

Blake stood up. "Even if that were true—and I'm not saying that it is—Wang Chan's wealth has increased a thousand fold from legitimate business in the last ten years. Why would he need money from drugs?"

"Isn't that what greed is all about?"

Blake put the photograph back on the bookcase and sat down. "I don't see any motivation for him to be involved in drugs now. I can't speak about the past."

Lai fiddled with a pen on his desk for a few moments. "The war among the triads has heated up. Has the DEA got anything new on that?"

"If you want I can make a call."

"I'd appreciate that, Blake."

The furrow between Lai's eyes deepened as they talked. There's more to this than he's telling me, Blake thought.

"Will Raymond inherit Chan Enterprises now?"

Blake nodded in his mind. There it was.

"As an adopted son, there's some modest provision for me, but virtually everything passes onto Raymond. If you're suggesting Raymond is a suspect, that doesn't make sense. He would have inherited everything when Wang Chan died of natural causes."

"What about Sabrina Chan?"

Blake's pulse quickened. "What about her?"

"What's her relationship like with Raymond? Is she included in Wang Chan's will?"

"That's a question you should ask them."

Lai smiled and stood up. "Well, I think that's all for now."

"Not quite. I've got a few questions for you."

Lai stopped in his tracks.

"How many men can you put on the case?" Blake asked.

"The usual for a homicide."

"Wang Chan was a prominent member of Hong Kong business community. He deserves more than the usual."

Lai looked at the shiny buttons on his coat. "I could request additional men."

"Then do it. I'd rather not go over your head."

Lai glared at Blake. "I'll look into it . . . Are you staying in Hong Kong for a while?"

"I have to return to the U.S. for reassignment, but I'll stay a few more days to give Raymond a hand with family affairs."

Lai shook Blake's hand. "I'd like to keep in touch until you leave. Thank you for your cooperation . . . and the advice."

Blake shook Lai's hand firmly.

Lai opened the door. "We'd better take them down to the Morgue."

Blake followed Lai, thinking. He had the distinct feeling that Lai didn't like the prospect of an unsolved, high profile murder on his record. Blake felt compassion for Raymond, who'd taken Wang Chan's death hard. To his surprise, he wasn't worried about Sabrina. She was strong and would survive anything, but he wondered how Wang Chan's death would affect her divorce from Raymond. But most of all, Blake was surprised that he didn't feel any sadness for Wang Chan's passing.

4

The white stucco mansion hung on the hillside amidst some of the most expensive real estate in the world. The multimillion dollar homes, with spectacular views of Kowloon, Hong Kong Central, Victoria Harbor, Aberdeen and Stonecutter Island, dotted the hillsides of Victoria peak, the apex of the fifteen-hundred foot Mt. Austin.

Simon Fung's home, a huge soaring mansion of concrete and glass, surrounded by manicured gardens, could have nestled easily into the Hollywood Hills. Inside, traditional Chinese antiques and furnishings stood in marked contrast.

Simon Fung, a handsome, athletic, medium-height man in his late forties, dressed in a white linen suit, sat at his antique cherry wood desk, looking carefully over several accounting ledgers. Ceremonial Chinese swords and Japanese *katanas* hung on the walls beside him and sat on a cradle on his desk. A photo of a younger Fung in a Peoples' Liberation Army uniform sat prominently among the *objects d'art* display case.

A servant entered the room and placed the tea service on the rosewood coffee table in front of two men, one young and the other, much older, both dressed in darker tailored suits.

"Drug business is down ten percent," the young man said, "and they've killed two of our best dealers." He had a wild-eyed look and sat on the edge of his seat, looking as if he were ready to pounce on someone.

Fung nodded, but kept looking at his papers.

"We should intimidate their buyers, make some hits in their distribution network," the young man continued, smacking his fist into his hand, "our survival depends on expansion and that means either taking business away from our competitors, or finding new markets."

Fung looked up and nodded.

"The other triads are fat and lazy. We can crush them in a war," the young man rambled on.

Fung held up his hands, palms outwards. "What do you think we should do?" he asked, looking at the older man.

The older man sat back and sipped his tea. "Sun Tzu said 'hold out bait to entice the enemy. Feign disorder and crush him.'"

Fung nodded at his old buddy from the Red Guard, then unsheathed the Japanese katana sitting on his desk and pointed it at the young man. "Invite two representatives from our chief rival to a meeting to negotiate. Then kill them and leave the calling card of one of the other triads."

The young man smiled broadly, jumped out of his chair, bowed slightly and left the room.

"You and I know this constant war with the other triads is taking its toll on our organization too. We need an advantage," Fung said.

The old man nodded. "Ramirez?"

"What have you found out about him?"

"His cartel is at war with the other more established cartels in Mexico. He worked in the Juarez cartel as a drug runner and assassin and then set up his own organization. They've tried to kill him several times, but he's managed to hold on, liquidating a handful of the competition."

"So, he faces the same problems that I do."

"Yes, but our business is heroin, not cocaine."

"That's true, but to win our war, we must look beyond what we've done before."

"Do you really want to be partners with a Mexican?"

Fung laughed. "Such sensitivities from a man who has a Thai wife."

"That's different."

"Nevertheless, my old friend, I want to look into this Ramirez possibility more seriously."

The old man stood up, bowed and then left the room.

Fung leaned back in his chair and ran the flat of the katana across the tattoo of a red dragon on the back of his hand, the symbol of the Hung Se Ying triad.

5

Once a honky-tonk town of bars and brothels serving San Diego's naval station, Tijuana, Mexico, with a population of two million, had become one of the fastest growing cities in the world. Huge shantytowns with shacks built from cardboard and shipping pallets lined dirty streets and sprawled down the slopes of desert mesas below the *maliquadoros,* the American border factories. The migration of thousands of people north to the border, looking for work and the creation of new elites from the enormous economies of drugs, has marred the efforts to build a viable economic and social structure. In a place where anything was for sale, the price of human life is on a razor's edge.

Once known as the "mules" for Columbia's powerful cocaine cartels, Mexico's drug traffickers had grown into drug lords in their own right and the front line of the drug war had shifted from the jungle of Central America to America's front door. Mexican drug cartels run their own distribution networks in the United States and now buy cocaine directly from producers in Bolivia and Peru. Because of this power shift, drug-related violence among the Mexican drug cartels and corruption at all levels of government and law enforcement has spiraled out of control.

A handful of bars and clubs in Tijuana, such as the Chicago Club and the Adelita Bar were choked with people that evening. Half a dozen street walkers from the *Zona Norte* had wandered down from *Calle 1A* to look for customers. The sound of blaring music and the laughter of drunken men accosting young women filled the air.

Special Agent Xtimal Mendoza, a middle-aged, short, barrel-chested man with reddish-brown skin and the flat facial features and thick coarse hair characteristic of Mexico's Indian population, sat with his back to the wall facing the entrance in the *Café Gato*. He was the lead agent in the Ministry of Public Safety's Drug Enforcement Unit, recently established due to the

United States government's pressure on the Mexican government. Known only to a few people in his agency, his mission was also to seek out Mexican police and government complicity with the drug traffickers.

Mendoza's unit had received a reliable tip that a bagman for the Juarez Cartel, a man on the most wanted list for the past year, would be at the Café to meet two of his associates. Mendoza had the Café and the surrounding streets staked out thoroughly.

Mendoza looked at his watch. It was ten p.m. "Check in," he whispered into the transmitter pinned to his lapel. A small, barely visible receiver sat in his ear.

One by one, his men, called in.

A black SUV with dark tinted windows pulled up in front of the Café. Two of the car windows rolled down, Uzis stuck out and fired on the two men under surveillance sitting at the sidewalk table. A hail of bullets struck the men, knocking one back out of his chair, blood spurting from bullet wounds in his chest and face.

Mendoza leapt out of his seat, his gun in his hand, at the sound of the first gunfire. "What the hell? All units, move in, move in!" he yelled into his transmitter.

The other man under attack stood up and pulled a handgun from the waistband of his pants and returned fire. His bullets shattered one of the SUV's windows. The Uzis continued to spray bullets at him. As though he was dancing in slow motion, a dozen bullets spun him across the table onto the sidewalk. All around, people first stared, frozen, then jumped up and ran, screaming. Several of Mendoza's agents ran from their positions behind the cars toward the Café, their guns drawn. The SUV pulled away, smashing the bumper of a parked car.

"Unit Two, block the SUV," Mendoza barked into his transmitter, as he reached the sidewalk. He fired his gun repeatedly at the SUV, the bullets clunking into the bumper of the vehicle.

Down the street, an unmarked police car pulled out into the street and skidded sideways to block the path of the SUV, but it was too late. The SUV sideswiped the police car, careened off a parked car and sped away.

"Unit One, pursue," Mendoza called out. "Unit Three, move into position at *Los Herdes* and *Calle 2A*. Unit Two, proceed to *Los Herdes* and *Calle Rodriguez*. We'll pursue."

Mendoza jumped into a car across the street and slapped the shoulder of his bulky driver, who slammed his foot on the gas pedal and sped after the fleeing SUV. The driver of the SUV drove recklessly along *Los Herdes* at high speed, forcing cars out of its path. Then it turned sharply onto *Ave Diego Rivera* toward the river, *Rio Tijuana*.

"We've got'em boss," a voice crackled on the police radio, "it's a dead end."

"All units block all exits from *Diego Rivera,*" Mendoza said with a smile.

By the time Mendoza's car caught up with the SUV, it had turned off its lights and sat motionless. Four police cars had blocked all possible exits, and the wire fence which ran along the *Rio Tijuana* had blocked the SUV's escape northward.

Mendoza grabbed the car's microphone and switched on the loudspeaker. "This is the police. Drop your weapons, get out of the car, and lie face down on the ground."

The red and blue lights of the police cars made silent sweeps in the night. A minute passed.

Abruptly, the SUV's doors flung open and three men jumped out, firing their Uzis at the police. They began to scale the wire fence as they fired their weapons.

"Return fire! All units return fire!" Mendoza yelled into his radio-microphone.

Ten policemen opened fire on the fleeing criminals. The whining and clunking sounds of bullets hitting concrete, metal and flesh reverberated amidst the smoke of discharged weapons. A policeman grunted loudly when a criminal's bullet struck him in the leg.

The three fleeing men were literally torn apart by the storm of bullets. Two of the men fell to the ground, the third hung from the fence, his fingers still caught in the chain link.

"Cease fire! Cease fire!" Mendoza barked.

The gunfire stopped. Only the sound of the policemen reloading their weapons hung in the air with the smoke from discharged weapons.

"Unit Two, move in!" Mendoza ordered. "Anyone hit?"

"Galinez took one in the leg, looks like a flesh wound," one of the other policemen replied.

"Get an ambulance here, *pronto*," Mendoza said. "Now, move in on the SUV."

Four policemen quickly ran toward the gunmen, their weapons ready. When they reached the SUV, they checked inside and then moved to the fence. They kicked away the Uzis and checked for the gunmen's' vital signs.

"All dead," one policeman called out.

Mendoza ran over to them.

"I recognize these two," one of the policemen said, shoving the toe of his shoe into the bloody shirt of a dead gunman, "bagman for the Ramirez Cartel."

"That explains the hit on the two Juarez men at the Café," another policeman chimed in, "territory warfare."

The policemen searched the bodies of the dead and wounded men. The sirens of the ambulances got closer and closer.

"Make sure Galinez gets to the hospital fast," Mendoza said, as the first ambulance rolled up.

The policemen loaded their wounded comrade into the ambulance.

"We found this in one of the dead men's wallet," a policeman said, handing Mendoza a torn piece of paper.

Mendoza looked at the paper, turning it in his fingers. "Looks like a piece of an envelope. Do you recognize the symbol?"

"No sir," the policeman answered.

"If only you could talk," Mendoza whispered, rubbing his finger over the embossed symbol of a red dragon.

6

Raoul Ramirez lounged on the deck chair of the white-tiled terrace overlooking the azure water of the pool which was cleverly cantilevered on the hillside so that the viewer's perspective from the pool deck carried naturally to the Pacific Ocean far below. The blazing red bougainvillea draped the ten-foot white stone walls that surrounded the palatial home. Several men in T-shirts, shorts and sandals and armed with Uzis, walked along the stone walls and guarded the metal gate.

Ramirez was a fat, greasy man with glasses. He was dressed in white cotton pants and a *guayabera* shirt won loosely outside his pants. His thick moustache was flecked with the remains of his last meal. Despite his slovenliness, he fancied himself a handsome man whom women couldn't resist. But the truth was that the only women who surrounded him were the ones he paid.

He clipped the end off a long fat cigar and lit it, taking in a couple of deep drags before the cigar's smoke coiled around his head. Ramirez, the head of one of the fastest growing drug cartels in Mexico, was embroiled in an escalating war with the three other largest cartels.

Across from Ramirez sat his right hand man, Raphael Salinez, a handsome man in his thirties, stylish and fastidious in a white linen shirt and pants.

"I just got the report," Salinez said, "we made the hit on the Juarez men in Tijuana, but the *Federales* killed our men.

Ramirez chewed furiously on his cigar. "Were they questioned by the police?"

Salinez shook his head. "It was Drug Enforcement people, not local police."

Ramirez smashed his fist on the table. "Find out who they are," he sputtered, "kill them or put them on the payroll."

"Easy boss, remember your heart," Salinez said.

Ramirez grunted.

"Every time we make inroads on the other cartels, we take a hit," Salinez said.

Ramirez pointed a fat finger at Salinez. "I haven't crawled out of the gutter in Tijuana, slaved in the slime and blood of slaughter houses, cleaned the crap in toilets, become a runner for street dealers and fought my way up the food chain for nothing." He was panting heavily and then stopped talking and took a deep breath. "That's why an alliance with Fung and his Hung Se Ying triad interests me."

"We don't know much about Fung."

"I know he's got the same problem that we do, competition. We both need an edge."

Salinez smiled. "I think I may have stumbled on one."

"What?"

"Instead of competing for cocaine, heroin and marijuana markets, we should go after a new drug—exclusive."

"What are you ranting about?"

Salinez turned and yelled back to the house. "Bring him here!"

One of the armed guards brought in a short, square-shouldered, barrel-chested man in his thirties, dressed in dirty cotton pants and shirt. His hawk-like nose and thick straight hair spoke of his *Zapotec* Indian origins.

"Please, *senõr*. I've done nothing wrong," the man begged, his eyes as big as saucers.

Salinez motioned to the armed man to release him. "Tell me about this," he said, waving a wrinkled piece of thin bark marked with symbols.

The man's knees quivered and his voiced cracked. "My grandfather gave it to me. He told us of the ancient Mayan ball game ceremony and of the drug, *jfuri,* that the warriors took. He said these symbols came from the Mayan ruins at *Chich'en Itza*."

"This drug, *jfuri*, as you call it, he said it was a powerful drug?" Salinez asked.

"Yes, yes. It makes you dream while you're awake. It makes you feel like a God, and you don't get sick from it," the man replied.

Ramirez looked at the man carefully. "Have you told anyone about this?"

The man was shaking. "No. No one."

"One of our informants heard him talking in the cantina about how he was descended from Mayan kings, waving this thing all around," Salinez said.

Ramirez clucked his tongue.

"You can have it, I won't tell anyone," the man said.

Ramirez looked at the piece of bark, then the man. "I know you won't." Ramirez nodded to the guard, who grabbed the man's arm.

"No! No! Please! I promise I won't tell," the man screamed, as the guard dragged him away.

"What do you think of this drug, what's it called— *jfuri*?" Ramirez asked.

Salinez adjusted his black-framed sunglasses. "There are many psychotropic plants in Central America—*Zacatechichi, Tupa, Teonanacatl, Oloiuqui*—but his description of *jfuri* sounds a lot like *Ayahuasca*. It's a powerful hallucinogen, but it's got violent after affects, so it's not popular. It seems this *jfuri* is a hallucinogen and seems to leave the user with the euphoria of cocaine without the nasty after effects."

"If this *jfuri* is what he says it is, we've got the edge to bury the competition."

"But we don't know where to find the plant that produces *jfuri*."

"We'll find that at *Chich'en Itza*. In the meantime, I want you to draft up a proposal to Fung, and enclose a copy of the symbols to show we're acting in good faith."

Salinez got up. "I'm on it." He got up and walked back to the house.

Ramirez grinned, relit his cigar, and blew a perfect circle of smoke.

7

The United States has engaged in foreign intelligence activities since the days of George Washington, but only since World War II have they been coordinated. Under the leadership of New York lawyer William Donovan, The Office of Strategic Services, or OSS, as it became known, was created in 1942, with the mandate to collect strategic information for the military. In 1945, the OSS was abolished and its functions were assumed by the various military branches, but Donovan recommended to President Truman that a new permanent organization be created. The National Security Act of 1947 created the National Security Agency (NSA) and the Central Intelligence Agency (CIA), which also became known as "The Company." The CIA's mandate was to collect, analyze and disseminate intelligence information. With the advent of the Cold War, these functions were expanded to include foreign covert activities intended to prevent America's enemies from endangering American national security interests. By the current day, the intelligence business had exploded to more than one hundred civilian and military agencies.

The small town of Fairfield, nestled along the coast of Connecticut, overlooking the Long Island Sound, has been the home of the rich and powerful for more than two centuries. The large New England-style home of Jack Cross, Deputy Director of Covert Operations for the CIA, sat on a small peninsula, had extensive gardens, a swimming pool and a private boat dock. Cross came from five generations of New England stock and had married into old money. His wife's family connections had helped pave the way for Cross' appointment to the CIA after his distinguished career in the Marines.

Benjamin Cranston, a stocky man with thick glasses, in his late sixties, wearing an open neck denim shirt and khaki pants, casually walked into Cross' book-and memento-lined study.

"I knew I'd find you in your bunker," Cranston said amiably. Cranston sat down in one of the big leather chairs in front of Cross' desk.

Cranston, Director of Covert Operations for the CIA and Cross' boss, was a career government bureaucrat, having worked his way up through the ranks in the State Department. Inside government circles, he was known for his political skill in dealing with Congress. His biggest fault, claimed his critics, was his overly cautious nature.

Jack Cross had a leathery face, worn by years in the inclement outdoors, steel-gray hair and a patrician's nose. His large angular physique had earned him the nick name of "stork" in the Marines, but only out of his earshot. Guile lurked behind his dull gray eyes like a Mako shark in the purple deep.

"I've really enjoyed this weekend, Jack, it's so relaxing," Cranston said. "How long have you been here now?"

"I don't know if I've ever told you, but this is actually my in-law's house. When they died, Margaret and I moved in and renovated it over the years, making room for the children. After Margaret died and the kids grew up and moved away it does seem a little big sometimes," Cross replied.

"Why don't you move into something smaller in Washington?"

Cross picked up a photograph of his wife on the desk. "Margaret loved this place. I feel like I'd be betraying her if I left."

"Jack, why don't you retire? You don't need the money and you've served our country well."

"I could ask you the same question, Ben."

Cranston shrugged. "I will soon. Unlike you, I'm not independently wealthy."

Cross got up and walked over to the credenza beside his desk, opened the door and took out a bottle and two glasses.

"Single malt, forty years old," Cross said, pouring some into each glass.

"You've always had a taste for the best," Cranston replied.

"*Salud!*" Cross said.

Cranston clinked Cross' glass and sipped the Scotch. "I could never understand why, with your family background and money, you never went into politics."

Cross smiled. "I'd rather be the power behind the power. Besides, I'm after your job, Ben."

Cranston laughed. "You can have it soon, and for what's its worth, I think you'd do a bang-up job, if you'd just learn to ease up now and then."

"Easing up is for the weak at heart and politicians . . . Ben, while we're on the topic and I know we said we wouldn't talk shop this weekend . . ."

"What is it?"

Cross looked intently into Cranston's eyes. "The Company's in deep trouble. We've endured the third year of budget cuts, while we watch the National Reconnaissance Service and the National Security Agency get fatter. Not to mention the damn Bureau."

Cranston nodded vigorously. "It pisses me off too, Jack. But since the collapse of the Soviet Union there's little interest in anything resembling the Cold War. It's difficult to get Congress, let alone the President, enthusiastic about covert operations."

Cross smacked his hand on his knee. "Damn it, we can't afford to just sit back and wait for the enemy to come to us."

"The military have convinced the administration, Congress and the American people that money needs to be spent on weapons to defend against rogue nations like North Korea or Iraq."

Cross looked up at the antique ceiling fan, its blades silently turning. "Our greatest threat is from terrorist groups in the Mid-East, Central America—hell, even in our own country. Covert Ops is now, more than ever, our country's best foreign policy weapon."

Cranston stared out the window into toward The Sound.

Cross got up and sat next to Cranston. "I'm not knocking you Ben. God knows you've tried." He put his hand on Cranston's shoulder. "Somehow, and somewhere, we've got to find more money for Covert Ops. Even if terrorists attack us, it'll only be a matter of time before politicians find a way to eventually lose interest and withdraw funding."

Cranston's hand clenched Cross' arm. "I'd welcome any creation solutions, Jack."

"I'll make it a priority." Cross smiled. "But enough shoptalk. Let's take the boat out. I know you can't swim so I've got two life preservers for you."

Cranston got up and walked to the door. "Thanks, you think of everything."

Cross walked out the door with Cranston. "I try to, Ben, I try to."

8

Chinese funerals in Hong Kong are a fusion of Buddhist, Confucian and Taoist rituals. In Taoist tradition, if the person dies violently or tragically, they may become vengeful spirits for a time, lingering around the place of their death. And if the dead person had performed misdeeds in his lifetime, his spirit is punished in the underworld. Chinese tradition visualized the dead person riding a dragon to paradise, a trip requiring a three day supply of food. Only the wealthy could afford a burial as useable land is at a premium in Hong Kong.

The Taoist priest, dressed in his ceremonial robe and skull cap, stood at the head of Wang Chan's coffin, repeating the same incantation, while two monks shook the discordant bells. To the right of the coffin, Blake, Raymond and several other distant male relatives and business associates, all dressed in dark suits, stood solemnly. Sabrina and the other women, dressed in white, stood to the left of the casket. White and yellow chrysanthemums decorated the coffin, while incense and candles burned around it. Then the priest's assistants burnt paper money to ensure Wang Chan's safe trip to the next world.

Honoring the Taoist tradition, family members placed personal items in the coffin along with food for the journey. Raymond placed a jade ring that his father had given him on his thirteenth birthday, while Sabrina had chosen an ivory comb. Blake found his selection a difficult one and finally settled on a tiny lead soldier, part of the set that Wang Chan had given him when he first arrived in the Chan home.

When the ritual chanting was finished, the flowers were removed from the lid of the coffin and it was lowered. According to custom all onlookers turned their faces away. When the coffin had been lowered all the way, firecrackers were lit to ward off evil spirits.

Blake was glad Raymond had chosen not to have the complete traditional Chinese forty-nine day funeral with formal prayer ceremonies every seven days and the scattering of small squares of colored paper, pierced by tiny holes to confuse evil spirits that supposedly had to pass through each hole before reaching the soul of the deceased.

Blake glanced over several times at Raymond and Sabrina during the funeral. Raymond's face had never looked so drawn nor his shoulders so stooped. But behind Sabrina's sad eyes Blake saw her strength, her indomitable spirit.

After the priest and the others had paid their respects and left, Raymond let out a big sigh and motioned to Blake and Sabrina to walk back to the car. "I know it's tradition to host a big feast now, but I don't want to."

"That's fine with me," Sabrina said.

"Sometimes, less is more," Blake said.

"It's been a week. Why haven't the police come up with any suspects? Father's death must be avenged, or my family will lose face!" Raymond said emotionally.

"Investigations take time, Raymond, but I'll keep the pressure on Inspector Lai," Blake said. "Look, if it would help, I'll stay longer, put off my reassignment for a week,"

Raymond shook Blake's hand. "Thanks, but you should go ahead with your plans. But if the police don't get results, I'll take matters into my own hands."

Blake studied Raymond's tense face. "Don't do anything foolish."

Raymond stared at Blake but didn't answer.

"Blake, with your inheritance and an early retirement pension, you could make Hong Kong your home again. I'm sure Raymond could find a place for you in Chan Enterprises," Sabrina said enthusiastically.

"Oh . . . yes . . . of course, Blake," Raymond stumbled, "I'd be glad to have you join me."

"I don't know what to say. I'd like to think about it. It goes without saying that I appreciate the offer," Blake said, "let's talk again after my next assignment is finished."

Raymond opened the car door for Sabrina. She'd replaced the look of irritation on her face with one of calmness and composure. Before stepping into the back seat, she held Raymond's and Blake's hands in hers. "Just remember, we're the only family left now."

Blake watched her and Raymond get into the car and drive away. The graveyard's silence wrapped around Blake. He was tempted by Raymond-- or was it Sabrina's-- offer. Yet the future of their relationship still lay in doubt. Still, to be part of a family again pulled at a place in his heart.

Later that evening, Blake walked onto the terrace of the Chan home in *Shek O,* with its panoramic view of the South China Sea. He walked over to the railing, looking at Big Wave Bay in the distance. A gentle breeze, with a scent of hyacinths in the garden, drifted across the white tiled terrace.

"I'd forgotten how beautiful it is here," Blake said.

"Father didn't want to move from Victoria Peak where we grew up. But I've always loved it here. It has a serenity that makes you feel like you're far away from one of the most congested cities in the world. I think he agreed to move to please me, but once he was here for a while, he loved it too," Raymond said, sitting in a white rattan chair.

Blake poured himself a cup of coffee. "You haven't had much sleep."

"Is it that obvious?"

"I know it's tough for you right now with father's death and your split with Sabrina."

"You know, I don't think I ever asked you if you were okay after father's death. Thinking about my own pain, I guess."

"I'm okay. Wang Chan was more like a big uncle to me than a father."

Raymond nodded.

"Can we talk about the divorce?" Blake asked.

"You've never been one to beat around the bush."

"Sabrina seems to really want reconciliation. Is that not possible?"

Raymond stood up and walked to the edge of the terrace. "She wants it only on her terms."

"Which are?"

"Being married but acting like she's single and independent."

"You mean single as in available to other men?"

"Not affairs, to my knowledge, but you know as well as I do, she loves the company of men."

"Sabrina's always loved to party . . ."

"But I need to have her by my side, all the time."

Blake opened his mouth to say something, but Raymond held up his hand.

"Let me finish. I know you were in love with her once. You never said if you'd asked her to marry you, and she's never said. That doesn't matter anyway. For whatever reason, she chose to marry that Scottish guy Duncan, with the shipping company."

"You don't have to . . ." Blake interrupted.

"You opened the subject."

Blake nodded.

"After Duncan's fortunes collapsed and they divorced, Sabrina and I got close. The first few years of our marriage were great. Then gradually, her desire for independence pushed us apart."

"She says there was pressure on her to play the role of the stay-at-home dutiful Chinese wife, with no aspirations of her own."

"There's some truth to that, I admit. But I gave in to her a lot. And she knew my expectations when we got married."

Seeing the anguish on Raymond's face, Blake paused for a moment, feeling both compassion and pity for him. "If you had an understanding with Sabrina when you got married, why was the prenuptial necessary?"

Raymond crossed his arms, the furrow between his eyebrows deepening. "Father insisted and you know Chinese customs well enough to know I couldn't go against his wishes. The prenuptial is generous to her."

Blake walked over to Raymond and put his arm around him. "Tough times, brother. I don't mean to sound like I'm second guessing you. I just thought talking it out might help."

Raymond smiled. "I know. But there's nothing you can do to change things." He refilled Blake's coffee cup. "So where's your next assignment?"

"Costa Rica. I'll be training some drug enforcement people there."

Raymond nodded.

"But I'll call as often as I can and keep in touch with Inspector Lai," Blake said.

"I appreciate that. It's been great having you home, despite the circumstances. Seems like we don't see each other often enough. And I want you to think seriously about my offer to join Chan Enterprises."

"I will."

An easy silence fell between them as they both stood at the edge of the terrace.

"Can I ask a favor of you?"

"Ask away."

"If Inspector Lai doesn't find father's killer, will you save our family's honor?"

Blake looked intently at Raymond. "You mean find him and turn him over to the police?"

"I mean an eye for an eye."

"I can't believe you would see me as a hired killer."

"You'd be doing it for family honor, not money."

Blake fought his rising anger. "I know you're upset about Wang Chan. He was my father too. But to ask me to kill someone out of revenge . . ."

Raymond threw up his hands. "You're right; I don't know what I was thinking. You have no idea the pressure I'm under in the Chinese community to save face. Blake, father's killer must be found and punished."

Blake grabbed Raymond by the shoulders with his strong hands. "And I'll do everything I can to help the police, but I won't kill for revenge."

Raymond's shoulders sagged and he sighed deeply. "I know, I know, it was stupid of me to ask." Raymond abruptly looked at his watch. "I've got a meeting in twenty minutes. Have a safe trip; I'll talk to you soon."

Raymond embraced Blake then left abruptly.

Blake turned to look out over the South China Sea. In an odd way, Blake had never felt closer to Raymond, yet at the same time so far away from him.

9

Blake wiped his forehead with his arm. The Costa Rican jungle was like a damp rotting blanket. A few drops of sweat leaked through his reddish-blond eyebrows into his eyes. He scrunched his eyelids shut, squeezing out the brine. He elbowed the huge shape in sniper camouflage lying beside him.

Jimmy Candelero, a young agent in the Costa Rican government's drug enforcement police, was a hulking, six-foot-three and two hundred and fifty pounds. He got his size from his German mother and his dark good looks from his Costa Rican father. He peered through a night vision lens aimed at a large wood and brick farm house and two metals sheds two hundred yards away. The farm was an eight-thousand acre cattle ranch owned by an American named Richard Bull.

"*Agua*," Blake whispered. He looked carefully at Candelero. "I thought big men sweat like pigs."

Candelero grunted and passed the canteen to Blake, tapping his forehead with a gorilla-like finger. "It's all in the mind, *gringo*."

Blake took a salt pill and downed it with a careful swallow of the tepid water, savoring it in his mouth like a fine wine. He squirted a small stream of water through his teeth onto Candelero's cheek.

Candelero grunted and crushed a large stick-like insect crawling across his sleeve.

"Your first field work?" Blake asked.

"No. When I was training in Peru, I took part in Operation Condor, the biggest bust ever with the Peruvian Guardia. I won't forget flying over the treetops, the Bell helicopter skids brushing the branches, scattering thousands of birds and monkeys. We hit a large cocaine operation run by the Cali cartel. They had dormitories for hundreds of people, a high-tech communications center, dozens of heat lamps to dry the cocaine, huge drums of coca chemicals, electric mixing vats—the whole nine yards."

"Did you find the stash?"

"Four tons of cocoa paste that could churn out five hundred kilos of pure cocaine a day. Estimated value at two hundred million. It was a sweet bust."

"Makes all the hours of surveillance worth while, doesn't it?"

"What pisses me off is the whole system. The peasants who grew the cocoa leaves, the *cocaleros*, made six times the money they could with any other cash crop and the other peasants, the *poseros*, who process the leaves into paste, made easy money. One hundred pounds of leaves to make one kilo of paste, four kilos of paste to make one kilo of pure white cocaine hydrochloride. And then the Columbia cartels make a killing on the distribution."

"Welcome to the reality of the war on drugs. It's a way of life not just for people but entire countries."

Candelero grunted.

"You mentioned your brother's in government service?" Blake asked.

"Diplomatic service. He gets all the ooohs and aahhs from the family," Candelero replied, then laughed, "but Jimmy gets all the women."

Blake laughed. He liked this raw-boned giant with his passion for life and sense of humor.

"I don't mean to be rude, but aren't you getting a little too old for field work?" Candelero asked.

Blake tapped his temple with his finger. "I may have lost a step or two, but I'm a lot smarter now than when I was your age."

"No offense intended. Most field agents are happy to take a desk job after a few years."

Blake smirked. "I'd clean your boots and wash your size thirteen feet before I took a desk job. But I am thinking about retiring. Maybe moving back Hong Kong."

"You've got family there?"

"A brother and sister-in-law. They're going through tough times right now."

"Oh, family squabbles?"

"My adopted father was recently murdered."

Candelero slapped Blake's shoulder. "Oh, I'm sorry, Blake. Do you know who and why?"

"Not yet."

"My father told me that people kill for passion or money."

"Or sometimes both. Anyway, when we finish here, I'll head back to Hong Kong and lend a hand in the investigation."

"How are your brother and sister-in-law taking it?"

"It hit my brother particularly hard. He was really an only child—I was adopted—and being traditional Chinese, father's death is seen as a loss of honor for the family."

"I gather you don't share his view."

"Only from the point of view of finding the killer and bringing him to justice."

Candelero slapped Blake's back affectionately. "Maybe this assignment will be a welcome rest for you."

Blake smiled.

"Give me the real scoop on our mission. I can't believe the DEA would bother to assign a veteran agent like you to do grunt work in the jungle with me," Candelero said.

"You're right. We've had good information that several Americans who own ranches down here may be involved in trafficking. If that's true, we'd like to extradite them back to the U.S. for prosecution."

"So this isn't a training assignment?"

"No, but I'll teach you plenty."

Candelero laughed.

Blake turned his attention to the ranch house, focusing his night vision binoculars. Two men dressed in shorts, T-shirts and sandals and carrying AK-47's emerged from the house, jumped into a pickup truck and drove onto the landing field. Within minutes they had lit fires at each end of the trip. A muscular man with a large handgun strapped to his side walked over to one of the sheds, disappeared inside and reappeared driving a small tractor with a forklift attachment. Richard Bull, a short fat man with a wide brimmed khaki hat, waddled casually over to the landing field with two dogs scurrying around his feet. The two men in the pickup truck drove down to join Bull after lighting signal fires.

The sound of a low-pitched, propeller-driven engine filled the air, and then a DC3 plane dropped out of the cloud cover and made a bouncing landing, before proceeding up to the pickup truck and tractor.

Once the plane had opened its doors, Blake and Candelero focused their camera lenses on the men. Candelero's motorized camera whirred into action. The pilot, a middle-aged man with thick gray hair and wearing a U.S. Air Force jacket, helped the muscular tractor driver and the other two men unload a dozen wooden crates and move them to one of the sheds. The pilot jumped into Bull's truck and followed the tractor into one of the barns.

Blake secured his snub-nosed MP3 submachine gun with Velcro straps, touched Candelero's arm and motioned toward the sheds. Like large balls of brush driven by the wind, they scrambled on all fours, trailing the green and brown camouflage netting interlaced with twigs and leaves. They stopped every thirty yards for a few seconds, motionless, waiting for signs of detection. And then they scrambled again. When they reached the rear of the feed shed, Blake pointed to the rope dangling from the loft loader above and gave the sign to climb. First Candelero, then Blake, scaled the rope. Once in the loft, they silently crawled through the crates and boxes until they could get a clear view below.

The fat man and his muscular assistant had pried open the lids on the wooden crates. Blake motioned to Candelero to take pictures with his video camera, and turned on a miniature tape recorder. He attached his earphone to pick up the details of the conversation below.

Richard Bull was nodding as his fat finger traced the items on the written manifest. "Six dozen M16 rifles, M16 and M60 ammunition, C4 explosives, compasses, military field radios, night vision equipment, GPS equipment and grenade launchers. Where are the Stingers?"

The pilot shrugged.

"The rebels want those Stingers."

The pilot shook his head. "I'm just the delivery man. Take it up with the Colonel. Let's load up; I've got to get out of here before daylight."

Bull motioned to his stocky associate, who threw a tarpaulin off a dozen military issue canvas duffle bags. Inside the bags, cocaine bricks were wrapped in plastic and coffee grounds and then wrapped with duct tape. He handed a brick to the pilot. "Finest Bolivian grade. Twenty million easy."

The pilot made a small neat slice in the brick with his pocketknife, stuck in his pinky finger and tasted the white powder and nodded. "Good shit."

Blake motioned to Candelero. They switched off the camera and tape recorder, swung their MP3s around and clicked off the safety catches. Blake motioned to Candelero to circle to the other side of the loft. Candelero nodded and moved quietly. When he was in position, Blake aimed his MP3 at Bull's chest.

"Police! Drop your weapons and freeze!" Blake called out.

"*La Poliçía!*" Candelero called out, repeating Blake's order in Spanish.

The men below looked up into the loft in shock. The two armed men in shorts fired their AK-47s blindly at the loft, the bullets missing Blake and Candelero while the pilot sprinted toward the door. Bull just stood there, frozen. Blake fired a burst of three bullets into one man's chest, knocking him backwards, and then opened fire on the other man, hitting him in the head. Meanwhile, Candelero took out Bull's muscular assistant with a round of three bullets.

"Stop shooting, I surrender!" Bull shouted, holding his hands in the air.

Candelero scrambled from his position and jumped down to the floor. "I'm going after the pilot!" he yelled.

"Stow that," Blake replied. "We've got who we want. Check the other three."

Candelero walked over and checked the vital signs of the men they'd shot and gave the thumbs down signal. He moved over to Bull and slipped on the handcuffs while Blake scaled down from the loft.

Candelero pushed Bull down into a sitting position on top of one of the wooden crates, pulled out his large field combat knife and pushed it against Bull's crotch. "You're going to tell us everything we want to know, or you'll be a soprano in five seconds."

A wet stain quickly spread on Bull's light colored shorts. "Please! I'll tell you everything."

Blake switched on the video camera. "Who's the pilot?"

"Michael Ransom, a pilot for AEROCO airlines."

Candelero nodded. "Now you've got my attention, go on."

Bull looked down at the knife. "AEROCO is run by the Ramirez Cartel in Mexico. They delivered arms, and picked up cocaine destined for the U.S. I'm just the middle man."

Candelero pointed the knife again at Bull's crotch. "What else?"

Bull pushed himself away from the tip of the blade, his eyes white with fear. "Someone in the Company provides the arms to Ramirez."

"The Company? Who?" Blake asked.

"I don't know. I'm just the cutoff, I tell you," Bull replied.

"Alright, now you're going to tell us every detail of your operation from day one, including names, dates the contents of the shipments, or my big friend there will do some shish kabob work on you," Blake said.

"Okay, okay, just put the knife away," Bull replied.

Candelero put the knife away, took out his canteen, took a swig and passed it to Blake. "Might as well relax while we listen to his story."

Blake took a mouthful and coughed. "That's good."

Candelero smiled. "The best *Agave*."

Blake looked at Bull. "When you're finished, we're taking you back to San Jose and I'll be arranging for your extradition back to the U.S. Your cooperation will affect what charges you face."

Bull nodded, faced the video camera and the story of his four-year involvement in drug trafficking spilled out of his mouth.

A day later, with Bull behind bars, Blake and Candelero filed their reports with the DEA station chief in Costa Rica, Robert Gates. His office was located in a warehouse area in San Jose.

Gates paced back and forth in front of a large fan on his desk. He took a handkerchief out of his pocket, removed his wire-rimmed glasses and wiped his forehead.

"Damn, it's hot. These damn fans just push the damn hot air around," Gates said.

Behind him were pictures of him on the wall shaking the hands of politicians in front of tables piled high with drugs and money?

"Why don't you get an air conditioner?" Blake asked.

"Budget, keeping a low profile, the usual bullshit," Gates replied.

Blake pointed at the plastic bag on Gates' desk, with the video and audiotapes they'd recorded at Bull's ranch. "It's obvious that Bull's the cutoff man. Do you know anything about this Ramirez?"

"Only that his cartel is at war with the other cartels in Mexico," Gates replied.

"So we're going to proceed with Bull's extradition?" Blake asked.

Gates nodded. "The Costa Rican government has been very cooperative."

"My government is anxious that our country is not seen as another banana republic that lives on the drug business," Candelero said.

"Looks like we've got a few days until the paperwork is done and then I've got to go back to Los Angeles," Blake said, then winking, "so my big friend, let's go have a good time."

"Exactly my sentiments," Candelero said.

"I'll be in touch when Bull is ready to travel," Gates said.

Blake and Candelero left Gates' office and walked several blocks down the *calésas*, the brick and cobblestone streets, to the Café Blanca. They wandered past four men in white wrinkled suits arguing over a coq fight wager and two working girls trying to hustle the last dollar out of a drunken tourist. Blake steered Candelero to a corner table with a view of the door and the street.

Candelero held up two fingers and circled them over his head. A minute later, the happy waiter, with two front teeth missing, brought four *cervazas* and four fingers of tequila.

Candelero downed a shot of tequila and followed it with a big gulp of beer. "Long life, *amigo*. The hell with the rest."

Blake drank his tequila and beer. "*Salud,* Jimmy. To making the bastards pay."

Two young women in short skirts and tight halter tops walked into the Café and sat at the bar. The toothless waiter bantered with them and pointed to Candelero and Blake.

Candelero watched every step and sway of the women's bodies. "Look at those *chichis*. Come on, Blake, let's go have some fun."

Candelero waved at the women. "Ladies, my name is Jimmy Candelero and this handsome gentleman beside me is

Blake Morgan. We would be honored if you would join us for a drink."

The ladies laughed and sauntered over to Blake's table. Candelero put his giant arms around both of them and laughed raucously.

This is just what the doctor ordered, Blake thought.

10

After a few days of rest and relaxation with Jimmy Candelero, Blake returned home to Los Angeles only to receive word that he'd been reassigned to a big case in Seattle. While he was packing his bags, the telephone rang. He picked it up.

"Blake, this is Jimmy Candelero."

"Jimmy, you miss me already?"

"Of course . . . but I've got bad news."

"What?"

"Gates just told me that Bull won't be extradited to the U.S."

"What? Why?"

"He wouldn't tell a peon like me. Maybe you can find out."

"That's bullshit. We had evidence, we had his confession."

"I know, I know. I can't figure it. And my government is being hush-hush about it."

"Okay, thanks Jimmy. I'll call Gates. Keep up the fight."

"Always, big brother."

Blake hung up the telephone, found Gates' number and called him.

"Robert, this is Blake Morgan."

"Hello, Blake, how are you doing?"

"Pretty pissed off. I just got a call from Jimmy Candelero and he said that Richard Bull is not going to be extradited back to the U.S. to face trial."

"That's right."

"What the hell is going on?"

"He's been declared an asset by The Company and given immunity from prosecution."

"Why?"

"All I was told is that it was a matter of national security. Apparently he provides The Company with valuable information about terrorist and insurgent movements in Central America."

"But to protect a self-confessed drug trafficker with tons of evidence?"

"Hey, I'm not thrilled about the idea either. But the Costa Rican government is cooperating and has dropped extradition procedures."

"This is bullshit, Robert. What are you going to do about it?"

"Nothing. I've got my orders. We just keep doing our job."

"That's not enough."

"It's a done deal, Blake."

"Maybe for you. I'm going to file a report with DEA Internal Affairs. This kind of thing makes a farce out of our work."

"Suit yourself, but count me out."

"Thanks Robert, for your support." Blake slammed the telephone down. He wanted to destroy something, vent his anger. He'd worked for twenty years trying to stop the spreading cancer of drugs. And now someone in his own government was aiding and abetting criminals that he'd caught red-handed.

He repacked his bags, still fuming about the news and took the first flight to Seattle. On the trip he wrestled in his mind with his threat to go to the DEA's Internal Affairs over the issue and then thought about Raymond and how the Wang Chan murder investigation was going.

11

Blake Morgan's fingers cramped. Heat will help, he thought. Better yet, a shot of vodka. No, several.

He'd been cooped up all night in the steel box, scanning the Seattle docks with his night vision binoculars.

Waiting. And watching.

Blake looked at the frayed Drug Enforcement Agency badge on the arm of his jacket. While twenty years of field work hadn't blunted his mind's eagerness for action, his aging body, with its years of scars and bruises, begged for retirement. He put the binoculars aside and sat down on the cold metal floor. He loosened the straps on his Kevlar body armor and *stretched* his six-foot lean body into a yoga stretch, sliding easily into *prana,* deep controlled breathing. He glanced at his reflection in the stainless steel wall. A long angular face of man in his late forties with large blue-gray eyes looked back at him. A two-day growth of reddish blond facial hair mirrored his thick wavy hair. He stretched his back and shoulders, letting the stiffness sink away. Soon a warmth like hot oil returned to his joints.

He glanced out of the crane's cab window to the docks below. The black sky of night was waxing into the pearl-blue of the morning. In the waters beyond, an eagle etched itself over the water, then blurred, then etched again.

"You awake, Blake?" a voice of James Redfield, another member of the surveillance team, squawked on Blake's headset.

"No, I'm sleeping," Blake replied, tightening the straps on his body, tucking a black sweater into his black rip stop nylon pants.

"We've been here ten hours now. Jamieson should call it," the voice came back.

Blake rubbed a long scar on his chin. "He said the informants were solid." Blake adjusted the cuffs of his pants into his Gortex and leather boots. "You'll be a hero on the six-o'clock news, Redfield."

"Yeah, yeah, I know."

"This is Jamieson. Cut the chatter and keep this channel open," a harsh Scottish highland baritone voice cut in.

"Yes sir," Redfield replied to the leader of the DEA special unit called Omega Strike Force.

Blake scanned the docks. Two loading cranes, like giant metal praying mantises, hung over the containers. Beside the behemoth ships, the eagle he'd seen earlier, burst from the water's surface, a fat wriggling salmon dangling from its talons. The white-crested predator climbed high to the power pole close to Blake's crane. There on its perch, the eagle tore the flesh from the fish, then suddenly jerked up its head. It abruptly flew away, alarmed by the sound of a large semi-trailer that had pulled up beside the containers. Blake relaxed his muscles, ready for action.

Four Asian men wearing long black raincoats jumped out. They looked nervously around the dock before approaching the containers. From under their coats they drew Uzi submachine guns. Upon a signal from the tallest of them, they opened the doors to the containers and moved cardboard boxes from the containers to the truck.

"Now, go, go, and go!" Jamieson's voice blared into Blake's headset.

Blake scrambled out of the small door of the crane cab, hooked the D ring on his belt onto a rope and rappelled down at full speed. He recoiled his knees and rolled on his shoulder when his feet hit the dock. He crabbed his way to a metal drum twenty yards from the gunmen and drew his handgun from its holster, checking the hollow point bullets in the magazine. The faceless shapes of a dozen DEA agents, helmeted, armor-clad and braced with weapons, surrounded the containers and the truck. A police boat in the water beside the dock moved into position.

"This is the Drug Enforcement Agency. Put down your weapons. Come out in the open with your hands behind your head," Jamieson's voice scraped through the megaphone.

Two Uzis stuck out of the container openings. The Asian gunmen opened fire in the direction of Jamieson's voice, the bullets chunking into the concrete, wood and metal.

"All agents, this is Jamieson," his voice rattled inside Blake's headset, "open fire."

A pause like the eye of the storm passed, and then the automatic weapon fire from a dozen agents joined the staccato bursts from the gunmen, the sound careening around the docks like the ricocheting bullets. Suddenly, one of the gunmen emerged from the container, one of his arms around the throat of a young woman.

"No! Help me! Please!" the woman screamed in Cantonese.

"What the hell? Where did she come from?" Redfield yelled.

"Cease fire! Cease fire!" Jamieson barked.

"The hail of bullets stopped. Inside the container, the muted screams of women sliced the silence like a knife scraped on concrete.

"Give us a safe passage to ship offshore," the gunman who was holding the girl yelled, "or we kill all of them."

"You're surrounded. Give yourselves up!" Jamieson bellowed on the megaphone.

"Jamieson, this is Blake. I think they've got a bunch of 'snakes' in the container," Blake said on his headset.

"Bring a boat in and take us to the ship offshore," the gunman yelled, "or we kill all of them, the first one in two minutes."

He dragged the girl back with him to the cover of the container.

Silence. Not even the bleating sound of seagulls.

"What now?" Blake asked.

"You know it's our policy not to negotiate," Jamieson snapped back. "Be ready to lay a cover of flash and smoke grenades, and then hit them."

"Sir, Redfield here. Couldn't we draw them out with their hostages first? Promise them something?" Redfield asked.

"You heard what I said," Jamieson said.

The gunman with his young hostage soon reappeared at the door and looked around for the boat he'd asked for. "Two minutes are up," he yelled.

He leveled his gun at the back of the young woman and fired a burst of three bullets. They ripped through her body, exploding blood and flesh out of her stomach and chest. She collapsed in a floppy doll heap at the gunman's feet. "Five minutes till the next one. Get the boat." He retreated back to the safety of the metal container.

"You bastards," Redfield cursed.

"Keep the air clear for my orders," Jamieson barked.

"Redfield, FQ6," Blake said.

He switched the frequency on his radio.

"We'll catch it for switching frequency," Redfield said, after switching frequency on his radio.

"They'll keep killing more hostages; we have to act," Blake replied.

"What have you got in mind?"

"Give me smoke cover."

"Better check with Jamieson first."

"By the time I get permission, the bad guys will be doing us like prison brides."

"Okay, it's your call."

Redfield threw two smoke grenades on the dock between Blake and the containers. In seconds a thick smoke cloud hung in the air.

Blake raced back to the crane and climbed up into the cab. He switched on the power and pushed the red lever. The crane moved backwards. Blake flipped the lever back. "Now's no time to learn." He flipped the green lever and the crane moved forward along its track toward the containers. He pressed the button with the symbol for the crane's grappling clamps.

Two steel arms descended from the crane toward the first container full of the hostages and two of the gunmen.

"Nothing to this," Blake chuckled to himself.

"Morgan, what the hell are you doing?" Jamieson bellowed into Blake's headphone.

Blake didn't reply, but moved the clamps around the container and pressed the lock button. Then the lift button. The crane clamps grappled the container and lifted it into the air.

A gunman appeared at the container opening and fired a burst at Blake. A bullet hit the cab's metal door and metal shard glanced off Blake's cheek. Blood dripped down his face onto the control panel.

The gunmen's' Chinese profanity melded with the screams of the hostages.

Blake pushed the other lever and the grappling clamps moved the suspended container toward the water.

"Come on, move faster," Blake said to himself.

The screams of the hostages in the container climbed high above the sound of the gunfire as the container swung in the air.

"Get the guys in the boat ready to recover people in the water," Blake yelled, "the container will sink fast."

"Police launch, move in!" Jamieson yelled.

Blake moved the container until it was over the water and lowered it to within several feet of the surface then hit the release switch. The metal box plummeted. The water rushed into the container's open door and it sank. First one, then the other gunman and the female hostages bobbed to the surface, struggling to stay afloat. Seizing the opportunity, the DEA agents on the police launch jumped into the water to save the hostages and subdue the gunmen.

Blake slammed the gears back and the crane rumbled back and latched onto the second container. Before he could raise it, the remaining two gunmen threw down their weapons and came out with their hands in the air.

"Lie face down, with your hands behind your heads!" Jamieson called into the megaphone.

The gunmen lay down on the dock. DEA agents rushed in, cuffed them and dragged them into the warehouse, which served as the command post. Jamieson emerged from cover, his hands on his hips, surveying the action like a proud football coach on the sidelines, barking orders left and right.

Blake rappelled down from the crane, ran over to the edge of the dock where the other agents were fishing the gunmen out of the water. He recognized the man who'd shot the young woman.

"I'll take care of this one," Blake told one of the other agents. He grabbed the soaking wet man and dragged him behind one of the containers. "Tough guy, hey?" Blake spit the words out through clenched teeth. "Like picking on women?" He punched the man in the kidney.

"I give up, I give up," the man screamed.

Blake took his gun and held it against the man's eye. He cocked the hammer.

"No please, please don't kill me," the man said.

"Blake!" Redfield called out from behind him.

"I was just asking him for directions to a good Chinese restaurant," Blake quipped.

Blake released the hammer on his gun and pushed the man toward Redfield. "Take him in."

Redfield pushed him toward one of the other agents. "Take him into the warehouse for questioning," then he turned to Blake, "you'd better come down to the second container. You speak Cantonese."

Blake walked with Redfield over to the second container.

An acrid smell like the one he'd breathed a lifetime ago attacked his nostrils. He stopped in mid-stride. "Get a medical team down here," Blake said.

"It's on the way," Redfield replied.

Blake reached the opening to the second container. "This is the police, you're safe," he said in Cantonese.

A jumble of hushed voices replied. He swept the beam of his flashlight around the small space. Three young teenage girls huddled with their mother, whose eyes were closed as she mumbled a prayer for deliverance. Another dozen thin and sick looking young women scrambled back into the corner along the slimy deck. Then Blake saw the little girl. Half-naked, seven or eight years old, she was clinging to the still body of an adult female.

Blake took off his sweater, put it on the girl, and gently enfolded her in his arms. "Let me look at your mother."

He moved the girl so he could feel the woman's carotid artery. The barest pulse of life coursed there. Grief sliced through him for the child, who leaned against him, shivering.

"We must take your mother away to take care of her. You'll see her later. Come over here," Blake said softly.

He carried the child over to a woman in the opposite corner. "Please take care of the child until the doctor arrives." The woman nodded and held the child.

Blake scanned the container one more time with his light and stopped on the source of the foul smell. A large metal bucket, full of human excrement and urine overflowed onto the metal floor. Blake stifled an impulse to run to the warehouse and kill the gunmen. He imagined putting his Glock to their foreheads and then pressing the trigger, hearing the hammer fall like the sound of his knuckle cracking. Blake stumbled out of the container, ashen-faced.

Redfield found Blake leaning against the metal container. He squeezed Blake's shoulder. "You okay?"

Blake took a deep breath. "Yeah, it just brought back memories."

"They're waiting for us in the warehouse."

The other DEA agents gave Blake good-natured abusive ribbing as he walked in.

Jamieson came over to Blake and put his face close. "You disobeyed orders."

"I stopped a bloodbath out there," Blake snapped back.

Jamieson poked his finger into Blake's chest. "That's your opinion. Now, you listen to me. You may boast a big arrest reputation but I don't need any lone rangers on my team. Is that understood?"

"I got the job done, didn't I?" Blake replied.

"You'll follow orders, or you're off the team!"

"Sure, sure, you're the boss," Blake said. He turned and sat down next to Redfield.

"Alright listen up, everyone," Jamieson's baritone voice bounded around the room. He walked over the white board where he'd written down some notes in point form. "We know that what appeared to be two standard metal containers were unloaded two days ago from the ship, South Ocean, owned by Indonesian business interests and registered in Hong Kong. That ship is now in international waters off our coast. The containers carried about twenty million, street value worth of high-grade heroin. What we didn't know until now is that each container also had fifteen illegal aliens. Many of them were suffering from dehydration, malnutrition, dysentery and heat prostration. Most of the aliens came from Fuzhou in China through Hong Kong to Vancouver, then here. Each of them paid fifty grand each for passage and forged passports."

"Who do the gunmen work for?" one of the other agents asked.

"My guess is Hong Kong triads," Jamieson replied. "We do know the triads in Hong Kong are involved in everything from street crime to international corporate crime. More recently, the Hung Se Ying triad, or the Red Dragon Boys, as they're called, is flexing their muscle. They were established by ex-Division 17 Peoples' Liberation Army soldiers, commandos famous for their work behind lines in the Vietnam War. Their operations have spread from China to Hong Kong to the Netherlands and Canada and now the U.S. These guys are hard cases that like to use heavy weapons. At this point, however, we don't know which triad is beyond the operation we busted."

"I'd like to question our prisoners," Blake said, "I speak Cantonese and Mandarin."

Jamieson stared at Blake and rubbed his chin. "Alright. But watch it."

"I want to talk to two of them separately. Keep the video on," Blake said.

Jamieson nodded and directed one of the other agents to set it up.

Ten minutes later, Blake walked into one of the interrogation rooms. A thin man in his late twenties, dressed in black jeans and tee-shirt, with a dragon tattoo on the back of his hand, sat motionless at the table, his eyes cast downward.

Blake wrapped his body around the table so he could control the man's line of sight. "I'm Agent Morgan, DEA," Blake said in Cantonese, showing his ID badge, "you've been caught red-handed smuggling snakes and heroin into this country. That's fifteen to twenty years in prison. That's U.S., not Hong Kong, prison time." He paused and let the last words hang in the air. "But we could cut a deal."

The man stared at the wall but didn't answer.

Blake slammed his fist on the table. "Did you hear me? The man didn't move or reply.

"Who's behind your operation?" Blake asked.

The man looked up at Blake. "I want a lawyer."

"Sure. You can make your call in a few minutes," Blake said, leaning over him, "first, think about this. If you tell me what I want to know, I'll cut a deal for you. A reduced sentence. Think about it."

The man looked at Blake with renewed interest.

Blake walked out of the room and leaned against the door. He knew he was taking a risk offering him a deal, but he also knew it would be a plea bargaining fest once the lawyers got involved.

Blake walked into the other interrogation room. A stocky middle-aged man with a short hair sat at the table. As soon as Blake walked up to him, the man shot a stream of obscenities in Chinese and English at Blake. This guy may be more manageable, Blake thought, he can't control his emotions.

Blake pulled up a chair and poked his finger at the man. "Listen, I'll say this just once. One of your buddies, next door, may be cutting a deal with us. He said that you ran the operation on this side. He said that his job was only to help the snakes relocate, but you ran the heroin operation. If you take the rap, it's fifteen to twenty years, hard-time in prison."

The man leaped out of his chair. "He's a liar!"

Blake leaned back in his chair. "Sit down and take it easy. Now why don't you tell me the truth?"

"They'll kill me."

"Look, good soldiers aren't stupid. You think your buddies will give a shit about you once you're in the joint? You think they'll take care of your family?"

The man crossed his arms and looked down at the table.

"If I have to, I'll go with what your buddy told me. So you can rot in prison for all I care." Blake got up and started to walk away.

The stocky man pounded his fist on the table. "My job was only to deliver the women and heroin."

"Your word against his. I need to know who ran the whole operation."

"Okay, okay. You'll get me a reduced sentence? Maybe witness protection after?"

"That'll depend on what you tell me."

The man slumped in the chair. "Simon Fung and the Hung Se Ying triad in Hong Kong ran the operation."

"Go on."

"Heroin is the real deal, the snakes are just cover."

"Anyone else involved other than Fung?"

The man hesitated. "A *gwai-lo* is a silent partner."

"Who?"

"He's in the CIA."

"The U.S. Central Intelligence Agency? You sure?"

"I saw him meet with Fung from a distance. Fung said later he was in the CIA."

"What's his name?"

"I . . . I don't know . . . Fung didn't say . . ."

Blake grabbed the man by his hair and slapped his face. "Tell me his name!"

"Get away from me!" the man screamed, blood streaming out of his nose.

"Morgan, come out here!" Jamieson's voice boomed over the loudspeaker.

Blake angrily looked at the loudspeaker and then walked out of the room back to Jamieson.

"I haven't finished with him yet," Blake protested.

Jamieson jabbed his finger in Blake's chest. "You're no super cop. You're part of a team and you've crossed the line back there. Now pack up your gear and clear out. We'll finish up."

Blake glared at Jamieson and then picked up his gear and walked out, motioning with his eyes to Redfield to follow. Together they walked to Blake's car.

"Why do you always have to push so hard, do it your way?"

"Hey, I thought you were on my side," Blake said.

"That's why I'm saying this," Redfield replied, "I've worked on a dozen cases with you and you always want to do it alone."

"I get results, that's what counts."

"One day you'll turn around and you won't have anyone to back you up."

"I watch my own back."

"Damn it, Blake, stop being such a hard case. I don't know why I even give a crap about you."

Blake slapped Redfield on the back playfully. "Because I'm always right."

"What are you going to do now?"

"Go back to Los Angeles and wait for my next assignment."

Redfield shook Blake's hand. "Keep your head up, buddy."

"I know, and my back to the wall."

Redfield smiled, turned and walked back to the warehouse.

Blake got into his car and looked at himself in the rear view mirror. He touched the dried blood on his cheek and glanced into his narrowed eyes. The enemy within, he thought. We win the battles, but the generals don't want to win the war.

12

Blake had returned to his condo in Los Angeles and was still ruminating over the Seattle case, when he received a call from Redfield.

"Blake, you won't believe this."

"What?"

"Those Asian drug traffickers that we busted were just released."

"You mean they made bail?"

"No, they were never charged."

"What? That's crazy. We got the evidence and their confessions."

"Jamieson told me that the CIA declared them as assets and granted them immunity from prosecution."

"Not again."

"What's that?"

"The same thing happened to me in Costa Rica. What was the reason given?"

"National security. Apparently, they were part of an organization that keeps watch on the Chinese government."

"That's bullshit. What did Jamieson say?"

"He was pretty pissed. Said he'd file a complaint, but he's close to retirement; I don't think he'll make waves."

"Sounds familiar."

"So what are we going to do?"

"Career advancement has never been a burning issue for me. I'm going to see someone in the DEA's Internal Affairs."

"I know a good man, David Quinn. He was a field agent for almost thirty years."

"Will he listen?"

"I think he's a straight shooter."

"It's worth a go. Well, thanks for calling."

"No problem. Be careful, Blake."

Blake put the telephone down; still astounded that The Company would interfere in two DEA operations. He'd made a decision. He couldn't turn a blind eye to the damning evidence pointing to someone corrupt in The Company and possibly the DEA. He was determined to talk to Quinn in Internal Affairs. He was just finishing that thought when the telephone rang again. He picked it up.

"Hello, Blake Morgan."

"Blake, this is Harvey Cezak. I want you to come down to my office right away," the voice at the other end said.

"Sure. What's up?"

"We'll talk about it when you get here."

Blake hung up, got in his car and drove to the DEA's regional offices in the financial district. He walked through the reception area and stopped at the door marked "Harvey Cezak, Regional Director, Drug Enforcement Agency." Blake knocked on the door.

"Come," a youthful voice answered from within.

Blake walked in and stood before Cezak's desk.

Harvey Cezak was a youthful looking thirty-eight, a thin man, dressed immaculately in a dark blue suit and white shirt, his hair and nails neatly trimmed. Cezak had a law degree and had been promoted quickly, having had little field experience. Blake recognized him for what he was, a man whose sights were on his next job.

"Sit down, Blake," Cezak said.

Blake sat in a chair across from Cezak and looked expectantly at him.

"I've been talking to Scott Jamieson and I'm a bit concerned about you," Cezak continued.

Blake continued to make eye contact with Cezak but said nothing.

"Nothing we haven't talked about before. You wanting to act alone, not following proper interrogation procedure, forgetting you're part of a team . . ."

Blake held up his hands. "I'll save you the time. Guilty. But I get better results than many of your so-called team players."

"Times have changed, Blake. The focus now is on team cooperation. We can't risk having loose cannons, regardless of how successful they've been."

Blake stared at Cezak. "Did you hear about what went down in Seattle?"

"Yes, it was one of our most successful busts."

"I mean the bullshit about The Company letting those criminals go."

Cezak pulled at his shirt collar. "It might not turn out that way. I've been talking to people in The Company and Justice Department about it, trying to impress upon them the importance of this case and . . ."

"Is The Company going to rescind the immunity from prosecution order and let us nail those bastards?"

"Well, that hasn't been worked out as yet."

"I thought so."

Cezak cleared his throat. "Well, that's out of our hands now, but that's not what I wanted to talk to you about. You've banked a lot of vacation time and I think it would be a good idea if you took a big chunk of it."

"I just took a vacation."

"I'm ordering you to take a six-week vacation. And during that time I want you to think carefully about what I said about being a team player. If you don't take the vacation time, there's a good possibility you'll be spending the balance of your career filing reports."

Blake leaped out of his chair, put his hands on Cezak's desk and stared down at him menacingly. "You're the boss, you make the decisions. I'll take the vacation time. But don't ever make the mistake of threatening me again."

Cezak looked up at Blake with fear in his eyes.

Blake turned and walked out the door, slamming it behind him.

A few minutes later, Blake had found the offices of the DEA's Internal Affairs, two floors above Cezak's office.

"Agent Blake Morgan to see David Quinn," Blake said to the receptionist.

"I'll tell him you're here," the young receptionist said. She walked back to the offices and returned a minute later with a tall woman in her late thirties with long blond hair and azure blue eyes, alabaster skin and a sensual mouth. Behind her came a short, stout man in his late sixties with gray hair and a beard and gray sparkling eyes.

"Mr. Morgan, I'm Angela Townsend, Special Prosecutor," the blond woman said, "and this is David Quinn, Director of Internal Affairs."

Blake shook hands with both of them. He found himself momentarily staring at Angela, taken aback by her physical beauty and presence.

"Let's go to my office, Mr. Morgan," Angela said.

"Blake, please," Blake replied.

She led Blake and Quinn back to her office. Blake found his eyes resting on her shapely buttocks and legs as she walked in front of him. Angela sat down at one of the chairs at the coffee table and Quinn sat beside her.

Blake sat down across from them after looking around the office, taking note of Angela's degrees from Harvard and Columbia Law School on the wall. Why would an Ivy League law graduate want to take a low paying job as a prosecutor, Blake wondered? His eyes wandered for an instant from the wall back down to Angela's legs. He looked up and his eyes met hers and she smiled. Then Blake realized Quinn had been talking.

"What can we do for you, Agent Morgan?" Quinn asked.

"First, tell me the status of our conversation and the actual power you have," Blake said.

"Internal Affairs investigates any allegations of misconduct by DEA employees. After our investigation disciplinary action and or prosecution could follow. The most common cases we deal with involve bribes or involvement in drug trafficking," Quinn replied.

Blake knew the answer to his question but he wanted to watch Quinn as he spoke. "And what does Ms. Townsend do?"

"I'm a Special Prosecutor assigned by the Justice Department to go after the money launderers," Angela said.

"I've worked for thirty years for the DEA and only recently have we targeted the real criminals—the banks and businesses that make the drug business possible," Quinn said.

"And government agents?" Blake asked.

"Them too, although there's a natural reticence to look for rot in your own house," Quinn said.

"Do I detect a note of skepticism, Blake?" Angela asked.

Blake liked that she was direct and to the point.

"I've found being skeptical has kept me alive all these years," Blake replied, "Being a whistleblower is not a popular occupation."

"You don't strike me as someone who cares about popularity," Angela said.

Blake laughed. "Next question. This discussion is off the record unless I say when we're finished, it's on the record."

"Are you here to negotiate or to give us some information?" Angela asked curtly.

Quinn reached over and touched Angela's arm. "Whichever way you want it, Blake. But if you say it's on the record, you could be subpoenaed as a witness."

Blake looked into Quinn's eyes for a moment. "On my last assignment in Costa Rica we busted an American rancher named Richard Bull for trafficking drugs and weapons. He confessed the operation was run by the Ramirez drug cartel in Mexico," Blake said.

"Sounds like a successful bust," Quinn said.

"Millions in cocaine and weapons. I returned to Los Angeles fully expecting that Bull would be extradited back to the U.S. for prosecution. Then I got a call from my station chief in Costa Rica, Robert Gates, who told me Bull had been declared a

Company asset and given immunity from prosecution," Blake said.

"Immunity?" Angela asked.

"What did Gates give as the reason?" Quinn asked.

"He said Bull was an important source of information for The Company regarding terrorist and insurgent groups in Central America," Blake said.

"Do you think someone in the DEA may be involved as well?" Quinn asked.

"Don't know, but he and the Costa Rican government were obviously cooperating with someone in The Company," Blake replied.

"Anything else you can tell us?" Quinn asked.

Blake nodded. "I've just returned from an assignment in Seattle. We busted a huge operation of heroin and illegal alien smuggling run by a man named Simon Fung and his Hong Kong triad, the Hung Se Ying.

"It sounds like it was another successful DEA operation," Angela said.

"Started out that way. During my interrogation of one of Fung's men, he said that someone in The Company met with Fung in Hong Kong. Before I could get more detail I was cut out of the loop for what my boss said was improper interrogation," Blake said.

Quinn nodded.

"When I returned to Los Angeles, I got a call from another agent who worked the Seattle case with me. He told me that Fung's men had been released because The Company had declared them assets and given them immunity from prosecution," Blake continued.

"My God, why?" Angela asked.

"I was told, national security. Something about Fung's men being important sources of information inside China," Blake replied.

"So what did you do?" Angela asked.

"I got put on a forced vacation for my improper interrogation and then I came directly here," Blake replied.

Quinn and Angela looked at each other, then at Blake, and a few moments of silence followed.

Quinn stood up. "Could you excuse us for a few moments, Blake?"

"Sure, I'm in no hurry," Blake replied.

Angela and Quinn left the office and returned a few minutes later.

"Are you willing to testify?" Quinn asked.

"What are you offering me?" Blake asked.

"Meaning?" Angela asked.

Blake smiled. "I need to know what I'm getting myself into. Am I going to be the sole witness for some attempt to prosecute someone, or will I be part of an inter-agency investigation. What protection can you offer me once I've exposed myself?"

"You seem like the kind of man who does the right thing despite the risks, Blake, or have I read you wrong?" Angela snapped.

"You don't know me well enough to judge what kind of man I am, Ms. Townsend," Blake said curtly.

Angela didn't respond, but looked at Blake intently.

"It's a fair question," Quinn said, "maybe this will help. We're currently investigating reports that someone is involved in laundering drug money. Your testimony would give us another piece to build our case."

"What are you going to do?" Blake asked.

"We're going to meet with some people in The Company and the Senate Committee on Intelligence Activities to get some allies before we take the step of full exposure or prosecution," Quinn said.

"Won't you be tipping your hand?" Blake asked.

"We believe there are some people we can trust, who'd want to ferret out any corruption," Angela said.

"What do you want me to do?" Blake asked.

"First, agree to make your story on record. Second, come with us to Washington and take part in the meetings that I referred to," Quinn replied.

Blake paused, letting his eyes scan Quinn's and Angela's for a few moments. "Agreed. In return, I want you to share with me all the other evidence you've got—and don't give me any of that need to know crap."

Quinn nodded. "Agreed. We're leaving for Washington tomorrow. Angela will give you the details and the information you want." He stood up and shook hands with Blake. "Welcome aboard, Blake. And now if you'll excuse me, I've got another appointment." Quinn walked out of the office.

"I think you've made the right decision," Angela said.

"That remains to be seen, Ms. Townsend," Blake replied.

"Angela, please."

"Angela."

Blake felt surprised by her sudden warmth. He guessed that she'd been testing him. The same thing he would have done.

"I'll bring the files with me so you can read them on the plane. Have you ever been to Washington?"

"Years ago."

"I love it. The energy, the culture, the restaurants. Different feeling than New York or Los Angeles."

Blake eyes quickly glanced at her law degree on the wall. "I see you lived on the East Coast for a while."

"Columbia was great and I practiced briefly for a New York law firm, but I got bored. This is more exciting."

"You like excitement?"

A slight blush appeared on Angela's cheeks. "I like challenge and this job is that and more." She stood up. "You'll have to excuse me, Blake, but I've got a lot to do before we leave. I'll arrange for a car to pick you up in the morning." She shook hands with Blake. "I want to thank you personally for agreeing to help us."

Blake shook Angela's hand, letting his eyes rest for a moment on her bright blue eyes. He realized he was still holding her hand when she withdrew it self-consciously.

"Until tomorrow then," Blake said.

He left the office feeling better about his decision to blow the whistle on The Company and confident about Quinn's and Angela's motivations. And he felt particularly good about meeting Angela, a feeling that he'd not had about a woman in a long time.

Blake returned home to his condo and packed his things. After he was finished he picked up the telephone and dialed.

"Sabrina, it's Blake. How are you doing?"

"Oh Blake, it's good to hear from you. I'm okay, but I'm worried about Raymond. The police still haven't come up with a suspect for Wang Chan's murder and Raymond's getting more agitated every day. He's neglecting Chan Enterprises and canceling social engagements."

"I was afraid of that. I wish I could do something to help."

"You could accept Raymond's offer to join Chan Enterprises and come home."

"I'm still thinking about it, but my hands are full right now."

"With what?"

"My last two assignments have uncovered government corruption. I'm working with some people in the DEA to do something about it. That'll keep me here a little while longer."

"Please finish that as soon as possible and come home. Raymond needs you. I need you."

A silence passed for a few moments.

"Tell Raymond that I called. Take care of yourself, Sabrina."

"Come home safely, Blake."

Blake hung up and sat down on the sofa, thinking for a few minutes. Then he picked up the telephone and dialed again. "Inspector Lai, please." He waited for a few moments.

"Peter, this is Blake Morgan. I called to see how the Wang Chan investigation is going."

"No suspects so far, Blake. We've interviewed all his current and past known business associates. The problem is that Wang Chan did a lot of business off the record," Lai said.

"Oh, you're back to the business with the triads."

"We have a witness who saw Wang Chan meet with Simon Fung the head of the Hung Se Ying triad. We've prosecuted some Fung's street dealers in the past, but we've never been able to get Fung."

"Simon Fung? We busted some of his men in Seattle for running a heroin and illegal alien smuggling operation."

"Is the U.S. government going after Fung?"

"No, and his men were declared assets by The Company and given immunity from prosecution."

"That doesn't sound right."

"An understatement . . . so can you tell me anything more about Wang Chan and Fung?"

"Nothing other than their meeting."

"Well, I should tell you that if you don't come up with a suspect pretty soon, Raymond's probably going to private sources to find Wang Chan's killer."

"You can tell him—no, I'll tell him myself—that I don't want any interference in our investigation."

"He's got a legal right to hire a private investigator. I might even be inclined to do it myself."

"I don't want any interference."

"Results would solve the problem."

"Did you call me to apply pressure or get information?"

"Pressure. And to make an offer to help when I return to Hong Kong."

"The offer's duly noted."

"I'll be seeing you soon, then."

Blake hung up the telephone. Lai's voice showed his growing frustration and tension over the case, Blake thought. He was sure Lai was getting pressure by his superiors and the thought of an unsolved case could be a disaster for his political ambitions. And the mention of Fung's name caused the little hairs on Blake's neck to stand up on end.

13

Seated in the middle seat between Quinn and Angela on the flight to Washington the next morning, Blake read through most of the information that Angela had given him about the money laundering investigation.

He put the file folder down. "I've never been good at reading or writing reports. Tell me about your work."

"Did you know where the term money laundering came from?" she asked, her eyes sparkling.

Blake shook his head.

"Back in the glory days of the Mafia, it chose Laundromats to get rid of their dirty money because it was a cash business."

"Something like casinos today."

"Exactly. Meyer Lansky, the mob's accountant, was the first to develop ways to launder illegal money. He discovered the Swiss numbered bank account."

"And I thought Swiss watches drove their economy."

Angela laughed. "What's surprising is that it's only in the 1980's that our government has taken steps to stop money laundering."

Blake nodded, fascinated by Angela's animated expressions.

"Money laundering is now a global problem, estimated at half a trillion dollars annually," she continued.

"Could you outline for me how money laundering works?"

Angela took out a pen and paper, drew a circle with three dots on it. "There are three stages. The first is placement, where illegal money is smuggled out of the country and placed in a bank, financial institution or business in a foreign country. Step two is layering or the attempt to conceal ownership by creating complex layers of financial transactions designed to disguise the audit trail and provide anonymity. Layers are created by moving the money in and out of offshore bank accounts of shell companies through electronic transfers or through complex transactions in stocks, commodities or futures brokers."

"Can't that be traced?"

"The volume of these transactions is so huge, it's virtually impossible to monitor them all."

"What's the third part?"

"Integration. The money is integrated into legitimate businesses or cleaned by the establishment of anonymous companies in countries where secrecy is guaranteed. The companies then grant themselves loans from the laundered money or send false export-import invoices overvaluing goods or make electronic transfers to legitimate banks back in our country."

"What a job to police all that!"

"You may have heard of the Justice Department's operations called Mule Train, Risky Business, Skymaster or Juno. They all targeted money launderers."

"Were they successful?"

"Partially. We face enormously complex problems such the lack of cooperation by foreign banks and the countries themselves who make profits on the dirty money deposits and even the complicity of some of our own institutions and businesses."

"I know what you mean: the enemy within."

"But we can't give up the fight."

"Well, for what it's worth, I admire the work you're doing."

Angela touched Blake's arm. "It means a lot."

"Can you fill me in on who we're meeting in Washington?"

"First, we're going to meet with Jack Cross, Deputy Director of Covert Operations for The Company."

"Into the dragon's lair?"

"He was my father's commanding officer in Special Forces for years. Jack is a highly decorated Vietnam veteran.

I've known him since I was a child."

"And you think he'll help us?"

"I believe he'd want to root out any bad apples in The Company. And that's our objective, isn't it?"

"And the other meeting?"

"We're meeting Senator Bryce Connor, Chairman of the Senate Intelligence Committee. He'd have the say on appointing a special investigator or holding hearings."

"You know much about him?"

"He's an ambitious and powerful senator despite his youth. Some say he has ambition to be President. But he's annoyed the administration and some veteran bureaucrats on the hill. Our read on Connor is that he's prepared to launch hearings if there's evidence."

Blake looked over at Quinn who was asleep, his head drooping down on his chest. Blake reached over, pushed the recline button on Quinn's seat and gently pushed it back all the way, took his blanket and covered him.

"He's a good man," Angela said. She was sitting beside Blake, dressed in a royal blue suit. Its color made the blue of her eyes like a tropical lagoon.

"I respect his courage and dedication. Is he like your father?"

She nodded. "My father's dead. He was away a lot in the forces, but when he was home, we had the best of times."

Blake reached over and held her hand. She looked up and smiled at him.

"And your mother?" Blake asked.

"She died last year of cancer. She was never the same after dad died."

"I'm sorry. Were you close to her as well?"

"She was more like a sister. We did everything together."

"Any brothers or sisters?"

"I'm an only child . . . what about your family?"

"Both my parents are dead. I have an adopted brother. But I'll leave that story for another time."

"I'd really like to hear it."

The Captain of the plane came on the cabin speakers announcing the plane's descent into Washington. His voice awakened Quinn.

"Are we there yet?" Quinn asked sleepily.

Blake laughed. "Yup, and you slept most of the way."

"Give me some slack, Blake, when you're my age, you'll need a little extra rest too," Quinn replied.

"You're secret is out. That's how you stay so sharp," Blake said, laughing.

The Central Intelligence Agency's Headquarters are located in Langley, Virginia, a short drive from the Capitol. Double chain-link fences stopped with barbed wire surround the CIA's compound. Each segment of fence is fitted with a tiny black plastic box, part of a system that sounds an alarm in the Office of Security's duty office when the fence vibrates.

Quinn steered the rental car into a separate lane upon entering the grounds, where a sign told them to drive up to a post equipped with an intercom and a closed-circuit video camera. He leaned out of the window and talked into the intercom. "David Quinn, Angela Townsend and Blake Morgan. We have an appointment with the Deputy Director of Operations."

A voice from the intercom said, "Your Social Security numbers?"

Quinn read off the numbers and a long pause followed.

"Pull up to the main guard gate," the intercom voice replied.

Quinn pulled the car up to a concrete and glass structure twenty-five feet beyond the intercom. A guard came out.

"Identification please," the guard said.

Quinn handed him picture identification for the three of them, which the guard examined along with their faces very carefully. Then the guard gave Quinn three visitors badges, a parking permit with a map and a form giving the CIA the right to search the visitor, for each of them to sign.

"If you're carrying any firearms, they'll have to be left here before you enter the building," the guard said.

Blake felt for his Glock inside his jacket. "Okay." He handed the gun to the guard, who had Blake sign a receipt.

Quinn then drove the car into the main parking area. Quinn, Blake and Angela got out of the car and walked through one of the fifteen doors at the main entrance of the new million square foot building with its green tinted glass into a large lobby of gray and white marble. Along the left wall was a statue of William J. "Wild Bill" Donovan, former director of the Office of Strategic Services, or OSS, as it was known, the forerunner of the CIA. On the wall beside the statue was a large inscription: "And ye shall know the truth and the truth shall make you free." Along the other main wall were more than fifty gold stars flanked by an American flag on the left and a flag with the seal of CIA on the right. Each star represented a CIA officer who had died in the services of the agency.

They walked up to the receptionist. "We have an appointment with Mr. Jack Cross," Quinn said.

The receptionist examined her computer screen, looked carefully at Quinn, Blake and Angela, then picked up the telephone and spoke to someone. Within a few minutes a young man in a blue suit came out of the elevators and joined them at the reception counter.

"Mr. Quinn, Ms. Townsend, Mr. Morgan, please follow me," the young man said.

They followed the young man to a turnstile where he inserted his identification card and punched in several numbers.

"Now please insert your visitor cards into the slot before you walk through the turnstile," the young man said.

They followed his instructions then he led them past armed guards to the elevators.

"Just remember to insert your visitor cards in the turnstile when you leave," the young man said in a businesslike but friendly voice.

After a short elevator ride, he led them to a meeting room into which he gained entry with his security card and punched numbers.

"Please make yourself comfortable; there's coffee, tea and water on the sideboard. Deputy Director Cross should be with you shortly," the young man said. He turned and left the room.

Blake, Angela and Quinn poured themselves a coffee and sat down at the table. A single green tinted telephone sat on the table at the end. The room was decorated in muted beige tones and had no windows.

They sat quietly until Cross entered, wearing a dark blue suit.

"Angela, it's good to see you again. You look wonderful," Cross said, warmly embracing her. "It's been a long time, but I hear you're doing a great job for the DEA."

"Too long, Jack, and thank you," Angela replied. "You look great, you never seem to age." She turned to Quinn and Blake. "I'd like to introduce you to David Quinn, Director of Internal Affairs, and Blake Morgan, a DEA agent."

"It's a pleasure, David, Blake," Cross replied, shaking their hands. He sat down at the end of the table by the telephone. "Your first visit here?"

"Yes, it's quite impressive," Blake said.

"We've renovated the original old building and connected it to the new one. Even then, this complex is a lot smaller than N.S.A.'s, or the puzzle palace as it's called by some," Cross said.

"Still, compared to our facilities, this is gigantic," Quinn said.

"Our job has gotten bigger and more important over the years, David. Our intelligence agencies are the most important part of America's defense and foreign policy," Cross said.

Blake looked over at Angela and noted the look of admiration in her eyes. "I'm amazed how big The Company and other intelligence agencies have become without much knowledge by the general public."

"Best to leave our business to the professionals, don't you think?" Cross replied, smiling, "but that's a topic for another day. You wanted to discuss something with me?"

"Is this off the record?" Quinn asked, glancing at Blake.

Cross shook his head. "Nothing is off the record here."

"The DEA is currently investigating drug money laundering and has received reliable reports that someone in The Company is interfering in DEA cases," Quinn said.

"Reliable reports, not just low-life traffickers turned informants trying to protect their sorry asses?"

"No, people like Blake Morgan here," Quinn replied.

Blake's eyes met Cross' for a long moment.

"Go on," Cross said.

"Knowing your dedication to The Company we felt you'd want to see any corruption ferreted out," Angela added.

"So we'd like to know if you would initiate an internal investigation," Quinn said.

Cross nodded. "First, give me some details."

Blake took a sip of his coffee. "On my assignment in Costa Rica we busted an American rancher, Richard Bull and confiscated a huge shipment of cocaine and weapons. He confessed that the operation was run by the Ramirez drug cartel in Mexico. We were about to extradite Bull back to the U.S. for prosecution when someone in The Company declared him an asset and granted him immunity from prosecution."

"Do you know why?" Cross asked.

"Apparently, he's a valuable source of information for terrorist and insurgent groups in Central America," Blake replied.

"That would make him a valuable asset," Cross said.

"Maybe, but he's a drug trafficker," Blake replied.

"Did you know anything about this?" Quinn asked.

"Even if I did, David, I couldn't discuss it with you," Cross replied. "Is there anything else?"

"My second personal experience happened in Seattle," Blake continued. "I was involved in a DEA team that busted a huge heroin and illegal alien smuggling operation run by a man named Simon Fung and his Hung Se Ying triad in Hong Kong. One of Fung's men that we arrested told us that someone in The Company had met with Fung in Hong Kong. And once again, Fung's men were declared Company assets and given immunity from prosecution."

"Why?" Cross asked.

"We were told they provided valuable information about the Chinese government," Blake replied.

"You sure this informer wasn't just trying to save his butt by seeing what would stick to the wall?" Cross asked.

"The point is that these guys were smuggling millions worth of high-grade heroin and two containers full of illegal aliens. How can information be worth that?" Blake replied.

"These are very serious allegations. If we could find out who in The Company may be guilty of misconduct or worse, we'd clean house," Cross said firmly.

"Meaning?" Quinn asked.

"That would depend on what we found," Cross replied.

"But we just told you what we found. What more do you want?" Blake snapped.

Cross stared at Blake.

"And if we went ahead with our investigation ourselves?" Quinn asked.

"Do you really want inter-agency warfare? That publicity would hurt both of us," Cross replied.

"I think the important thing that I hear you saying is that The Company would do something," Angela interrupted calmly.

Blake looked at Angela. She's too anxious to exonerate The Company because of her personal feelings for Cross, he thought.

"I can give you my word that I'll do my best to find who in The Company has gone astray and do something about it," Cross said, "but give me some time before you act."

"Well, we can't give any promises that would tie our hands, but we appreciate your cooperation," Quinn said.

Cross looked at Angela and smiled. "Thank you for coming to me first." He picked up the green telephone and punched two buttons. "You'll be escorted out."

Blake and Quinn got up and shook hands with Cross and Angela embraced him. The young man who had escorted them to the room appeared and led them back to their car.

"So how did that go?" Blake asked after Angela had driven the car out of the CIA complex and back toward the Capitol.

Quinn put his fingers to his lips, took out a piece of paper and wrote on it the words "car could be bugged," and showed it to Blake and Angela. They nodded.

"As well as I could have expected," Quinn replied, "At least Cross wasn't antagonistic."

"We've got a few hours before our next meeting," Angela said.

"So let's eat, that's what I was thinking," Blake said.

Quinn and Angela laughed.

When they reached their hotel, Angela parked the car and Quinn motioned them to walk to an open area in the hotel parking lot.

"You really think Jack would have the car bugged?" Angela asked.

"Maybe not him personally, but it's the kind of thing The Company does," Quinn replied.

"I took him at his word. I think he wants to help," Angela said.

"Or he wanted to give the appearance of doing so," Blake said.

Angela shot him an irritated look.

"Either way, I'm not prepared to just drop the whole matter and wait forever for the results of The Company's internal investigation," Quinn said, "I still want to meet with Senator Connor."

"Let's eat first. I know this wonderful Italian place. We can walk from here," Angela said enthusiastically.

"Lead on McDuff, or should I say Lady McDuff," Blake quipped.

Angela laughed and playfully smacked Blake's arm with her notepad.

"Let's return the car to the car rental for another one," Quinn said, "just in case."

Angela and Blake nodded and walked back to the car.

After a leisurely lunch, they drove to the Senate building and met with Senator Bryce Connor, Chairman of the Senate Committee on Intelligence Activities. They were escorted into Connor's offices where they waited for a few minutes before he walked in.

Bryce Connor was a man of medium height in his late thirties, with chiseled, handsome features, sparkling Irish green eyes and thick black hair. His Hollywood good looks and a charismatic personality had helped to propel him into a successful political career. He'd made a name for himself by aggressively expanding the scope of his committee's investigative powers, sometimes at the embarrassment and displeasure of the White House.

"Mr. Quinn, Ms. Townsend and Mr. Morgan, it's a pleasure to meet you," Connor said in a thick Boston accent. He shook hands with them. "You said on the telephone this is a matter of some urgency," Connor said, pouring a glass of water.

"We believe so, Senator," Quinn said, "we have reliable evidence that implicates someone in the Central Intelligence Agency in laundering drug money and interference with DEA cases," Quinn said.

Connor's eyes opened wide. "You've identified specific people in The Company?"

"Not yet," Quinn replied.

"And you're prepared to testify to my committee?" Connor asked.

"If I thought the testimony would lead to finding out who in The Company is responsible, yes," Blake said.

Connor rubbed his chin thoughtfully for several minutes. "Mr. Quinn, the last time we talked, you said there's a history of the CIA crossing the line. Can you elaborate?"

Quinn nodded. "When I worked for the Office of Naval Intelligence or ONI as it was known, during World War II, I found out that Meyer Lansky and Lucky Luciano, famous Mafia bosses, were asked by the ONI to assist it in fighting the Communist-leaning unions on New York's waterfront docks. In return, Luciano was paroled from prison and deported to Italy, where he proceeded to build up his criminal organization. After the war, our government allowed Luciano to return to New York, where he rebuilt his criminal empire. Lansky settled in Cuba to run mob activities there and support Cuban dictator, Juan Batista. When Castro came to power, Lansky returned to Miami to run the mob rackets."

"Are you saying, Mr. Quinn, that the U.S. government worked with known criminals?" Connor asked.

"I'm saying that the ONI had a cooperative relationship with Luciano and Lansky for the avowed purpose of fighting Communism," Quinn replied.

"Go on," Connor said.

"After we began our investigation into the current matter, I decided to do some more historical research. I interviewed retired General Maurice Montagne, former head of the SDECE, the equivalent of the CIA. Dubbed Operation X, the French intelligence service controlled most of the opium trade in IndoChina in cooperation with Corsican gangsters. The SDECE financed most of its covert activities in the region in this manner," Quinn said.

"How does that relate to the CIA?" Connor asked.

"Montagne told me that when France left IndoChina, The Company took over the SDECE's assets and pursued the same policies," Quinn said.

A look of mild shock passed over Connor's face.

"My research revealed that in 1968-69, Company assets opened a cluster of heroin labs in the Golden Triangle. The Hmong tribes in Laos loaded opium on The Company's Air America planes to supply U.S. troops in Vietnam. In a secret report by The Company's Inspector General in 1972, he admitted that The Company turned a blind eye to the drug trafficking because the heroin drug lords were useful in the fight against Maoist communists," Quinn said.

"So you're still talking about people not directly employed by our government?" Connor asked.

"We know that huge quantities of heroin and opium were smuggled into South Vietnam during the war, with the assistance of high-ranking officers in the South Vietnamese Army, some of whom later become prominent political figures," Quinn replied, "and by 1971, according to the Pentagon report that I read, almost thirty percent of American troops in Vietnam were addicted to heroin."

Connor poured himself a glass of water and took a sip. "So you're saying that The Company was involved in supplying heroin to our troops?"

"There's evidence to show that The Company had working relationships with known drug traffickers such as the KMT and the Hmong tribes and that a Company proprietary company, Air America, was involved with the South Vietnamese armed forces in transporting large amounts of heroin," Quinn replied.

"Was proof of this provided to the proper authorities?" Connor asked.

"Yes. In 1971, the DEA sent a team of agents to Laos. Upon their arrival, they were prevented from conducting their investigations by the U.S. Embassy, The Company and the Laotian government," Quinn replied, "and our army's Criminal

Investigation Division uncovered incriminating evidence that South Vietnamese armed forces officers were drug traffickers. These reports were sent through channels to the U.S. Embassy in Saigon, which took no action."

A heavy quiet filled the room, with only the sound of Angela's pen drawing small circles on her notepad, breaking silence.

"Even if all this is true, and I must admit, I'm somewhat taken aback, that was a long time ago, Mr. Quinn. Is there anything more recent?" Connor asked.

Quinn nodded. "A few years ago, an Australian Federal policeman named Dobson stumbled across a dead body in the desert. It belonged to Frank Regis, CEO of the Regis Prescott bank. His partner was Michael Prescott, a former Company man. It turns out that Dobson was already investigating them for laundering drug money."

"Did the police move in on the bank?" Connor asked.

"Too late. Prescott and about five billion dollars in bank assets disappeared. And Regis' death was ruled a suicide, even though Dobson swore that he'd been murdered," Quinn said.

"What happened to Dobson's investigation?" Connor asked.

"He was removed from the case. The Australian FBI, called the ASIO, took over the investigation, claiming it was a matter of national security," Quinn said, "but Dobson persisted on his own. He found out that The Company had pressured the ASIO to intervene, which wouldn't have been the first time it had exerted its influence in Australia," Quinn said.

"What do you mean?"

"I found out from one of Dobson's associates that years before, the Australians had elected a left-leaning Labor Party as the government under their leader, Roger Wilson. He was immediately in The Company's bad books because he withdrew Australia's support for the Vietnam War, and publicly confronted The Company over the Pine Gap surveillance base in Alice Springs," Quinn said.

"Our allies don't always agree with our policies, Mr. Quinn," Connor said.

"Yes, but listen to this. The Governor General at the time, a man named John Farr, who had worked with the OSS and had close ties to American intelligence, used a little known technicality to dissolve Wilson's government and appoint the opposition party which was friendly to The Company," Quinn said.

Connor's eyebrows rose. "What happened to Dobson's investigation?"

Quinn shook his head. "Dobson was found dead, floating in his swimming pool. Police ruled it a suicide. All his evidence disappeared."

"These are serious allegations, Mr. Quinn. What would prompt The Company to do these things?" Connor asked.

"Good intentions gone awry," Quinn replied, "when President Truman created The Company, he gave it a clear mandate to stop Communism. But the fear of Communism became the excuse for unprincipled covert intelligence activities. The people who had been given the public trust for intelligence began to believe that they no longer had to justify their actions. They believed that they were a law unto themselves," Quinn replied.

"Since the collapse of the Soviet Union, and the decline of the Cold War, hasn't the Communist threat disappeared?" Connor asked.

"That's true, Senator, but now terrorism and the perceived threat of so-called rogue nations have replaced it," Quinn said.

"So how does all this tie in with your present investigations?" Connor asked.

"It's my belief," Quinn replied, "that a mindset of misguided patriotism, of an ends justifies the means philosophy, has pervaded The Company and perhaps other intelligence agencies, a belief that in the fight against America's enemies and the protection of our national interests, working with criminals is justified."

Connor stood up and walked to the window. "And you want to tell this whole story to my committee?"

"No, but you wanted me to provide background to the current situation," Quinn replied.

"Which is?" Connor asked.

"Blake Morgan can outline two recent incidents," Quinn said.

Blake nodded. "The first is in Costa Rica. We busted an American rancher there named Richard Bull. We confiscated a large cache of cocaine and weapons. He confessed to ties to the Ramirez drug cartel in Mexico. We were about to extradite him back to the U.S. for prosecution, but The Company stepped in, declared Bull an asset and granted him immunity from prosecution."

"Why?" Connor asked.

"I was told that he was a valuable informant regarding terrorist and insurgent groups in Central America," Blake replied.

Connor scratched his head. "And the second example?"

"A few days ago in Seattle we broke up a heroin and illegal alien smuggling operation run by a Hong Kong triad. Our interrogation revealed that someone in The Company had been seen meeting with Simon Fung, the head of the triad. Before we could pursue prosecution, The Company takes declared these men assets and granted them immunity from prosecution," Blake said.

"Why?" Connor asked.

"I was told they too were valuable informants inside China," Blake said.

"Don't you think that's too much of a coincidence?" Quinn asked.

"My experience with our intelligence agencies has taught me they may be involved in things which on the surface look fishy," Connor said, "but . . ."

"But this doesn't smell right?" Blake said.

"How can the DEA do its job if it's being compromised?" Quinn asked.

"I see why you have your suspicions," Connor replied.

"We'd like to get an indication from you regarding your willingness to pursue further investigation of The Company if we provide evidence and testimony," Quinn asked.

Connor sat down again. "I can give you this assurance. My committee will be prepared to subpoena anyone to testify who can shed light on any intelligence agency misconduct. I'm sure I don't have to tell you that's a difficult task sometimes because of the national secrecy laws."

"We understand that, Senator, but we feel encouraged that you support our effort to bring the light of day on any misconduct or corruption," Angela said, "and I might add in fairness to those honest and dedicated people in The Company, they'd want to clean out the rot as well."

"I'm sure that's true, Ms. Townsend. We can talk again to set up a possible timeline for your testimony before a closed session of my committee. Of course, you'll provide some documented evidence for me to review first," Connor said.

"Certainly," Quinn said, patting his briefcase.

Connor looked at his watch. "If you'll excuse me, I have a meeting to attend. I appreciate very much your dedication and candor." He shook hands with Quinn, Blake and Angela, and showed them to the door.

Outside they stopped on the Senate offices steps.

"Well, how did it go?" Blake asked.

"I was encouraged by Senator Connor's response. If his committee is on our side, it'll make our job a lot easier," Angela said.

"We have to remember that he's a politician with aspirations for the White House. I think he'll be prepared to hold the hearings but I'm not sure he wants a nasty fight with The Company," Quinn said.

"So I'm to testify?" Blake asked.

"Yes, and we'll submit all the other evidence that we have," Quinn said, "and I might just have something which exposes this shadow in The Company," Quinn said.

"What's that?" Blake asked.

"An undercover cop named Pantages claims he can identify someone in the Company who is laundering drug money in an off-shore bank," Quinn replied.

"If he's legitimate, this would boost our case immensely," Angela said.

"I've arranged to meet him at the Holiday Inn off the Maryland Turnpike in a few hours," Quinn said.

"You want us to come with you?" Angela asked.

Quinn shook his head. "He insisted that I come alone. I've agreed to pay him if his evidence pans out."

Blake looked at his watch. "In a couple of hours I'll be hungry again. Why don't we have dinner together?"

"You two go ahead, I'll join you after my meeting with Pantages. Hopefully, I'll have some good news by then," Quinn said.

"Sounds good," Angela said, "I know this great French restaurant, Chez Michel, just a few miles from our hotel. You know where it is David?"

Quinn nodded.

"Why don't you come by my room about seven, Blake?" Angela continued.

Blake scratched his head. "French restaurant. That sounds fancy, so I guess I should wear my one and only suit?"

"I'd offer mine, but I don't think it would fit," Quinn said.

14

Back in his hotel room, Blake poured himself a Vodka on the rocks, sat in the overstuffed sofa and reflected on the meetings with Cross and Senator Connor. It was obvious that his discovery of misconduct or criminality in The Company was not a single isolated incident. Blake hoped that Quinn's meeting with Pantages would give them more than a case of interference with the DEA's investigations. Blake took a short power nap, and then got up, showered and put on his dark suit. He chuckled to himself as he changed his tie for the third time. And then he walked over to Angela's room.

Blake knocked on Angela's hotel room door, holding a single rose behind his back that he'd taken from the vase in his room. When she opened the door, Blake stood in teenage shock with his mouth open. Angela was wearing a black dress with a plunging neckline. Her hair was done up and her neck was simply adorned with a gold chain.

"You look very dashing in your one and only suit," she said, looking appreciatively at him.

"I wear it for weddings and funerals and now, for special dates," he quipped, then handed her the rose.

"Thank you, Blake, that's sweet of you." She leaned over and kissed him lightly on the cheek.

The feel of her warm breath on his face made Blake's heart speed up.

She grabbed a small vase from the counter, put some water in it and placed the rose on the coffee table. "Deep red, my favorite color."

"The hotel seemed to know that," he said impishly. He helped her put her coat on, his hand lingering for a moment on the bare flesh of her neck.

The brief taxi ride brought them to an old building with a brick façade. Inside, the warm of woven carpets on brick floors, old wood and white linen table cloths completed the intimate ambience. They were greeted enthusiastically by the head waiter, who showed them a small table in the corner by the fireplace. Angela ordered a bottle of French red wine and then the waiter quietly disappeared into the background.

"You said that you'd tell me about your family history. Do you mind?" Angela asked.

Blake hesitated for a moment. "I was born in Hong Kong. My father, Trevor, a Welshman, was in the Hong Kong police force and my mother, Alicia, was a Mexican-American from California."

"Now there's an interesting combination. How did they meet?"

"I don't want to bore with a long story."

Angela reached over and touched his hand with hers. "I'm not bored . . . Please?"

"My father ran away from my abusive grandfather when he was fifteen. He stayed with his aunt until he was sixteen and then he joined the British Army, lying about his age."

Angela leaned forward toward Blake, in rapt attention.

"After basic training, he was shipped to Palestine and spent seven years in police action."

"This is fascinating," Angela said, her eyes sparkling.

"He got tired of the military, retired from the army and took a job in the Hong Kong police force."

"I would have loved to have met your father. He sounds like he was a courageous and independent man—like you."

Blake smiled. "He was a great man . . . but I never got to grow up with him."

"I'm so sorry. What happened?"

"Here's the rest of the story. My mother's family was originally from Sonora, Mexico, where a lot of Spanish people settled. Mexicans from there look a lot more European. Her mother and father settled in San Diego, where she grew up. My mother was a warm, loving woman, but very frail. She seemed to give away her life force to others. Everyone who knew her loved her."

"How did she end up in Hong Kong?"

"She worked for a travel promotion company. She was in Hong Kong on business. One night while she was eating at a restaurant, my father walked in. He sat down at the table next to hers and casual conversation led to several dates the next few nights and then father proposed. She accepted."

"Love at first sight. Do you believe in that?"

Blake looked intently into her eyes. "It's one of those things you can't prove other than by asking the people it happens to."

Angela looked thoughtfully at him for a few moments. "How did you lose your parents?"

"My parents and I were prisoners of the Japanese in WW II. My mother died while escaping from the camp with me. She was very ill from disease and malnutrition. My father was killed helping us to escape."

A tear formed in Angela's eye. "I'm so sorry. That must have been horrible for you as a child.

"Many people don't understand this, but as a child, the experience was often surreal. I still played games with the other children, with sticks rather than toys and we made faces at the Japanese guards just like they were the postman or newspaper boy."

Angela leaned back holding herself with her arms.

"I remember that I used to pretend I was on watch for my father and the other camp leaders. I used to crawl through a hole in the wallboards of our hut onto a beam on the roof and watch."

"Watch what?"

"The guard changing, the trucks delivering food supplies and the camp commandant, Colonel Yakishita, beat the hell out of one of the soldiers in Kendo practice every morning. Of course, the soldiers never dared to hit back."

Blake took a sip of his wine and stared into the glass. "And I remember the daily roll call. Every day at noon, the two thousand prisoners in Stanley camp had to line up and be counted, called the *tenkos*. We stood there, often in the blazing sun for hours, until *tenkos* was done."

"And you were there for four years?"

Blake nodded. "This one time is burned in my brain forever. We lined up on a brutally hot day with high humidity. I was standing with my mother and father, playing in the dirt. Our captors took their time. They liked to use the sun and heat to torture us. Then suddenly a voice cried out, *Keirei!* the Japanese word to bow. And then the voice yelled, *Naore!*, which meant we all had to straighten up."

"And if you didn't?"

"You were beaten or rifle-butted if you didn't lower your eyes and look at the ground when they passed."

"Oh my God, I had no idea."

"To finish my anecdote, in comes Colonel Yakishita with his officers, all wearing shiny riding boots and sword, called *katanas*. They climbed up on a platform in front of us to supervise the count and make speeches. Yakishita bellows this out on the microphone: 'You are all enemies of the great Nippon Empire. It is only through the goodness of the Emperor that you are housed and fed. You have no home, no country and no religion. You must be obedient, polite and self-disciplined. It is your duty to work hard. If you do not do these things, you will be punished.'"

"You remember the words?"

"Only because of what followed. When the roll-call was completed, seven prisoners were missing. Yakishita ordered an immediate search of the camp and we had to wait. About twenty minutes later the guards dragged the seven men in front of Yakishita. He told us the men had tried to escape during roll call and that the punishment would be immediate execution."

"In front of everyone?"

Blake swallowed hard. "The guards forced the men to kneel on the ground and the officers took out their *katanas* and cut off the prisoners' heads. I stood there, no more than twenty feet away, watching their bodies twitch."

"Oh my God, they made the children watch?"

Blake nodded. "But the full impact of what I saw hit me many years later. I remember my father telling me that our Japanese captors were butchers, not *samurai*, as they liked to think of themselves. They didn't consider us human and worthy of respect because we had surrendered. According to their code, we should have committed *hara-kiri*—suicide---despite the fact that we were civilians."

"I don't know how you survived all that," Angela said, with tears in her eyes.

"Survival against great odds gives you a great inner strength, but in a way it also makes you more detached from people."

"I really want to hear more, Blake. Can you talk about how your mother and father died?"

A lump formed in Blake's throat and he looked away. "I don't know."

"I've got to take a bathroom break. Can you think about it?"

Blake stood up and watched Angela walk to the restaurant washroom. He was surprised that he'd opened up so much to her. His mind flashed back to the time of the father's and mother's death.

Flies buzzed relentlessly around Blake's face. Sometimes, he just got tired of swatting them and he let the filthy creatures land. "Father, how much longer will we be in this place?"

"Not much longer if I can help it," his father, Trevor, replied.

Blake and his father walked along the barracks past women and men dressed in mere strips of rotting clothing with broken teeth, tufts of hair growing on bald heads and huge boils and ulcers on their legs. Trevor picked Blake up in his arms and walked back toward their quarters, humming a Welsh lullaby. Blake loved to hear his father's velvet lilting voice. He nuzzled his head in the crook of his father's muscular neck, closed his eyes, and swayed in time with the motion of Trevor's step and the beating of his strong heart. After a minute, Trevor put Blake on his feet and pointed to a large hut.

Blake tried to imitate his father's long stride. A larger dust cloud devoured the little dust clouds that billowed around Blake's little bare feet. Reddish-black shadows fingered their way across the compound toward the huts. His father reached back and pulled Blake beside him with strong, wide hands.

"What are we going to do?" Blake asked.

"We're going to take your mother out of the infirmary and back to our quarters."

"Can't they help her here?"

"No. And they won't allow the English doctors to treat her."

Trevor held Blake by the shoulders and looked into his eyes. "Just remember, most of the people in here are dying. Only great love or great hate will save them now."

Tears welled in Blake's eyes. "Can't we get Mum some medicine?"

"There's little medicine for prisoners. So I'm trying to buy some on the black market through Ballantine, the camp trader."

The giant shadows of dusk painted the huts a filthy brown. The infirmary's windows and doors were shut, despite the sweltering heat. Hand in hand, Blake and his father walked up the stairs into the infirmary.

Blake saw his mother, Alicia, lying on the floor mat against the wall. He ran to her and embraced her tightly. He could feel the protruding bones and burning skin.

"You shouldn't have come," Alicia said weakly. She was a petite Mexican-American with large liquid brown eyes and smooth olive skin. Her once lustrous black hair was gray and lifeless; the skin on her cheeks a sickly pallid color, the bright spark flickering in her eyes.

Blake's father kneeled down close to her, his eyes full of love. "I'm taking you out of here."

Trevor lifted Alicia's gossamer body into his arms and walked out of the infirmary, Blake in tow, holding his mother's hand. Once inside their hut, Trevor quietly led them to the corner of the hut that was their home. He laid Alicia down gently on the blanket that was their bed, asked Blake to turn around and then changed her soiled garments for clean strips of cloth.

"Alicia, if you stay here any longer, you'll die," Trevor said softly, "your only chance is to escape. I know when the soldiers have their guard down. We can do it." He enfolded her in his arms.

"Go on," she said weakly.

"The guards are most relaxed every other morning when the supply trucks arrive. The gates stay open when the Chinese workers are unloading the trucks and the guards are busy dickering black market purchases. You and Blake will dress as Chinese workers as best you can. Your skin color is close and Blake's is dark from the sun. Your small bodies will fit in."

"What about you?" Alicia asked.

"I'm not going with you," Trevor answered.

Alicia grabbed Trevor and held him tightly. "No. We always said we'd stay together, no matter what."

Trevor gently stroked her cheek. "The only way I can guarantee that you and Blake will escape is by creating a diversion across the yard. In a few weeks, I'll make my escape. I've arranged for you to stay with Wang Chan's family until I come to get you. He owes me a big favor."

"I don't have the strength to fight you," Alicia said weakly, collapsing back on the blanket into sleep.

Trevor stroked her brow gently.

"You must help me get ready, son," he said, gripping his arm.

Blake met his father's eyes like a man, but inside he still felt like a boy.

Two days later, they made their escape.

Blake and Trevor held Alicia up as they moved along the shadows of early morning toward the supply hut. They stopped and flattened themselves against the rear wall. Alicia was moaning deliriously.

"Everything's going to work out fine," Trevor said.

"Won't the Chinese workers give us away?" Blake asked, full of apprehension.

"Don't worry, they're loyal to Wang Chan," Trevor replied.

Blake was shaking. "I'm afraid."

Trevor embraced Blake. "Fear is good, son, it gives you an edge, as long as you don't let it swallow you up."

"We'll be fine dear," Alicia said thinly, "go now."

Trevor embraced them, kissed Alicia and Blake and melded into the shadows.

In a few minutes, the sky was alight with the morning sun and Blake heard the trucks pull up and the voices of the soldiers and the workers. The soldiers didn't bother to inspect the goods or crates and burlap sacks, but were anxious to get on with their black market purchases. Suddenly, Blake heard Sergeant Tanaka's high-pitched shout and his father's baritone Welsh voice.

"You yellow scum, that's the last time you'll put your boot on me," Trevor bellowed.

The guards posted by the supply hut ran to toward Trevor and Sergeant Tanaka.

"Now, Blake," his mother said.

Blake helped his mother into the supply hut, unnoticed. From behind the sacks of flour Blake and his mother changed into the loosely fitting clothes, sandals and hats that his father had left for them. Two of the workers entered the hut carrying big baskets of produce, dropped their load and ignored Blake and his mother. They followed the workers back to the truck. The short walk seemed like the length of a football field to Blake. He felt his mother's muscles sag with each step. He tried to lift his mother up over the tailgate onto the truck. And failed.

"I can't, I'm not strong enough," Blake cried out.

"Here, I'll help you," a voice came from behind Blake. A medium height man in his mid-thirties appeared.

"Are you Wang Chan?" Blake asked hopefully.

"Yes, now, help me lift her. Hold her head," he replied.

Together, they lifted Alicia onto the truck. Blake jumped up and helped his mother to the front behind the driver's cab and covered them with empty burlap sacks.

"We made it so far, mum," Blake whispered, hugging his mother. But her eyes were closed. He fumbled to feel her neck and found a weak pulse. The truck suddenly lurched to a start and stopped momentarily at the gate and then gained speed. Blake heard the guards closing the gates behind the trucks. He was shaking uncontrollably, fear sucking at his insides like the tentacles of an octopus.

Blake counted under his breath to thirty and then lifted the sacks covering him to look back. Through the wooden slats of the truck's sides, he saw Sergeant Tanaka lying on the ground with his own katana impaled in his chest. Beside Tanaka, Blake's father was on his knees, held by two soldiers while a third repeatedly rifle-butted him. And then they dragged him away. As the truck picked up speed, Blake saw only the blurring strands of the barbed wire fences between the wooden slats of the truck. He reached out with his arm, clenching his fist to hold onto his father. He let the tears come but swallowed his deep sobs so his mother wouldn't hear.

For the next half-hour, the truck lurched and bumped its way through the Stanley Gap Road toward Hong Kong Central. Blake periodically checked on his mother, who remained asleep. Her pulse was weakening and her breathing got shallower. Panic suddenly smothered Blake. He pounded on the cab roof to get Wang Chang's attention. The truck pulled over to the side of the road and Wang Chan got out. He waved the other trucks on and then climbed onto the back of his truck.

"What is it boy?" Wang Chan asked, looking around nervously.

"My mother's very sick," Blake replied.

Wang Chan felt her pulse and touched her burning skin. "We've got to get her to Dr. Yang, fast."

Wang Chan jumped back into the cab and drove the truck at high speed into the city. He parked it in an alley with leaking water pipes and makeshift electrical wires criss-crossing above. Blake helped Wang Chan carry his mother through the alley door of a rotting building. They emerged into a dark room lit by a bright light over a table. They placed her on it. An old man with a long white beard walked into the room. He nodded to Chan and looked at Blake.

"What's wrong with her?" the old man asked.

"Camp fever," Wang Chan replied, "see what you can do for her."

The old man examined Blake's mother, checking on her breathing several times. He turned to Wang Chan and Blake and shook his head. "I'm afraid you're too late."

Blake threw himself on his mother. "No, she'll be alright, she's just asleep." He shook her. "Mum, wake up, wake up!"

Blake slumped to the floor, sobbing, still holding his mother's hand.

Wang Chan grasped Blake's shoulders. "Boy, listen to me. I owe your father a great favor. I've agreed to take you into my family until he can join you. Now, we must go. Life is for the living."

Blake barely heard his words. The pain of his mother's death had cleaved his soul. And little did he know he was all alone now.

"Blake, are you alright?" Angela said her hand on his shoulder. "You look a bit pale."

He looked around him and realized he was still in the restaurant in Washington. He took a big drink of water.

"Memories. Maybe one day I can tell you. All I can say is that they were both killed when we escaped from the camp."

"I understand . . . And you were left alone?" she asked, holding his hand.

"I was taken in by a Chinese businessman, Wang Chan, who helped me and my mother escape. He was in debt to my father. So I was officially adopted and became a brother to his only son, Raymond."

"Thank God, you became part of family again."

Blake nodded and paused. "Tragically, Wang Chan was murdered a few weeks ago."

"Oh no, I'm sorry."

"Sometimes I think a black cloud follows me."

"I'm sorry if I dredged up painful memories."

"That's alright. You know, I've never talked to anyone like this before, except to Sabrina."

"Sabrina?"

"Sabrina Chan, my sister-in-law. She was with me in the POW camp. Her name was Sinclair then."

"It sounds like you two were very close."

"We promised to get married when we grew up. Never worked out that way . . . she married my brother, Raymond."

"Considering what you've gone through, you . . ."

"Don't sound paranoid?"

"I was going to say you're incredibly grounded and strong."

Blake looked down into his glass. "Except for the nightmares."

Angela looked at him expectantly.

"About a dragon chasing me, trying to kill me. I've gone to a therapist. He says the dragon is in me . . . but, ah hell, that's another dinner conversation." He refilled Angela's wine glass. "But that's enough about me, let's talk about you."

Angela leaned back and sighed. "Give me a moment to recover from what you've told me . . . well, let's see, nothing as exciting as your life. I grew up in Montana, a cowgirl."

"Funny, with your tailored suits and polished manner, I can't see you on a horse."

"There's more to me than meets the eye, Blake," she said softly, "I'm as comfortable riding a horse as riding a bench in the courtroom. Because I had no brothers and my father was in the Marines and away a lot, I learned to be top hand with horses, cattle, mending fences, digging wells . . ."

"A lot of male kind of things."

"Funny, a penis never seemed to be a requirement to get the job done. Just like it isn't now."

"Ouch! I didn't mean . . ."

Angela laughed. "I know, I just wanted you to know you won't get away with any sexist remarks . . . I think you'd love Montana, Blake. There's a peace to the wide open spaces that's good for the soul."

"I'm a city boy, but I'd like to go there some day."

"I'll take that as a promise."

"How did your father die if you don't mind me asking?"

"He died of a heart attack during a field training exercise. It's the way he wanted to go. I'll never forget the long rides he'd take me on. Just the two of us in the open country."

"Your mother didn't go with you?"

"She had a bad back and couldn't ride."

"Did she suffer long before she died of cancer?"

"No, thank God. Liver cancer. But watching her in pain was horrible."

Blake looked deeply into her eyes. "Seems like we have a lot in common . . . So tell me why a man hasn't snared you yet."

Angela laughed. "There you go again. I'm not the kind of woman who gets snared. Besides, I'm told I scare them off. Either way, I haven't found one that I could see as a partner."

Blake winked. "So the field is still open."

"Ah . . . yes," she stammered.

Angela looked at her watch. "I don't mean to break this wonderful conversation we've had, but I don't understand why

Quinn's not here. He was on his way to meet Pantages, and he said he'd join us directly."

"Give him a call."

Angela took a cellular telephone from her purse and called. "No answer. I'm worried, Blake."

"Where are they meeting?"

"At Pantages hotel, the Holiday Inn, about a half hour from here."

"Let's go."

Blake left some money on the table, and they left the restaurant.

15

The clerk at the desk put down the telephone. "Mr. Pantages doesn't answer."

Blake took out his identification case. "DEA. Give me the key to his room."

The clerk handed him a key. "Yes sir. Room 115, first floor, at the end of the parking lot."

Blake and Angela walked outside and through the parking lot toward the end of the building. A few feet from Pantages door a tall man in a dark overcoat burst out of the room and jumped into a car parked directly in front. The car suddenly accelerated and came directly at Blake and Angela. The high beams of the car's headlights blinded Blake momentarily.

"Angela, look out," Blake yelled. He knocked her onto the ground and rolled with her out of the path of the car. Blake looked up to see the car race out of the parking lot. He noticed the car had no rear license plate.

Blake and Angela lay on the pavement in a heap, panting heavily.

"Are you alright?" Blake asked, still holding her in his arms.

She looked up into his eyes. "You saved my life."

"Instinctive." He helped her up. "Could you see who that was?"

"It was too dark and he was moving too fast. But he came out of Pantages' room."

"Let's see what he was running away from."

Blake approached the door of Pantages' room cautiously, keeping Angela behind him. He wished he thought of packing his gun. He reached inside to the wall by the door and flipped on the light switch and then walked in.

On one of the beds lay a man with a bullet hole in his head, his blood soaking the bedspread. In his outstretched hand was a handgun. Beside him was a duffle bag partially opened, with a white powdered substance in a plastic bag cut open.

"Oh my God!" Angela said when she saw the body.

Blake took out a handkerchief from his pocket, examined the body for vital signs, and then took out the man's wallet. "It's Pantages and he's dead . . . don't touch anything." Blake tasted a sample of the white powder. "Cocaine."

Angela walked around to the bed and froze. "Oh no, it's David!" she exclaimed.

David Quinn was lying on the floor in a pool of blood, his hand clutching a handgun. Beside him, a briefcase full of money lay open.

Blake came over and checked Quinn's body for vital signs and shook his head. Angela sat on the bed and burst into tears. Blake came over and held her tightly.

After a minute, Angela took a big sigh. "I'm okay now." She looked around the room. "I don't see Quinn's briefcase with all the evidence," she said.

Blake and Angela searched the room.

"If he brought it here, it's gone," Blake said.

Angela looked at the dead bodies. "I have to go outside." She stumbled out the door and leaned on the wall outside.

Blake put his arm around her. "Breathe deeply."

"Quinn would never have been involved in any drug deal," she said.

"It's too perfect, with the drugs and cash and the police will probably find their guns killed each other. Their deaths and the drugs are a cover for the theft of his evidence."

"Who would do such a thing?"

"You know anything about this informer, Pantages?"

"David kept that information to himself."

"Pantages must have had something a lot more damaging to The Company than anything we've got so far."

"I just wish I knew what that was."

Blake looked at Angela intently. "You didn't tell Cross or Senator Connor about David's meeting with Pantages?"

An angry, hurt look crossed Angela's face. "No, and if you're insinuating that Jack would have anything to do with this . . ."

Blake held up his hands. "Someone obviously knew where to find him and knew that the evidence that Pantages and Quinn had, was dangerous."

A silence fell between them for a few minutes.

"We'd better call the police."

Angela leaned against Blake. "I still can't believe this is happening."

He put his arm around her and held her for a few minutes, then went inside and called the police.

After an hour of police interrogation, Blake and Angela returned to their hotel.

"Please come in for a while," she said, opening the door to her room, "I'm still a bit shaken."

"Sure, I'll make us both a drink," Blake replied.

She threw her coat and shoes off, and curled up on the sofa, holding herself and rocking back and forth.

Blake checked the mini-bar. "Vodka okay?"

"Fine, anything."

He poured two drinks, sat beside her and handed her a glass.

She took a long drink. "I've seen lots of action in the courtroom, but the reality of violence up close . . . I still can't believe that Quinn is dead." Tears welled in her eyes.

Blake put his drink down and held her, gently rocking her in his arms.

"You're so calm about all this," she said.

"It's not that I don't care. But I've seen so much death and violence in my life. I guess I try to keep at arms length to maintain my sanity." He brushed her cheek with his hand. "You should probably rest."

She finished her drink and put the glass on the table and then looked into Blake's eyes. "I'd feel safer if you stayed with me tonight."

Blake pushed the sofa cushion with his hand. "It's comfortable. Give me a few minutes to change."

"Take the room key," she said, pointing to the table by the door.

He walked to the door and stopped, looked back and smiled. "I'll be right back. Lock the door behind me."

Blake returned to his room to collect his toothbrush and change into a sweat suit. He took his gun and a spare ammunition clip from his suitcase and returned to Angela's room. He knocked, and then opened the door with the key. "Angela, it's Blake."

There was no answer, but the noise of the shower came out of the partially open bathroom door. He saw Angela's naked body as she climbed out of the shower, wrapped a towel around herself and walked out of the bathroom. She straightened up, surprised, and then smiled when she saw Blake.

"I didn't mean to startle you. I called out but you probably didn't hear me," Blake said.

"It's alright. I'm still a bit jumpy."

"Would you like another drink?"

"Love one," she replied, walking into the bedroom.

Blake walked to the mini-bar and poured two glasses of Vodka with ice, and walked back to the bedroom, knocking lightly on the door.

"Come in," Angela called out.

She was lying in bed, the sheets pulled up to her neck.

Blake sat on the bed beside her and handed her a drink. "To better days."

She touched her glass against his. "Better days."

A few moments of silence passed.

She took his hand in hers. "I'll never forget that you saved my life." She pulled him towards her and kissed him passionately on the mouth. He took the two glasses and placed them on the bedside table and returned her kiss with equal passion.

"I want you here with me," she whispered.

Blake pulled the sheets from her. The silver light of the moon through the window glinted off Angela's naked body. She tore at his sweat suit while kissing him deeply. Blake's slow moving hand brushed her cheek, her lips and neck, and then rounded her shoulder as if he were drawing her in silhouette. His lips touched hers, his tongue sliding softly into her mouth so that as she inhaled, she breathed him in deeply. His lips traced the line of her neck down to her uplifted breasts. She moaned and ran her fingers through his hair. Angela pulled herself up onto him and then slowly crashed back down. Blake arched his back and groaned sharply, the veins and muscles in his neck and arms distended. She clawed at him with her frenzied nails. Their cries together were choked and primitive. And then suddenly, there was lightning, white, hot, jagged. They collapsed the sound of their rapid panting splitting the quiet of the room.

Blake awoke early the next morning, rolled over in bed and looked at Angela's graceful, naked back and her thick blond hair cascading down over her neck and shoulders. He lightly touched her neck with his lips and she moaned softly in her sleep.

He quietly slipped out of bed into the bathroom, showered, dressed and ordered room service. Twenty minutes later he answered the knock on the door, his hand on his gun behind his back. He tipped the waiter in the hallway, rolled the service cart into the room and locked the door. And then he quietly rolled the cart into the bedroom beside Angela. He poured a cup of coffee and held it close to her nose.

"Room service ma'm," he said.

She opened her eyes. "Ummmm, that smells good."

She sat up, the sheet falling off of her to expose one of her naked breasts. She self-consciously pulled it up. "You give good room service."

He laughed, his eyes following the lines of her body beneath the sheet. "Fruit, toast, yogurt."

She leaned over and kissed Blake. "I'm ravenous," she said, helping herself to a bowl of fruit and yogurt.

Blake watched her with amusement.

"Did last night happen, or did I dream it?" she asked.

"It was no dream . . . but listen, I understand that you need to feel safe and . . ."

"I wanted you to stay. It wasn't gratitude or fear."

Blake smiled.

"I've thought about what we should do," Angela said, "we'll return to my office in Los Angeles. I'll try to retrieve the copies of Quinn's files."

"Sounds good. Have you got a spare room in your place?"

"Yes, why?"

"I'd like to stay with you; I think it would be safer. But I don't want you to think I'm suggesting . . ."

"Oh, thank you, Blake. I was going to ask you that. And no, I don't have any expectations."

"Good! Well, I'll let you get dressed and pack."

Blake leaned over and kissed her lightly on the lips and returned to his room. While he was packing, his mind was flooded with a visual replay of the spontaneous love-making with Angela. But it wasn't just the sex. Life just felt better when he was with her.

16

After Blake and Angela returned from Washington that evening, Blake grabbed a few things from his place and settled comfortably into the spare bedroom of Angela's townhouse in Redondo Beach.

As was his custom, he arose about five-thirty a.m. the next day. The dawn bathed his bedroom in a cool, blue light. He took one deep cleansing breath and then dragged himself to the edge of the bed. Blake's fingers traced the line of two scars, a jagged one on his freckled shoulder and the other, a thin red line along his jaw. The price of years of field work. He walked over to the closet and threw on a sweat suit and running shoes and quietly left the townhouse, careful not to awaken Angela sleeping in the next bedroom. He ran down to the ocean walk and found a small patch of grass.

He placed his feet shoulder-width apart and with bent knees, raised both hands in front of his chest, as if he was embracing a tree. With each successive deep breath a sound unfolded from the pit of his stomach like wind racing through a deep cave. A warm glow rolled from the center of his palms, moving outwards until his mind's eye saw ice-blue sparks leap between his hands. He moved gracefully with his arms and legs to the left followed by the "grasping of the bird tail" movement and the remaining movements of the short Yang form of Tai Chi. And then he swung silently to his resting position and bowed to the sun.

Invigorated, Blake ran back to Angela's place. He quietly returned his room and decided to make a few telephone calls before he showered. He picked up the telephone and dialed.

"Hello, Sabrina? It's Blake."

"Oh Blake, it's so good to hear from you," the voice at the other end said, "I'm worried about Raymond. The police still haven't come up with any suspects for Wang Chan's murder and Raymond is getting more agitated every day. He's neglecting Chan Enterprises and cancelled his social engagements."

"I was afraid of that. Can't you talk to him, calm him down?"

"I've tried. He avoids me and when we do talk, all he talks about is revenge. He refuses to discuss our reconciliation."

"I know it's difficult for both of you."

"It's like ten years of my life have been taken away from me."

"But both of you have told me there were good years."

"I know that. I'm referring to the divorce settlement. I agreed to the prenuptial thinking we'd never split up. Now I think it's grossly unfair, given the fortune that Raymond has inherited."

"Can't you renegotiate?"

"He refuses to discuss it."

"I don't know what to say."

"I feel so alone, Blake. Can you come back soon?"

"I'm involved in an important case right now. It turns out that my last two assignments in Costa Rica and Seattle have uncovered possible CIA connections to laundering drug money."

"The CIA? You've got names and witnesses?"

"We're still working on it. In Seattle, one of the men we arrested worked for Simon Fung's Hung Se Ying triad. You heard of him?"

"Only what I've read in the newspapers . . . so now what are you going to do?"

"Angela and I are going to try to take what we've got to the Justice Department and maybe the Senate Intelligence Committee."

"Who's Angela?"

"Angela Townsend, Special Prosecutor for the DEA. We're working closely together."

"How closely?"

"We have a good working relationship . . . why do you ask?"

"Oh, no reason. Listen Blake, I'm sure your work there is very important. But Raymond is in a bad way and needs you. And I need you too. Please come home as soon as you can."

"Be patient, I'll see you soon."

Blake hung up the telephone feeling disquiet about his conversation. Now he was as concerned about Sabrina as he was about Raymond. Her voice had sounded so weak and thin, like a child's, despite her effort to sound strong. He sat on the floor, letting his mind wander back to the time when they were children together in the POW camp.

The dome of the orange sun shattered the night sky's black tranquility. The chatter of insects faded into the shadows as a breeze carried a whiff of the heat that would soon engulf the camp. Rainbows flashed on a dragonfly's wings as it darted and devoured a mosquito bloated from its night-time feast. The smell of dying flesh drifted like a fog across the prison camp.

Blake sat on a large wooden beam just below the jutting corner of the roof, his long spindly legs tucked beneath his prepubescent body. Dirty smudge marks framed his blue eyes and unkempt strawberry blond hair.

A large two story building and a dozen wooden huts, remnants of an abandoned prison, spread out over a rocky peninsula, surrounded by the sea on two sides. A barbed wire fence interspersed with guard towers encircled the camp and a single road connected it to the city of Hong Kong. The soldiers' huts and the large commandant's quarters stood close to the entrance gate. The fence swung down to the water to the south where a series of boards had been built over the water to serve as toilets.

Three flatbed trucks with boarded sides rattled up the camp entrance. The guards opened the gate and waved the trucks through to the supply shed. Five Chinese "coolies" dressed in greasy singlets and black baggy shorts unloaded provisions under the watchful eyes of the guards. The driver of the first truck, in his mid-thirties, talked to Sergeant Tanaka, the highest

ranking non-commissioned Japanese solider, or "toad," as Blake
and the other children in the camp called him because of his
bow-legged swagger. The driver and Tanaka talked to each
other, waving their arms and then Tanaka slapped the driver on
the back and bellowed with laughter. The driver bowed,
unsmiling and then retrieved a package from the truck. Tanaka
handed him an envelope.

"Whatya doing, Blake?" a melodic child's voice called
out from behind Blake.

Blake spun around. A young girl knelt behind him, her
big green eyes sparkling. The morning sun glinted on strands of
her dirty auburn hair.

"Sush, Sabrina! I'm on watch," Blake replied.

"Watching what?"

"It's stealth."

"What's stealth?"

"It's watching others without being seen."

"Teach me, Blake, teach me."

Blake puffed himself up to look bigger. "You're too
young and it's too dangerous. Besides, this is work for men, not
girls."

"You're a boy."

"I'm much older than you," Blake snapped. He waved
his hand. "Don't bother me."

She twisted the braids in her hair with her fingers. "Oh
please, Blake, please."

"Oh, alright, but don't make any noise and do everything
that I tell you."

"I promise, Blake, I promise."

The soldiers in the compound jumped to attention when
a small, bald man with a Hitler-like mustache, wearing riding
pants and leather riding boots, emerged from the Commandant's
quarters.

Blake recognized Colonel Yakishita swagger. "My
father says he walks like that American actor, John Wayne."

"Who's John Wayne?" Sabrina asked.

Blake rolled his eyes upward.

A soldier followed Yakishita, teetering under a mountain of *Kendo* gear. They stopped in an area lined in a square with white stones. Yakishita and the soldier donned their *Kendo* padding and helmets and took up their bamboo swords. After a ceremonial bow, Yakishita attacked the other man, smashing him with his sword on the shoulders and head. The soldier parried defensively, but did not strike an offensive blow. After twenty minutes of retreating under Yakishita's blows, the soldier collapsed. The two bowed again and then Yakishita threw his pads at the soldier. He strutted proudly back to his quarters, the soldier stumbling behind him with the heavy load of gear.

Blake swung his arms with an imaginary *kendo* sword to simulate a head strike. "I'd smack him but good."

"Yeah, I bet you'd kill him," Sabrina said.

"Okay, that's enough for today," Blake said abruptly.

"But I just got here . . . please let me stay."

"Do as I say or you can't come back."

Sabrina whined a little and then turned around and climbed back down into the space between the walls. Blake scrambled after her. They climbed through the loose wall boards and exited into the prisoners' quarters. Most of them were still asleep on the hard floor without blankets.

"Walk like I taught you. That's stealth," Blake whispered.

Sabrina reached up and kissed him on the cheek and giggled. "I'll see you at roll call."

Blake wiped the kiss off of his cheek and watched her rice paper walk that left no marks or sound. His eyes followed her little thin body until she reached her father who was still asleep on the floor, and then Blake climbed back through the wall opening to his favorite spot that he called his Eagles' Perch, to continue his watch.

The sound of a dog barking loudly outside shook Blake from his remembrance of the POW camp. He took a shower, dressed and went into the kitchen. He had cut up some orange slices when Angela walked in wearing a royal blue terry towel bathrobe.

"Good morning, Blake, have you been up for a while?" she asked.

Blake smiled. Even though Angela had no makeup on, she looked radiant. "I'm an early riser. I've made coffee and fruit. Do you want an omelet?"

"Thanks, Blake, just some yogurt, fruit and coffee would be great." She sat down on the stool at the kitchen counter and her robe fell away from her leg, revealing bare flesh up to her hip.

Blake glanced at her leg, their eyes met and they both smiled.

"I feel so much safer with you here," she said.

Blake took her hand and kissed it. "I am your willing servant."

She laughed. "You may regret that offer."

"I doubt it . . . so what's your plan?"

"I'm going to go through all of Quinn's files and computer records."

"I'm set to go. I'll wait for you to eat and dress. Twenty minutes?"

"Blake! Do I look like a man? I've got to shower, put my makeup on. Forty minutes is the best I can do."

"Sorry," he said, looking down at her exposed leg again, "and you definitely don't look like a man."

She reached over and playfully smacked his shoulder.

Blake laughed heartily like he hadn't laughed in a long, long time.

Thirty minutes later, after Angela was dressed and ready, they drove to Quinn's office. They searched Quinn's filing cabinets.

"The files on the money laundering case are missing and I can't find any reference to Pantages," Angela said, sinking heavily into a chair.

"What about your files?" Blake asked.

"All I've got is my notes. He kept all the originals with the affidavits."

"Let's check his computer."

They searched his computer files for several minutes. Angela slammed her hand on the desk. "Nothing. Wiped clean. Someone's been in here."

"Can you get your other witnesses to give you replacement affidavits?"

"I'll try. I just hope to God we can find them again."

"If not, it looks like I'm your only witness."

Angela held her face in her hands. "Oh Blake, I've got a bad feeling about this."

He put his arm around her shoulders. "Let's think through this. You'll get those affidavits again and I'll testify to Senator Connor's committee. In the meantime your friend Cross is doing his internal investigation. All is not lost."

Angela took a big sigh. "You're right. I'll get on it. Why don't you go back to my place and write out your statement. My computer is on my desk. I'll join you later."

Blake nodded. "Sounds good."

Angela walked Blake to the door. "Blake?"

"Yes?"

"Oh nothing, just thanks for sticking by me."

He suddenly embraced her and kissed her passionately on the mouth. She returned his kiss lustily. After a long minute they broke apart, breathless. He walked out the door and drove back to Angela's condo, his step a little lighter and the sun seeming a little brighter.

17

The stucco mansions of Victoria Peak materialized, then disappeared, among sculptured trees and fortified walls. At the end of the twisting, narrow road, a large red-tiled pagoda towered above gray granite walls.

"We're here, sir," Ho Tang said.

Tang, the Chan family's ancient, grizzled family servant and driver, stopped the green Rolls Royce thirty yards away from two massive metal gates.

Raymond Chan sat in the back seat, twisting his father's twenty-four carat gold ring on his middle finger. Long delicate fingers smoothed his Hong Kong Jockey Club tie under his white linen suit. The jacket collar stuck up a few inches above his shirt and ruffled the nape of his neatly rimmed salt and pepper gray hair. He shifted in his seat to see himself in the rear view mirror. Worry lines etched a thin and pasty looking face.

Tang drove along the exquisite gardens of bauhinias, roses, ponds and painted bird statues. Victoria Harbor spread across the horizon far below like a glossy photograph from an expensive travel magazine. Everything seemed surreal except the dark hills above Kowloon, called the Nine Dragons.

"Turn up the air conditioning," Raymond said.

"It's on high, sir," Tang replied.

Tang steered the car up to the garage and parking area past a dozen Rolls Royce's and Mercedes-Benzes'. The limousine drivers were in a circle, kneeling around handfuls of paper money and *Pai Kau* cards. A hulking bald man in a suit one size too small and sitting on his haunches nodded to Tang. He nodded back.

"*Sei gau jais*—triad foot soldiers," Tang said.

Tang parked the car and Raymond followed him on foot up a dozen stone steps and along a wooden bridge that curved over a large pond. A thirty-foot stone dragon undulated in the water, its gaping jaws and bulging eyes warning all who approached. Soon they stood before two weathered wooden doors. Tang help up his hand to be still and quiet. He glanced up at the video camera above the door. The door opened and a muscular young man in a leather jacket and blue jeans stepped forward.

"Raymond Chan to see Fu Chun Lee. He's expecting us," Tang said.

The young man nodded and motioned them to follow him. Dust-covered, century-old vases and silk wall tapestries adorned the dark hallway. Two expressionless men in black robes stood beside the door at the end of the hall. They opened the double doors to a large room thick with the smell of burning incense. A hunched old man in a long white robe walked forward to meet them. Tufts of wispy white hair crowned a liver-spotted head. Raymond and Tang bowed and the old man returned the bow.

"May I introduce you to Lee, Fu Chun, the *Heung Chu*—Incense Master," Tang said formally, "Honorable Incense Master, may I introduce to you Chan, Raymond, son of Chan, Wang Sung."

"You will remain here until our business is concluded," Lee said, pointing to chair on the other side of a wooden screen." He pointed at Tang. "Your man must wait for you outside."

Tang's face registered a protest, but Raymond touched his arm gently. Tang bowed and left. Lee walked back to the other side of the screen and Raymond took a seat. He peered through the carved rosewood screen.

Half a dozen men gathered around a large black cherry table, all wearing black robes. A tiny middle-aged man with one hand was standing at the middle, waving his stump in the air while talking wildly to another man, who just nodded repeatedly. A younger man with slick-backed hair and a tranquil expression on his youthful face sat quietly in the middle, seemingly oblivious to the pandemonium around him.

Lee stood at the head of the table. "Order! Come to order!"

The band of dangerous men, looking more like a traveling theatrical group, paid no attention. Lee smashed the large copper gong by his chair, the signal to sit down and shut up.

Lee brandished a parchment document written in Chinese script. "We, the chosen representatives of Hong Kong's oldest triads, are united in our resolve to destroy the usurper, Simon Fung and his Hung Se Ying triad." He jabbed his crooked finger at the bottom of the page. "Each *Lung tau* will sign."

He passed on the document for signature and left the room, returning quickly, carrying a black canvas bag. The bag shook and wiggled, accompanied by the sharp squawking of an animal. He pulled out of the bag a box of matches and a bottle of brandy. When the signatures were complete, he held the yellow parchment over the bowl and set fire to it. Flames licked at his fingers and a bluish yellow smoke curled in the air. The Dragon Heads, or leaders of the triads, seated at the table watched, stone-faced and silent.

"This is the breath of the God of Vengeance, *Kwan Kung*. May he strike down anyone who is not true to our cause," Lee announced.

The red-faced old warrior held the burning paper between his yellowed thumb and forefinger until the paper's ashes floated into the bowl. He uncorked the bottle of brandy and poured some into the bowl, then unsheathed the ivory-handled knife in his sash and held it over the foul mixture.

"Blood will purify the truth," he said.

He reached deep into the black bag and pulled out a wildly flapping, black-feathered chicken by its feet. He slammed it down on the table and gripped the chicken's upper body. And then with the other hand, he drew the knife blade across the chicken's neck. It squawked and thrashed, feathers flying helter-skelter, while its life-blood splattered onto the bowl and table. Lee's grip was strong and he waited until the bird was still before dropping its carcass into the bag. He wiped the spattered blood from his hands and then picked up the bowl with the mixture of ashes, brandy and chicken blood, held it close to his chin and swirled its contents.

With his eyes fixed on the other men at the table, Lee sipped the mixture and said, "Who so ever breaks the oath and betrays our trust given this day will die by the ten thousand cuts."

He passed the bowl to the other Dragon Heads. The one-armed man held the bowl with his stump and good hand, spilling some of the liquid down his chin as he drank. He wiped it with his sleeve and passed on the bowl.

When it came to the last Dragon Head, he paused for a moment, looking at the bowl and said. "And may their families be broken as this bowl is broken." He threw the bowl on the floor and crushed it with his foot.

Lee wiped the bloodied knife on his sash and walked over to Raymond on the other side of the wooden screen. "Whatever you may have seen or heard must remain in this room. Do I have your word?"

Raymond nodded.

"You have a request to make of us?" Lee asked.

Raymond bowed and followed Lee back to the table. He cleared his throat nervously. "I am Raymond Chan. The death of my father, Wang Chan, has not been avenged. I am asking for your help in restoring my family's honor."

Raymond's words were met with indifferent expressions on the faces of the Dragon Heads.

"We've anticipated your request. We agree to help you, but in return you must do something for us," Lee said.

"What?" Raymond asked.

"Help us get some information from Simon Fung's triad in Guangzhou," Lee replied.

Raymond frowned. "What kind of information?"

"That is not your concern," Lee said.

"You mean steal it?" Raymond asked.

"We have some people you'll be working with. As a respected businessman, you will not raise suspicion."

Raymond rubbed his chin, but didn't reply for a few moments. "I agree."

"You will go to Guangzhou immediately. Stay at the Guangdon International Hotel. Our people will contact you there," Lee said.

Raymond bowed and left the room. He climbed into the car and sank into the back seat, holding his head in his hands. "Book a train to Guangzhou and make reservations at he Guangdon International Hotel."

"I should go with you," Tang said.

"I'm handling this by myself. And as far as Sabrina is concerned, I've gone to the mainland on business. Tell her nothing else."

"As you wish, sir."

Raymond looked up at his face in the rear view mirror. It was pale, and rigid, like a death mask.

18

Guangzhou, also known as Canton, is the largest and most prosperous trading city in southern China, approximately one hundred miles from Hong Kong on the Pearl River. In addition to close economic ties, the people of Guangzhou shared the Cantonese language with the Hong Kong population.

Raymond took the high speed train from Hong Kong to the Guangzhou train station where more than one hundred thousand people a day moved on one hundred trains. From there he took a taxi to the Guangzhou International Hotel. He sat in the lobby bar, drawing circles on the wood with his wet finger.

Two men, one tall and one short, in dark, rumpled suits, entered the lounge and walked up to Raymond.

"Raymond Chan?" the taller of the two asked.

"Yes, who are you?" Raymond replied.

"You don't need to know. Fu Chun Lee sent you. Please come with us," the tall man said.

Raymond paid his bar bill and followed the men into a waiting car. Ten minutes later, the car stopped at a restaurant along the river. Raymond and the two men got out walked into the restaurant and sat down at a table in the corner.

"You want to tell me what's going on?" Raymond asked.

The taller of the two men leaned over to Raymond. "We're waiting for someone."

"Look, I was told that I was here to help steal some information," Raymond whispered.

The shorter man grabbed Raymond's arm and squeezed it hard. "Just shut up and listen."

"We're expecting one of Simon Fung's men who we believe has information of great importance to Fu Chun Lee and the other Dragon Heads," the tall man whispered.

"And we're going to ask him to give us that information?" Raymond asked.

The tall man smiled. "Something like that. The restaurant owner is friendly to us. He'll introduce you as a potential buyer of Fung's heroin. We want you to get him to relax enough to put him off guard. We'll do the rest."

"Why didn't you just wait for him in some dark alley?" Raymond asked.

"He and his bodyguards would be expecting something like that. His guard will be down here," the tall man said. "Now listen. You'll be asked to join them. Tell the old man you want to buy ten kilos of high grade heroin. He'll probably ask for ten million. Offer eight and agree to nine. He'll ask to see the money. Tell him you've got only half but it's in your car up the street. Insist that the old man go with you alone to the car."

The restaurant owner appeared at the table and had a whispered conversation with the tall man. When they'd finished, the tall man said, "Bring us the house specialty and some beer." As he leaned over to talk, a handgun was clearly visible under his jacket.

A waiter appeared in a few minutes with several steaming plates of food and bottles of beer. Raymond and his two companions ate and drank heartily. Twenty minutes later, three men in business suits walked into the restaurant, one, and an older, short man, the other two men were younger and athletic-looking. The restaurant owner steered them to the table next to Raymond.

The restaurant owner had been talking the three men at the table next to Raymond. He motioned for Raymond to join them. Raymond shook hands with the old man and nodded to his body guards. The men who had accompanied Raymond left the table and walked back into the kitchen with the restaurant owner.

"Sit down, have something to eat," the old man said.

"Thanks," Raymond replied helping himself to a plate of food and a beer.

For the next forty minutes, Raymond ate and drank with the men, trading stories and getting drunk. By then all the other customers in the restaurant had left.

"So I'm told you'd like to buy," the old man said, looking at Raymond's gold Rolex watch.

"How much can you supply?" Raymond asked.

"How much do you want?" the old man replied.

"Ten kilos," Raymond said.

"That will cost you ten million," the old man said.

Raymond shook his head. "Eight million."

The old man spit out a chicken bone. "Nine. Take it or leave it."

"Not before I see a sample," Raymond said.

The old man nodded to one of the bodyguards who got up and left the table. He returned in a few minutes and gave Raymond a small plastic bag. Raymond opened it, wet his finger, touched the white powder and tasted it.

"Alright, nine million," Raymond said, "I'll give you half the money now and the other half on delivery."

"Let's have another drink to toast our arrangement," the old man said, "but I want to see the money."

Together, they drank several more beer.

"You wanted to see the money," Raymond said, "it's in my car down the street. But you've got to come alone with me."

The old man laughed and pointed to his bodyguards. "He thinks you'll rob him." He turned to Raymond. "Alright."

The old man and Raymond got up and staggered, drunk from the beer and made their way out of the restaurant out onto the deserted street.

"Which car is it?" the old man asked, walking a bit wobbly.

"That one," Raymond replied, pointing to a Mercedes parked on the curb fifty feet ahead.

When they reached the car, Raymond's accomplices appeared suddenly out of the darkness with their guns drawn.

"What is this?" the old man asked.

"Put your hands on the trunk, now!" the tall man said. The short man spun the old man around and slammed him onto the trunk.

"You'll pay for this," the old man shouted.

"Shut up, you old fool," the short man said, smacking the old man's face with the barrel of his gun.

The old man screamed in pain.

The tall man searched the old man's pockets and took out a small plastic cylinder. "Got it."

Just then the old man's two bodyguards burst out of the restaurant with their guns drawn. They ran toward Raymond, yelling.

Raymond's accomplices opened fire at the two men who returned fire. Bullets whined and chunked off of the concrete sidewalk and metal of the cars. Raymond ducked down behind the car to shield himself from the bullets. The two bodyguards and Raymond's short accomplice were struck down, fatally shot. The tall man held his gun to the old man's head and pulled the trigger. His body recoiled, blood and brain matter splattering the car. Raymond slowly stood up. The tall man reached inside his jacket to feel his stomach and his hand came away smeared with blood. In the distance, the sound of sirens could be heard.

"Here, take this, make sure it gets to Fu Chun Lee," the tall man said.

Raymond took the blood-stained plastic cylinder from his hand and ran down the street as the sirens got closer and closer. He glanced back to see the tall man slump to the ground.

Around the next corner, Raymond flagged down a taxi and rode back to his hotel He packed his bags and took a taxi to the train station. When he arrived at the station, a large number of police were checking passengers before they got on the train. Raymond left the station and took a taxi to a car rental agency, rented a car and drove it to the Hong Kong border.

When Raymond arrived at the border he parked the car and walked toward the border check point. The usual Chinese border guards were checking the travel documents and identification of a throng of people. And then a black car pulled up and several policemen got out and talked to the border guards. Raymond left the lineup and walked two hundred yards from the checkpoint. The moonless night provided a cover of darkness as he scrambled toward the Hong Kong territories.

He stumbled, falling face first into the muck. The heavy rains had turned the scrub brush into a swamp. He huddled behind a clump of tall weeds at the sound of staccato, shouting voices a hundred yards behind him. He held his breath and waited in this no-man's land bordered by sixteen-foot high fences, guard towers and patrolled by Hong Kong's Girkha soldiers. Opaque and shimmering, the morning light started to paint everything silver. High above, the morning mist slithered its way down the steep gorges of the dark hills.

Raymond pulled himself up and stumbled toward the Hong Kong side of the border. The wet scrub brush grabbed his legs. Exhausted after fifteen minutes, he collapsed face down into shallow water. A middle-aged Chinese man with intense black eyes and a deep furrow between his eyebrows reflected back at him.

A black sky opened and released a sea of rain, pummeling his head. He cupped his hands over his head and closed his eyes. Twenty minutes later, as if by command, the heavy rain stopped. Raymond got up and ran as fast as he could, the mud draining his strength with every step. And then, flashing silver in the mist, a fence appeared. He tripped and lunged his way the last fifty feet, then collapsed into the mud.

Double-length, ten-foot high coils of barbed wire blocked his way like a steely death trap. The barbed wire ran for twenty-five miles along the Sham Chun River between Deep Bay and Mirs Bay, marking the boundary between Hong Kong and the Peoples' Republic of China. A narrow road ran beside the wire on the other side. The wire and the border police on the Hong Kong side of the river were the barriers preventing a flood of Chinese immigrants from entering Hong Kong.

Raymond got up and followed the fence for a few hundred feet until he came to a place where the ground dipped and the fence seemed higher. He kneeled in the muck and breathed deeply. After a few minutes, he slid beneath the water and felt carefully for the fence wire. He grabbed handfuls of mud under the last wire and surfaced from the water to throw them aside. Repeatedly he dug and threw the mud aside only to have it slide back into the hole. He filled his lungs with air and then flopped on his back and wriggled from side to side to create a temporary trough in the mud. He turned his head sideways, collapsed the air from his lungs and with all his strength pushed with his heels and hands. He slide beneath of wire but it caught on his pant leg. He tugged hard to free it. The wire sliced through the cloth and deeply into the flesh along his shin. He screamed in pain as he stumbled out of the ditch onto the road that ran parallel to the fence. Raymond looked in both directions and then started limping down the road.

Suddenly a truck came around the corner, swerved to avoid hitting Raymond and stopped on the shoulder of the road. A young man in a grease-spotted shirt with long hair tied back in a pony tail eyed Raymond suspiciously. He staggered to the truck and grabbed the driver's door.

"Can you drive me to Tai Po?" Raymond pleaded. He looked anxiously over his shoulder.

"Someone chasing you?" the driver asked.

"I'll pay."

"How much?"

"One hundred dollars."

"Okay, get in!"

Raymond took out several bills and thrust the money into the driver's hand and then crawled into the passenger seat. "Now go!"

After a few minutes, Raymond drifted into sleep. In half an hour, he was awakened by the driver shaking him. The truck driver had stopped in Tai Po's market square. Raymond scrambled over to a nearby shop and slumped against the stone wall. Farmers were unloading open-bed trucks and pushcarts full of vegetables and fruits. Small bamboo birdcages full of chickens were hung from hooks along the storefronts. Braziers already stoked white-hot with coal, spat hot fat from the ducks and pigs rotating on spits. Large frogs lay motionless on their backs neatly spread out on plastic trays.

Raymond got up and stumbled his way along the crates and trucks lining the narrow back streets. He fell hard once and grunted in pain. He pulled himself upright again and careened into the Ling Po Incorporated sign on the wall of a building. Suddenly, out of the shadows a man stepped out, holding a gun. He fired shots at Raymond at point blank range and then ran back into the alley. The bullets struck Raymond in the chest and stomach, slamming him hard against the warehouse door. Raymond yelled in pain and pounded on the door with his fists. He grabbed the plastic cylinder out of his pocket and pushed it through the mail slot in the door and then collapsed on the pavement in a scarlet smear of blood.

A man in his twenties with messy hair and a wrinkled business suit opened the door.

"Ayeeyah! Uncle Ling, come quickly!" he yelled over his shoulder.

"What is it nephew?" and old man with a straggly white beard said as he hurried to the door. Then he saw Raymond.

Ling Po knelt down beside Raymond and felt for a pulse in his neck. "May the Gods protect his soul."

19

Sabrina Chan paced back and forth in her study. She had all the features of a classic European beauty—erect carriage, meticulously applied but understated makeup over the porcelain skin of high cheekbones and clothes carefully chosen to tastefully accentuate a curvaceous body. With one hand she fidgeted with the gold buttons on her peach-colored linen suit and with the other hand she pulled the long telephone cord free from the corner of the antique cherry-wood desk. As she walked barefoot across the Chinese rug onto the cool tile floor, her auburn hair, twisted into a single long braid, swayed across her back.

"I'm not going to lose this bid. This is our chance to enter the European market in a big way," Sabrina said, jabbing her finger at an imaginary person. She nodded, listening to the response at the other end. "I have faith in your persuasive abilities, but let's try a different tack. Find out what Gerhardt wants most in life and we'll give it to him."

The telephone cord caught on the corner of the desk. She gave it some slack and whipped it. The cord caught a glass picture frame on her desk, knocking it to the floor. It shattered into a myriad of pieces. "If that doesn't work, we'll have to appeal to his self-protective instincts."

Sabrina bent down and picked up the broken picture frame. "Damn it! No, I'm not talking to you . . . We don't have much time. I want action in forty-eight hours."

She replaced the telephone on the desk, sat down in a carved wooden chair and stared at the photograph in the broken frame of Raymond, Blake and her together. She and Blake were all smiles while Raymond looked very serious. She looked up when she heard a light knock at the door.

"Come," Sabrina said.

Tang came in and bowed. "Excuse me, Mrs. Chan."

"Yes, Tang?"

Tang stepped closer, glanced at the broken glass on the floor, then cast his eyes downward. "While you were on the telephone, your uncle, Ling Po, called on the other line. I think you'd better call him back."

"I haven't talked to him in months. What did he want?"

"It's about Mr. Chan."

"Why so mysterious?"

"Please call. I'll wait outside if you need me." Tang bowed and left the room.

Sabrina picked up the telephone and dialed. "Uncle Ling, what a pleasant surprise. Tang told me to call you but wouldn't say why." She listened intently to the voice on the other end. Her facial muscles sagged and her eyes widened. "No, it can't be. How? When?" She sagged back into her chair. "Tang!" she yelled.

Tang scurried quickly back into the room to her side. Sabrina passed him the telephone, turned her chair to the window and sobbed.

"May the God's protect Mr. Chan's soul. I am deeply sorry for your loss, Mrs. Chan," Tang said softly.

Sabrina touched Tang's arm. "Thank you. I know this is a great pain for you as well." She looked at the curtains billowing from a sudden wind. "A storm is coming."

Tang closed the window. "Shall I put up the shutters?"

"No, leave it for the other servants and bring the car around. Take me to Raymond before the storm breaks," she said calmly.

Twenty minutes later, the Chan limousine was moving along the Stanley Gap Road high above the South China Sea. The black waters signaled the approach of the storm and winds buffeted the car. Sabrina sank deeply into the leather seat and continuously twisted the gold wedding ring on her finger.

"Mr. Chan's body . . . his injuries might be upsetting for you," Tang said.

"It's something I have to do."

Ling Po's warehouse was located two blocks from the market square in Tai Po. Tang parked the car behind the warehouse. Sabrina stepped out onto the concrete and looked at her feet. She was standing on a large bloodstain. She stared at the stain.

Ling Po appeared at the door. "I am so sorry, my child, it's a terrible tragedy."

Sabrina embraced Ling Po, who gently stroked her hair.

"Where is he?" she asked, pulling away.

"I'll take you to him," Ling Po answered, "be prepared."

"Take me to him," Sabrina said.

Together, Ling Po, Tang and Sabrina walked down the hallway and into one of the storage rooms. A human shape covered by a blood-stained sheet lay on a table. Beside the body, a middle-aged man with wire-rimmed glasses waited.

"Dr. Tsui, what happened?" Sabrina asked calmly.

He bowed. "First, may I express my sincere sympathies for your husband's death?"

Sabrina nodded. "Thank you."

"Mr. Chan had been shot several times. Any of the bullets would have been fatal," Dr .Tsui said.

"Let me see him," Sabrina said. She walked up to the table and flipped back the sheet.

Raymond's face was clean and his hair combed and for the first time in along time, Sabrina gazed upon a peaceful face. She stood there, in silence, looking at him, and then brushed his cheek with the back of her gloved hand.

Dr. Tsui bowed and left the room.

"One other thing, Mrs. Chan," Ling Po said.

"Yes?"

Ling Po handed Sabrina the plastic cylinder. "Raymond must have pushed this through the mail slot before he died."

"What is it?" she asked, turning it over in her fingers.

Ling Po shook his head. "I don't know, but it must be valuable for Raymond to have protected it with his life."

Sabrina nodded and looked at Ling Po "I'll take it with me. And after Tang and I leave, call the police. Don't mention that Raymond was examined by Dr. Tsui or that I was here and don't mention the plastic cylinder."

Ling Po bowed. "As you wish."

Sabrina turned her attention back to the body on the table. "Please leave me alone with my husband."

Ling Po and Tang left the room. After they were gone, Sabrina stared at Raymond's face for a long minute. "You selfish bastard. Even in death you betrayed me."

20

Blake returned to Angela's condominium, sat down at her computer and began to write his statement. Thirty minutes later, the telephone rang. He answered it, thinking it would be Angela.

"Blake, this is Peter Lai," a serious voice said on the telephone.

"You've got news about the investigation?" Blake said.

"Uh . . . no . . ."

"Still no leads in the case?"

"Blake, there's no other way than to tell you outright. I'm sorry to inform you that your brother, Raymond, has been killed."

Blake grabbed the corner of the desk to steady himself. "Oh God, no, not Raymond?"

"His uncle, Ling Po, found him outside the door of his warehouse. He'd been shot."

"I . . . I still don't believe it . . . Does Sabrina know?"

"I called her already."

"Thank you, Peter, for calling . . . I'll return to Hong Kong immediately."

"We'll do everything we can to find out who did this, Blake."

"Thanks . . . I'll see you soon."

Then the connection was dead. Blake sank into the chair, an invisible hand clenching his throat. After waiting for a few minutes to collect himself, he dialed.

"Sabrina, it's Blake."

"Oh thank God, Blake . . . I was about to call you . . . I don't know how to tell you this, but . . ." Sabrina replied.

"It's alright; Inspector Lai called and told me about Raymond."

"Uncle Ling called me . . . he found Raymond's body at the warehouse . . . he'd been shot many times . . . Oh, Blake, it was horrible . . . I'm so sorry . . . I knew how much Raymond loved you."

"It's a great loss for both of us."

Several moments of silence fell between them.

"I want to get all the details when I get back," Blake continued.

"I'm so glad you're coming home. I feel so alone."

"I'll be there as soon as I can. And Sabrina?"

"Yes, Blake?"

"I promise you that I'll find out who killed Raymond."

"Hurry, Blake, hurry."

Blake put the telephone down, went into the kitchen, rummaged through the cupboards and pulled out a bottle of Vodka. He got some ice cubes from the freezer and poured himself a big glass, walked back into the bedroom and lay on the bed. He allowed the pain to settle into his solar plexus. He'd lost his real parents and then Wang Chan and now Raymond. Sabrina was the only person that could be called a family now. He reached over and took his gun from the bedside table and looked at it. What had a life of chasing criminals given him? No appreciation from his superiors for his work, no family, and no-one he could call a partner in life. He took another drink and cocked the hammer.

"So easy and the dragon will be still," he whispered.

Angela opened the front door, walked in and put her briefcase on the hall table. "Blake, I'm home," she called out in an effervescent voice. "Blake?"

She walked into the living room and then the kitchen and finally into Blake's bedroom. He was lying sprawled across the bed, face down. In his hand, he held his gun.

Angela ran to him. "Oh, Blake, what . . .?"

"Urgh," he grunted.

"Thank God." She embraced him, kissing him on the neck and face.

Blake rolled over and half-opened his eyes. "Sabrina?"

Angela pulled back. "No, it's Angela."

"Oh Angela," he said with slurred speech, "what time is it?"

She took the gun from his hand, put it back on the table and grabbed his shoulders. "It's time to sober up."

Blake's arm flopped back on the bed. "That's easy for you to say."

She dragged him into the bathroom and turned on the shower.

"You gonna have a shower with me?" he asked, putting his arms around her.

"I don't think so," Angela replied. She shoved him into the shower under the cold war, slammed the shower door and walked out of the bathroom.

Twenty minutes later, Blake, dressed in his bathrobe, shuffled into the kitchen and sat on the counter stool.

She handed him a cup of coffee. "You want to tell me what that was all about?"

Blake took a big gulp of coffee and groaned. "Just had a little too much to drink."

She leaned forward and put her face a few inches from his. "Don't play games with me, Blake. You drank the whole bottle and you had a loaded gun in your hand."

Blake looked down into his coffee cup. "I feel like a comic book character that has a black cloud over his head."

"Now you're feeling sorry for yourself."

He narrowed his eyes. "That's not allowed?"

"What's wrong, Blake? Talk to me!"

"It got a call from Inspector Lai of the Hong Kong Police." A lump formed in Blake's throat. "Raymond's dead."

Angela's eyes opened wide and her mouth fell open. "Oh, no Blake, not Raymond. What happened?"

"He was shot. I don't know why or have any details."

She came around the counter and held him tightly. "I'm so sorry, Blake, and I'm sorry for jumping on you the way I did."

He buried his face in her chest and held her tightly. "You couldn't have known. It just seems like everyone close to me, dies. Only Sabrina is left now."

"And me, Blake, and me."

He kissed her gently. "And you . . . you know it would probably be safer for you if you had nothing to do with me."

"I'm with you because I choose to be."

"Look at the situation realistically. My career has ended under a cloud. I can't convince people there's a conspiracy between organized crime and The Company and all my family has been killed."

"My heart goes out to you for your losses. If anyone can understand, I can. And there's no way I can take the pain away for you. But you do still have Sabrina and now me in your life."

He stroked her hair. "You understand that I can't make a commitment to you. There's too many uncertainties right now."

She held his face in her hands. "I know. But I'm here right now and that's all that matters."

He kissed her softly on the lips. She returned the kiss more passionately and took one of his hands and placed it on her breast. He continued to kiss her deeply and then pulled up her skirt and lifted her onto the counter. They made love there, gently and lingeringly.

Much later, lying in Blake's arms on the cool tile, Angela traced the outline of his lips with her finger.

"Blake, I'm in love with you," she said softly.

He looked intently into her eyes. "You don't have to feel sorry for me."

She smacked his shoulder. "I didn't say that out of pity, you idiot. I said it because that's what I feel."

"I don't know what to say. I'm flattered that someone like you would feel that way about me."

"Yes, so what's the problem?"

"I love the time we're together. I'm happy when I'm with you, which is saying a lot for me. But I've got to focus on Raymond right now."

Angela brushed his cheek with her lips. "I understand, Blake . . . what are you going to do now?"

"I'm going back to Hong Kong and find Raymond's killer."

She propped herself up on one elbow. "You mean help the police?"

"This is personal now."

"You don't mean revenge."

Blake didn't answer.

She slipped her clothes back on. "And going to jail doesn't accomplish that?"

Blake looked into her eyes.

"I can't believe this of you, Blake, after all your years in law enforcement."

"I'm not willing to take the chance of letting Raymond's killer go free."

She held his hands. "Let me go with you."

"This is something I've go to do alone."

"That's the problem, Blake. You do everything alone. It's like there's this raging dragon in you that you've created to fight evil, but it's also devouring you from the inside, piece by piece."

"I've got to pack," Blake said. He got up quickly and walked back into the bedroom.

21

Blake shouldered his way among the throngs of travelers in Hong Kong's airport, looking for a familiar face.

"Mr. Morgan," Tang called out from the crowd.

Blake recognized Ho Tang, the Chan family servant and driver. "How are you, my old friend?" he when he reached Tang.

Tang bowed. "I am fine. Welcome home, Mr. Morgan."

They walked a short distance to where the car was parked.

Tang stopped at the car and bowed more deeply. "I am shamed that I could not prevent Mr. Chan's death. I am no longer worthy of serving the Chan family."

Blake touched Tang's shoulder. "Sit in the back with me and talk."

They got into the limousine's back seat.

"The police were not getting results fast enough for Mr. Chan. He became very withdrawn and agitated. He felt great pressure to restore family honor himself," Tang said.

"Pressure from whom?" Blake asked

"His business associates, his family."

"Sabrina and me?"

Tang was silent.

"Go on," Blake said.

"Mr. Chan met with the heads of several of Hong Kong's oldest triads to ask them for help."

"What happened?"

"He wouldn't say. When he came out of the meeting with them, he asked me to book a train ticket to Guangzhou. I should have gone with him."

"You once told me that regrets can't change the past," Blake said softly.

Tang nodded.

"Did Raymond ever do business with the triads before?" Blake asked.

Tang looked at Blake through old narrowed eyes. "No."

Blake nodded. "You were a triad member in your youth before Wang Chan gave you a job, right?"

"That was a long time ago."

"I don't judge you for it. You can help me understand the triads better. Tell me what it was like."

Tang nodded and rolled his eyes up and to the left, searching his memories.

"I was twenty-four years old. The full initiation ceremony into the triad is rarely followed now, but in my day it was steeped in ritual. I arrived at the temple in bare feet. Triad members in black Buddhist monk robes messed up my hair and ripped open my coat and then gave me five joss sticks and I recited five ritual poems. They announced my name out loud and I was led to the first gate which was draped with a long sheet of yellow paper."

"You remember all this detail after more than forty years?"

"Like it was yesterday."

"Go on."

"At the gate, I did a ritual dance and was given a secret handshake. And then the members formed an archway with steel and copper swords and I walked through it. I was handed three red stones. Three men in red robes, called Generals, escorted me to the *Heung Chu,* the Incense Master, who gave me permission to enter. I knelt to the Generals four times and then the Incense Master gave me a lecture on loyalty to the triad. I entered the next gate called the Circle of Heaven and Earth, which was guarded by two more Generals and then I walked over to the East Gate of the City of Willows and knelt twice before a General there. I walked through the gate to a separate room where senior members of the triad, dressed in white robes were gathered. More ritual poems were recited and I was asked questions about the triad," Tang said.

"That was it, you were in?"

"No. They cut a piece of my hair, combed my hair and washed my face, took off my jacket and pants; made me put on a white robe and tied a red sash around my head. I was led to the altar while all members held nine blades of grass in their hands. The Incense Master took a silver wine jug and three jade cups and made a pledge to worship Heaven and Earth. Three lamps were lit, the last, a red one. The Incense Master recited a long series of Buddhist and Taoist prayers, a list of oaths were recited from parchment and they cut my hand and dripped the blood on the oaths. They gave me a bowl of wine and made me drop my blood into the wine. They took the yellow paper hanging in the entrance gate and burned it, dropping the ashes into the wine and then cut the throat of a rooster and let the blood drip into the bowl. And then they directed me sip the mixture in the bowl. Finally, they led me to West Gate and burned the oath list, gave me a knife and three coins."

"That was the end?"

"No, after, everyone went to a restaurant for a big meal."

Blake laughed. "And I thought DEA training was tough."

Tang grunted in such a way to say that his talk was over. "The Chan house?"

"Not straight away. Swing over to Kowloon first."

Soon Tang had the dark blue limousine moving down Nathan Road, often called the Golden Mile for its endless hotels, shops and restaurants. And people everywhere.

"Do you know why the other triads are united against the Hung Se Ying?" Blake asked.

"Drug trafficking territory, I would imagine."

Blake stared out the window into the streets. Two bare-chested deliverymen on bicycles, carrying cylinders, swerved suddenly in front of Tang. He adroitly avoided them, leaned out his window and yelled profanities at the men. Blake smiled.

The rattle of double-decker buses echoed in the streets. A man in black shorts and rubber boots carried a whole gutted pig over his shoulder, dragging behind him the entrails that he'd tied together. Butchers with bloodstained shirts chopped away at a fresh carcass with cleavers, ripping out steaming guts and throwing them into wicker baskets. A young housewife pointed at a pile of stripe. One of the butchers wrapped up her choice in a pink plastic bag. A child in a starched white bloused strapped to the woman's back giggled and played with her mother's pigtail. Dozens of cages full of clucking chickens hung from lines outside the shop. The woman opened a latch on top of one of the cages and yanked out one of the birds by its wing. The chicken squawked and tried to peck her as she squeezed its breast. She swung the bird upside down by its legs and paid for the evening's dinner.

As Tang drove on, the thriving market and shopping area became ranks of shabby tenements and outside bars with their pimps and toughs dealing number three grade reddish granular heroin called "red chicken." It was packed tightly into yellow plastic straws and sealed by heat at both ends. A customer would specify an amount to be purchased and the street dealer would heat up his knife, slice off a portion of the straw, which would be automatically resealed from the heat. Street dealers were experts at being able to shoot the straws up into waiting hands in second and third story windows. Anything could be bought here: drugs, prostitutes and even assassins. And no questions would be asked.

"Drop me off at the Hot Whispers Disco," Blake said.

Tang nodded and turned right at the next corner. A few minutes later the car stopped at a popular two level hangout for *gwai los* and Chinese businessmen.

"Wait for me," Blake said and then got out of the car.

A big-boned red-haired man with the tattoo of a red tiger on his arm guarded the door of the Hot Whispers Disco. He looked at Blake carefully and then motioned him to pass. Inside, the floor vibrated from the bass-driven disco music. The floors and walls undulated under the flashing strobe lights. The black, shiny forty-foot bar flanked by giant video screens ran the length of the room. Clusters of tables and a small raised dance floor book-ended the bar. Young Filipina dancers in gaudy bathing suits and pantyhose gyrated with mechanical, yet childlike innocence on the dance floor. Beautiful young Chinese women in *cheon sans*—tight dresses with slits up to mid-thigh—raced to the sides of old men with cigarettes hanging from their lips and drank cold tea while running up a bar bill and promising to fulfill their fantasies.

Blake took a seat at the curve of the bar so he could see the room.

"Hello, handsome, my name is Lucy, why don't you buy me a drink?" a young voice called out from behind Blake.

Blake felt a soft hand on the back of his neck and turned to see a young woman in a jade green dress. She looked like she was no more than sixteen.

Blake smile. "I'm just getting over my prostate surgery."

"Prostrate, standing up, I can do all positions," Lucy replied, smoothing her dress over her breasts and down her loins.

Blake laughed. "Perhaps another time, Lucy." He turned away from her and called to the nearest bartender. "Vodka on the rocks, please."

Lucy looked nervously at a middle-aged woman at the bar. She was the *mamma-san*, the bargirl minder. "Please, mister, please."

Blake glanced over at the *mamma-san*, who was glaring at Lucy.

"Cold tea and champagne," he called out the bartender. Lucy breathed a sigh of relief.

"So tell me about yourself, Lucy," Blake asked when the drinks arrived.

Lucy took a sip of her tea, glancing over at the smiling *mamma-san*. "I was born in Guangzhou."

Blake saw the pain beneath the innocence in her eyes.

"I ran away from home with my boyfriend, who was a red chicken dealer," she continued nonchalantly, as if she were reciting a recipe. "Then he made me work in fish-ball stall. But he beat me too much, so I ran away."

"How old were you then?" Blake asked.

"Fourteen. I moved in with a man who owns the Golden Rooster Motel. I work there for two years but got pregnant so he kicked me out."

"You have a child?"

"My daughter died at childbirth. One of my customers took me in; give me good food, good clothes, teach me how to get *gwai los*."

Blake looked carefully at Lucy. She's better off than before, he thought, but her years were numbered in a business that values only the look of childlike innocence. He waited until *mamma-san* was looking again then he took out two hundred Hong Kong dollars. "I know it won't do any good to tell you to get out of the business, but do it anyway."

"You have a place to go?" Lucy asked happily.

"Just tell her you're meeting me later at my hotel. She won't know the difference."

Lucy giggled, leaned over and kissed Blake on the cheek and then turned her attention to a tall European sitting a few seats from Blake who had been staring at Lucy's legs during their conversation.

Blake scanned the bar. Middle-aged men in rumpled blue suits clung to the bar and teenaged hostesses slung their arms around them. They drank cold tea with the men, cooed into their ears and massaged their necks. This would be an expensive night for some of them, Blake thought, but they'd boast of their conquests in the morning, real or imagined. One of the bartenders came over, a woman in black silk pants and jacket and a large gold broach on her chest.

"Mei-Lei, my God, it's you," Blake called out, "forgive these old eyes."

"Blake, people say you killed stateside. You not look dead," Mei-Lei sputtered, laughed, leaned across the bar and embraced him.

He hugged her back, laughing. "I wouldn't get killed without telling you first. It's been at least ten years. Remember the Happy Valley racetrack?"

"*Ayeeyah*! I won five thousand in the first five races and then lost it all on the sixth. I could have had my own bar. Then I quit gambling!" she said.

Blake shook his head and looked at her questioningly.

Mei-Lei rolled up her eyes. "All except *Mahjong*."

The both howled in laughter.

"I have a break now. Let's go sit down at that table." She pointed to a table in the corner.

Blake grabbed his drink and followed her to the table.

"You're as beautiful as ever, you never seem to age," Blake said.

Mei-Lei laughed and slapped him on the shoulder. "I'm still not married you know."

"They must all be blind."

Blake looked carefully at her. She still had the same zest for life and boundless energy that he'd known years ago. Back then she and her husband owned a restaurant that was burned down because they'd refused to pay protection money to one of the triads. Her husband, whom Blake had known from playing rugby, was killed in the fire. Blake helped her out by getting her a job.

"Well, every single man must be an idiot then," Blake said.

Mei-Lei took Blake's hand in hers. "I'm sorry to hear about your brother."

"I think he was murdered."

"Oh no! May the Gods protect his soul."

"I'm here to find out who did it."

Blake looked over her shoulder into the mirror behind the bar. Two men had just walked into the bar, the first, a handsome, middle-aged man wearing a tailored white linen suit and the second, a young man wearing a leather jacket and jeans.

Mei-Lei nodded toward them. "Simon Fung, Dragon Head of the Hung Se Ying and his bodyguard."

"Fung! What do you know about him?"

Mei-Lei shook her head. "A dangerous man. When he took over, the Hung Se Ying started a war with the other triads. Bad blood now."

"Anything else you can tell me about him?"

"He has many connections with people in government and moves in prominent social circles."

Mei-Lei looked at her watch. "I've got to go back to work. Wish me luck in the Mark Six Lottery. Then I'll own my own place." She reached across the table and kissed Blake on the cheek. "And you be careful."

"It was good to see you again," Blake said, "and don't worry, you'll get that bar sooner than you think."

Mei-Lei got up and returned to the bar. Blake finished his drink and walked over to Fung's table.

The young bodyguard stood up blocking Blake's path. "What do you want, *gwai lo*?"

"I want to speak to Mr. Fung," Blake replied.

The bodyguard put his hand on Blake's chest and pushed, ripping the pocket on his jacket. "He doesn't know you, so shove off."

Blake stepped forward quickly. His right arm swung sideways and upward. The heel of his hand smashed the cartilage of the bodyguard's nose. He staggered momentarily and in that moment Blake spun around behind him and applied a chokehold. Within seconds the man slumped to the floor.

"Like I said," Blake snapped, "I want to talk to Mr. Fung."

"Who are you?" Fung asked, his dark eyes assessing Blake carefully.

"Blake Morgan."

"What do you want Mr. Morgan?"

"I'm Raymond Chan's brother."

"Oh yes, I read in the papers about his and his father's tragic deaths. My condolences."

"Did you know them?"

"Not personally."

"Did you ever do business with Wang Chan?"

"You sound like a policeman, Mr. Morgan."

The bodyguard had awoken. He groggily got to his feet and started toward Blake.

Fung held up his hand. "Mr. Morgan and I are having a conversation."

The bodyguard backed away, glaring at Blake.

"I'm in Hong Kong to find out who killed them," Blake said.

"Isn't that a police matter, Mr. Morgan?"

Blake stared at Fung. "It's also a personal family matter. You'd understand that, I'm sure."

Fung nodded. "I'm afraid that I can't help you." He looked at Blake's torn pocket. "But please be my guest for a complimentary tailor-made suit at my tailor shop." Fung handed Blake a business card.

Blake flipped the torn pocket on his jacket. "I'm pretty handy with needle and thread." He took out a pen and piece of paper from his jacket and wrote down a number. "If you hear of anything, I'm staying at the Chan home. I can be reached at this number."

Fung studied the number for moment. "Good idea to give personal protection to Mrs. Chan."

"Are you offering?"

Fung smiled. "Goodbye, Mr. Morgan. It was interesting talking to you."

Blake nodded. "I imagine we'll be talking again." He turned on his heel, left the bar and got back into the limousine.

Tang looked at him quizzically.

"What do you know about Simon Fung?" Blake asked.

"Dragon Head of the Hung Se Ying triad for the past eight years. He has a reputation for being mean and ruthless."

"Did he ever do business with Wang Chan?"

"I only know that they've met at least once."

"And Raymond?"

"He would never associate with a man like Fung."

Blake looked at Tang thoughtfully. "Let's go home."

Tang headed the car back toward the tunnel and the road to Shek O.

Blake's thoughts turned to Sabrina. He remembered long ago when he first had thoughts of love for her. He was fifteen and she was thirteen, but physically mature. She'd come to the Chan home to receive lessons along with Blake and Raymond in the Chinese game, *Go*, from Tang. Blake recalled that Tang had said Sabrina had great mental toughness but needed more finesse in her game. Blake walked in the garden later with Sabrina. Their hands touched, raising the hair on Blake's forearm. Once, when they were playing *Go*, Sabrina reached across and kissed him on the cheek. The tingle of adolescent love was effervescent in his blood all that day. The next day, they exchanged a lingering first kiss.

Blake looked out of the window of the limousine, surprised at the detail of his memories of their young romance.

The car jerked to a halt in front of a large pink colored mansion in Shek O, high above the South China Sea. Tang gathered Blake's bags and walked with him up stairs to the front entrance. Sabrina ran to the entrance to greet them. She flew into Blake's arms and embraced him tightly.

"Thank God you're home, Blake," she said breathlessly. She kissed him passionately on the mouth.

Blake's lips yielded momentarily and then he released Sabrina and stepped back. "Tang, take my bags up to my room."

Tang nodded and left.

Blake waited for him to disappear out of sight. He turned to Sabrina. "What the hell was that all about?"

Sabrina touched his arm gently. "I know, I'm sorry, I've been so mixed up. Please don't be angry."

Blake's countenance softened. "I'm not angry. I'm really tired, why don't we talk in the morning." He kissed her on the forehead and walked upstairs.

21

The next morning, Blake found Sabrina out on the tiled terrace, sipping tea. She sat in a rattan chair, wearing a simple short, black-knit dress, her thick auburn hair falling in waves over her neck and shoulders.

She pointed to the Jasmine tea, coffee and sticky buns on the glass table. "Good morning. Help yourself."

Blake poured himself some coffee and settled into a chair across from Sabrina. "Are you okay?"

Sabrina nodded. "I'm sorry about last night. I'm still upset about Raymond."

Blake took a deep breath. "Tell me what you think happened."

She sighed and looked out into the sea. "He changed after you left. We rarely talked or spent time together. He became obsessed with family honor and revenge and neglected Chan Enterprises. And then one day, he went on business to Guangzhou. That was the last time that I saw him."

Blake reached across and touched Sabrina's hand. "Did he say what kind of business in Guangzhou?"

"No, but he has extensive business interests in China."

"Had he been threatened by anyone?"

"Why would he be threatened?"

"Did you know that he'd met with the triads?" Blake watched Sabrina's face.

"I knew nothing about that!"

Blake leaned back sipped his coffee. "It seems to me like he decided to act on Wang Chan's murder and went to the triads for help."

Sabrina turned away and looked out to the sea again.

"Did Wang Chan have business dealings with the triads?" Blake asked.

Sabrina stared at him. "If you recall, we weren't on the best of terms, so he never talked business with me. You lived in his home for years, did you ever see anyone?"

Blake looked into his coffee cup, trying to search his memories. "There was a time when I was about thirteen. Raymond and I used to chase each other around the house, sliding on the tiles with our stocking feet. That day I was running on the garden terrace at full speed. I crouched like a surfer, whipped around a post and headed into the first room."

"Raymond was chasing you?"

"Yes, and he yelled at me—don't go in there—but it was too late."

"What happened?"

"I went crashing through the shutter doors and suddenly I was on my back, looking up at a stocky man with a propeller on his head, smiling at me."

"Propeller?"

"He'd clotheslined me. The propeller was the ceiling fan circulating over his head. I could taste the blood in my mouth from hitting his arm. I looked around. There was a younger man in a white suit sitting at Wang's desk."

"Who?"

"I don't know. His back was to me. Wang Chan was standing nervously beside the desk looking at a man behind me who was on his knees, his hands tied behind him, blood flowing from cuts to his arms and shoulders."

"Why?"

"I don't know. Another young man was standing over him holding a small hatchet."

"Isn't that the weapon of choice for triad enforcers?"

"At least to make an example of someone. Just then, Raymond burst into the room. Wang Chan's face was flushed and he yelled at me to leave and Raymond to wait outside in the hallway. I didn't need much convincing to get out of there."

"Then what happened?"

"I just remember standing outside the door with Raymond and hearing the man at Wang Chan's desk say 'make sure his family sees him,' and a few minutes later, Wang Chan came out, pulled Raymond inside and told me to go to the kitchen and wait for him."

"And?"

"I listened at the door and could hear the sound of a bamboo stick whistling through the air and landing and Raymond's muffled cries. And then I ran to the kitchen before Raymond came out."

"Did Raymond tell you what happened?"

"I guessed that Wang Chan had beaten him for barging into his study. I asked Raymond why I didn't get punished as well and he said that I was an honored guest, a debt that Wang Chan owed my father and that Raymond was to take my punishment for me."

"It's funny how you see things later . . . you mentioned Wang Chan owing a debt to your father."

"Yes, but I never knew what."

"I think I know. Raymond told me once that when your father was on the Hong Kong Police force before the war, he saved Wang Chan's life. He'd got caught in the middle of a gang fight and your father stepped in."

"That explains a lot." Blake kept eye contact with Sabrina, probing. "Was Raymond involved with the triads?"

Sabrina slapped her thigh, visibly upset. "Blake, why are you grilling me?"

"I'm just asking questions that the police will probably ask you."

"As far as I know, Raymond was not involved with the triads."

Sabrina picked up a document sitting on the table beside her, walked over and tossed it into Blake's lap.

"What's this?" Blake asked.

"I found it last night. It's Raymond's will. And I thought I was angry about the prenuptial agreement."

Blake glanced through the pages of the will, his eyes opening wide when he read the second page.

"That's right, the entire Chan estate and Chan Enterprises goes to you," Sabrina said flatly, "I get only what's specified in the prenuptial."

"To say I'm surprised is an understatement."

Sabrina crossed her arms. "This is Raymond hurting me again."

Blake looked at the will again. "He never told you about this?"

"He wouldn't discuss it. He just said I'd be well taken care of. As his wife, I could probably challenge this successfully in court."

Blake shook his head. "That's not necessary. How much do you want?"

Sabrina looked at him intently. "I'll let you decide that."

"How about fifty-fifty to start."

Sabrina came over and kissed Blake's forehead. "That's one of the reasons that I love you, Blake. Your generosity."

"I don't know about that."

"You know there's a way we can both get one hundred percent."

Blake looked at her quizzically for a moment.

Just then Tang entered the terrace and cleared his throat. "Inspector Lai is here."

"Let's continue our talk later, Blake. Show him in, Ho," Sabrina said.

Tang left and returned with Lai.

Lai bowed. "Mrs. Chan, Blake, may I offer my sincere sympathies on the death of Mr. Chan? I'm sorry that you've suffered another loss."

Sabrina nodded. "Thank you Inspector."

"Thanks, Peter," Blake said.

Sabrina waved her hand to a chair. "Inspector, please help yourself to sticky buns and Jasmine tea."

Lai poured some tea and sat across from Sabrina. "Thank you." He paused for a moment. "I need to ask you some questions." He took out a pad of paper and pen from his jacket. "Where was Mr. Chan for the past week?"

"He went to Guangzhou on business a few days ago. I hadn't heard from him since," Sabrina said.

"What kind of business?" Lai asked.

"Chan Enterprises does extensive business interests on the mainland. Mostly import-export," Sabrina replied.

"Why didn't you accompany him?" Lai asked.

"I don't usually," Sabrina answered.

Lai nodded and looked at Blake. "Did your brother have any enemies?"

"Raymond was not the kind of man who made enemies," Sabrina replied.

"Do you think, Mrs. Chan, there's a connection between your husband's death and Wang Chan's death?" Lai asked.

"I don't know," Sabrina replied.

"Inspector, do you have a murder suspect for Wang Chan's murder yet?" Blake asked.

Lai stared at Blake. "We're still working on it." He wrote in his notebook at some length. "Well, I'd like to talk to your man Tang on the way out. Regrettably, you'll have to come down to the station to identify the body."

Lai got up, bowed, walked toward the doors and stopped. "Oh, one other thing, Mrs. Chan. Have the details of your husband's will been reviewed as yet?"

Sabrina leaned forward, her eyes wide open. "For God's sake, we've not even buried him yet, Inspector."

"Yes, of course, forgive me. But when the will is read, I'd like to know the details."

"Details of a private estate are not public information. You can issue a subpoena if you wish, Peter," Blake snapped.

Lai nodded. Then he bowed and walked out.

Sabrina smacked the arm of the chair with her hand. "Why was his tone so suspicious and insinuating?"

Blake waved his hand casually. "It's his job to poke and prod. Besides, we've got nothing to hide, have we?"

Sabrina reached behind the cushion of her chair. She walked over to Blake and held out a small plastic cylinder.

He took it from her hand. "What is it?"

"Uncle Ling said that Raymond had pushed this through the mail slot before he died. I don't know what it is."

Blake turned the cylinder over in his fingers. "It's sealed tight. I'll need some good tools."

"We can go to Cybertronics."

"Cybertronics?"

"It's one of the companies that Raymond set up. Communications technology."

"Let's go."

"Why don't we relax for a while? Go for a walk at Repulse Bay."

Blake looked at Sabrina's face and saw her need for moral support. "Alright. A little exercise might help."

Sabrina hugged Blake excitedly. "I'll tell Tang to bring the car around."

Twenty minutes later, Tang dropped them off at Repulse Bay beach and parked the car.

Blake and Sabrina walked along the dirty white sand, the waves gently rolling in a few yards away.

"You remember how beautiful the Repulse Bay Hotel was before the war, compared to those?" She pointed at a group of modern condominiums overlooking the bay, with their unique Feng Shui holes in the buildings.

Blake kicked a pile of small shells in the sand with his shoe. "I remember afternoon tea in the lobby. But my parents made me dress up with long pants and a bow tie."

Sabrina nudged him with her elbow. "Now the truth comes out. You don't like wearing pants." She laughed, kicked off her shoes and started running. "Come on, Blake, you never could catch me."

Sabrina sprinted, hiking her dress up to her hips. Blake ran after her, catching her in twenty yards. He grabbed her and they fell to the sand in a heap, rolling and laughing.

Sabrina rolled on top of Blake, breathing heavily, looking into his eyes. "It's been so long since I've laughed like this."

"We've always been able to play."

She kissed him hard on the mouth and for the briefest moment, Blake returned it, and then pushed her off of him.

"What? It's not as if we're cheating on Raymond," she pleaded.

Blake sat up and looked out at the waves. "You're turning to me out of grief and need."

"Is that so wrong?"

"I just don't feel right about it."

Sabrina sat up and rubbed his shoulder. "There's always been something special between us, Blake. I think we were fools not to have followed our feelings when we were young. I made a mistake marrying Raymond and an even bigger mistake with my first marriage to Duncan. I've got a chance now to make the right decision, the one I should have made all along."

"I admit that I've often though about what it would have been like—you and me—but . . ."

"What?"

"I told you that there's someone else in my life—Angela Townsend."

"Are you in love with her?"

"I don't know. I do know that she means a lot to me."

Sabrina grabbed a handful of sand and threw it. "We've shared loneliness and pain together. We've been the closest of friends. Can she offer you that?"

"She's a fine woman with many of your qualities."

"So you're saying no to us."

"I'm saying that you're turning to me because of stress and that Angela is in my life right now."

Sabrina got up and walked away, angrily.

Blake caught up with her. "Look, can't we concentrate on finding Raymond's killer?"

Sabrina sighed. "Alright, Blake. I'm sorry. But please don't close the door on the prospect of our future together."

Blake didn't reply.

They walked back to the car in silence.

"Let's go to Cybertronics," Blake said a few minutes later.

Cybertronics was a steel and glass building in the business district of Wan Chai, surrounded by fences and security gates.

"Most of Cybertronics is underground. It makes security easier," Sabrina said, pointing to the brightly lit building. "Raymond always used to say that technology, not retail goods, is Hong Kong's economic future."

Tang stopped the car at the gate and rolled down the tinted windows. The guard stepped forward, immediately recognizing Sabrina and Tang.

"Good evening, Mrs. Chan," he said, waving car through the gate.

Tang drove the car up to Cybertronics' front door where Sabrina and Blake got out.

Sabrina put her hand on Tang's shoulder. "Why don't you eat something at your favorite Shanghaiese restaurant? Check back in two hours," Sabrina said.

Tang nodded and drove away.

Sabrina and Blake walked past the security guards at the door, across the black tiled lobby and then took an elevator down to the research lab. When they entered the lab, a middle-aged, stocky man greeted them.

"I'm sorry to hear about Mr. Chan," Sung said, bowing.

"Thank you," Sabrina said, "this is Blake Morgan, Raymond's brother."

Sung bowed and Blake shook hands with him.

"Sung, we have a mysterious plastic cylinder we'd like opened very carefully. And you must not mention what we're doing here to anyone. Is that clear?" Sabrina asked.

Sung bowed. "Yes, of course, Mrs. Chan."

Sabrina and Blake followed Sung to a work bench.

Blake handed Sung the plastic cylinder. "Can you open it without damaging its contents?"

Sung turned the cylinder over in his fingers, then examined it carefully under a large magnifying glass. "I think so. Give me a few minutes."

Sung fixed the plastic cylinder in a small vise and then took a sharp blade and scored the four inch long cylinder. And then he donned goggles. "Turn your eyes away."

Blake and Sabrina looked away.

Sung turned on a low-powered laser, set the cutting depth and followed the cut line he'd already made.

"Got it open," he said, switching off the laser. He pried open the casing to reveal a thin strip with three dots.

Blake leaned over to look at the strip under the magnifying glass. "Microdots."

"I'll try to transfer them onto the computer," Sung said.

Within a few minutes Sung had been able to scan the microdots and they were clearly visible on the computer screen. "Looks like encrypted code and ancient symbols."

"Are you familiar with encryption?" Blake asked.

Sung nodded. "Encryption is achieved with algorithms that use a key to encrypt and decrypt messages by turning text into digital gibberish and then restoring it back to its original form."

Blake and Sabrina looked at Sung with interest.

"A fifty-six bit key requires seventy-two quadrillion possible combinations, whereas a hundred and twenty-eight bit key needs a thousand times that. A fifty-six bit key is considered decodable. At least for now," Sung said.

"So we should hope that the microdots have a fifty-six bit key," Sabrina said.

"Exactly," Sung replied.

Sung booted up the encryption software program. "I'll run the code through our program and hope for the best."

A few minutes later, Sung sat up in his chair and pointed to the computer screen. "I think I've got it. Mandarin characters. I'll run it through English translation so we have both."

Blake pointed to a large screen on the wall. "Can you project it onto that?"

"I think so," Sung said. He made some adjustments as soon as the decrypted code appeared in large format on the screen.

A copy of an accounts ledger, with sums of money and the names of people appeared on the screen.

"What is it?" Sabrina asked.

"It's a record of drug shipments and bribes paid to public officials," Blake replied. "Let's look at the rest."

Sung made some adjustments and another page appeared on the screen.

Sabrina moved closer and read it aloud. "Simon Fung, Dragon Head, Hung Se Ying: As a token of our good faith in our proposed business arrangement, I am sending you a copy of my recent rediscovery of an ancient drug that will set our business on its ear. This drug, called *jfuri* by the Mayans, can be the force that we both need to defeat our competitors. The symbols describing the nature of the drug are enclosed. I look forward to discussing my proposal with you and concluding our business arrangement. Yours truly, Raoul Ramirez."

Blake let out a whistle. "This is big enough to blow the balance of power among the triads and the Central American drug cartels. What do you make of those symbols, Sung?"

"Mayan or perhaps Aztec," Sung said, "but you'd need an expert to decipher them."

"Thank you, Sung," Sabrina said, "we'll clean up here."

Sung bowed. "Yes, Mrs. Chan." He got up and left the lab.

Blake looked again at the decoded message on the screen.

"What are you thinking?" Sabrina asked.

"I'm just trying to piece it together. The message foreshadows a partnership between Fung and Ramirez. It appears that Raymond stole this information from Fung for the other triads in return for a promise to find his father's killer. The other triads were probably after the accounting ledger and bribe information and didn't know anything about the symbols or this new drug."

Sabrina tilted her head, her eyes fixed on Blake. "Do you think Fung killed Raymond?"

Blake rubbed his chin. "Maybe one of his men did, trying to get the microdots back or maybe someone in the other triads trying to erase evidence of the theft."

"Should we turn this over to Inspector Lai?"

"I made a promise to find Raymond's killer myself."

"So what now?"

"I think I'll first pay a visit to Lai. See if he's come up with anything yet."

"Do you have the feeling his heart isn't in the investigation?"

"I was thinking the same thing, but can't figure out why . . . After I see Lai, I want to talk to Fung."

Sabrina touched Blake's arm. "Why?"

"Propose a trade—the microdots for Raymond's killer. The police are getting nowhere with Wang Chan's investigation and there's no suspects for Raymond's death. Fung's got the contacts and resources that I couldn't get."

"What if he's responsible for Raymond's death? Or Wang Chan's?"

"I know it's a bit of a bluff, but I don't much else to work with."

Sabrina put her arms around Blake. "I couldn't bear to lose you too."

"Hey, remember what you told me. I'm a survivor."

Blake picked up the microdot strip and stared at them. "There's still the matter of the Fung-Ramirez partnership."

"Can't you leave that to the police?"

"I am the drug police."

Sabrina sighed. "What are you going to do?"

"It's unlikely that Fung has received this message, although it's a just a matter of time until Ramirez contacts him again. Fung would want to have that incriminating accounting information back."

"The Mayan symbols?"

"I want to find out what they say, especially if they can tell us the source of this drug, *jfuri*."

"I know just the man who can help us."

"Who?"

"Dr. Rodrigo Bivar, Professor of Anthropology at the *Muséo Naçional de Antropología* in Mexico City."

"How do you know him?"

"I met him at a social event; we dated for a while before Raymond and I got married."

"Will he help us? Can you trust him?"

"Yes on both counts. I think he'll do anything for me."

"Still in love with you, is he?"

Sabrina laughed. "Aren't all men?"

"You do have a mesmerizing effect on men, I must admit . . . okay, let's call him."

Sabrina got Bivar's telephone number through the directory and dialed the number.

"!*Hola!*, Rodrigo. It's Sabrina Chan."

"!*Hola!* Sabrina. Have you finally come to your senses and decided to leave Raymond and marry me?" Bivar asked at the other end of the telephone.

"Rodrigo, I'm calling because Raymond has been killed."

"Killed? !*Mi Dios!* I'm so sorry, Sabrina. Please forgive me for the bad joke. I had no idea," Bivar said contritely.

"How could you have?" Sabrina replied, "I'm here with Raymond's brother, Blake Morgan. I'll put you on speakerphone."

Sabrina punched the speakerphone button and put the telephone back on the receiver. Blake pulled up a chair close to her.

"Hello, Professor," Blake said.

"Hello, Mr. Morgan, I'm very sorry about your brother."

"Rodrigo, I've called you to ask for your help," Sabrina said.

"How can I help?" Bivar asked.

"We've stumbled across some Mayan or Aztec hieroglyphics that we think might help us find Raymond's killer," Blake said.

"Hieroglyphics? What do they look like?" Bivar asked.

"We'd rather show them to you in person. Could Blake and I come to see you?" Sabrina asked.

"Why aren't the police handling this?" Bivar asked.

"I work for the DEA and I'm providing whatever assistance that I can," Blake said.

"I see. Well, I have some classes next week . . . I could reschedule." Bivar said, pausing. "But of course, Sabrina, I'll help."

"Thanks, Rodrigo. We'll take the first plane to Mexico City and come directly to see you," Sabrina said.

"I'll see you both then," Rodrigo said.

Sabrina cut the connection.

"Can you make the travel arrangements?"

Sabrina nodded and pointed to the microdots. "Do you want me to put that in the safe."

Blake shook his head. "It's best if I hold onto it." Blake put the microdot strip back into the plastic container, printed a copy of the microdots and then deleted the file from the computer.

"Shouldn't we have another copy?" she asked.

"No. And it might be better if I go to Mexico alone."

Sabrina shook her head vigorously. "Absolutely not. We're in this together."

Blake recognized that resolute look in Sabrina's face. "It looks that way."

Sabrina called for Tang to pick them up and they left Cybertronics.

Alone in his bedroom back at the Chan home, he picked up the telephone and walked to the bay window overlooking the gardens. He dialed.

"Angela, it's Blake," he said.

"Blake, I was hoping you'd call," Angela replied at the other end.

"The police haven't come up with any suspects for Raymond's murder, but Sabrina and I have stumbled on something important."

"What?"

"Raymond took his father's murder investigation into his own hands. He worked out a deal with the other triads: find his father's killer and in return he helped them steal drug shipment and public official bribe information from Simon Fung."

"The same Fung that you mentioned was connected to the Seattle bust?"

"Yup. Raymond somehow managed the steal microdots from Fung's men in China. He got the microdots to his uncle's house before he died and Sabrina recovered them."

"And they say there's no coincidences. Anything else on the microdots?"

"A letter from Raoul Ramirez who runs a Mexican drug cartel to Fung, proposing a partnership."

"Why?"

"To join forces against their competition. Apparently, Ramirez has rediscovered some ancient Mayan or Aztec drug which he plans to market exclusively. A set of symbols in the microdots should hopefully lead us to the details of this drug and its plant origins before Ramirez and Fung."

"My God, this whole thing gets more complicated by the minute. Are there any clues yet as to Raymond's killer?"

"It could have been Fung's men or the other triads."

"Are you taking the information to the police?"

"I want to handle this myself."

"What are you going to do?"

"I'm going to meet with Fung, propose that he give me information regarding Raymond's killer in return for the microdots."

"Blake, you're taking a big risk. How do you know he'll take the bait? He could just get another copy of the microdots from Ramirez before you see him."

"I think I've got a little time. It's worth a try."

"Do you want me to take the information about the Fung-Ramirez partnership to the DEA?"

"No, not after my experience with the Costa Rica and Seattle cover-ups. I don't want to take the risk the information will leak back to someone in The Company. Sabrina and I are going to Mexico to get those symbols deciphered first. Professor Bivar, an expert on ancient Central American cultures, has agreed to help us."

"Sabrina's going with you?"

"She insisted."

"Why don't you contact someone in Mexican drug enforcement to help?"

"Same problem as with the DEA . . . wait, my old friend, Xtimal Mendoza."

"Who's he?"

"Used to be with the Mexican Federal Police but he's in drug enforcement now. We attended some DEA training sessions together years ago and became friends."

"Good! You know I don't like to see you handling this alone."

"I know."

"How are you doing, Blake, I mean about your brother?"

"I'm alright I guess. Sometimes I feel like it hasn't hit me yet."

"You've suffered so many losses. My heart hurts for you."

"That means a lot to me."

"How is Sabrina doing?"

"She's pretty shaken. What's made it more difficult for her is that she and Raymond were on the verge of a divorce."

"Oh, she initiated it?"

"No, Raymond did. She's bitter about the prenuptial agreement and the fact that Raymond didn't make her the prime beneficiary in his will."

"Who is?"

"I am."

"I can see how she'd feel burned. Is she resentful toward you?"

"No, I've promised her that she'll get at least half of the estate."

"That's very generous of you, Blake."

"Hey, I'll still have more money that I'll know what to do with."

"I hope you don't mind me asking, but has Sabrina suggested that the two of you get back together?"

"Well, not exactly . . . I mean, she needs me more than wants . . ."

"I thought so. Are you considering it?"

"I told her that there's someone else in my life."

"Someone I know?"

"She's interesting, beautiful, intelligent, although sometimes a little opinionated."

"Sounds like my kind of woman. Who is she?"

"Special Prosecutor for the DEA. I think I'm stuck on her because she likes horses."

"You'd better not let her go."

"Not a chance."

They both laughed.

"Well, I've told people about you," Blake said. "I guess we'll have to do something about this when I return."

"I've got a few ideas."

"Hmm. I'll keep that thought . . . Listen, I've got to go. I'll call you from Mexico."

"Alright, Blake. Please stay safe. And remember that I love you."

"I know. I'll miss you."

Blake hung up the telephone and sat down in his chair. Finally declaring his feelings, as best as he could, for Angela, left him with an odd sensation. One of release, as though the valve to a huge reservoir had not been just turned on, but broken open and at the same time he felt anxious, for that reservoir had been a huge bulkhead of protection for his heart. He knew for certain now that he loved Angela, even if he couldn't tell her yet.

Blake left that thought and decided to call Xtimal Mendoza. He dialed DEA information and got the number.

"Xtimal, this is Blake Morgan."

"Blake, you old dog! You still owe me a hundred bucks," Mendoza said on the other end of the line.

"Give it up. My shot was a good half inch closer to the bulls eye."

"Bullcrap. That was an old bullet hole on the target sheet."

They both laughed loudly.

"It's been a long time, Blake. When are you going to come down for a visit?"

"Soon. How's Mary and those wonderful kids of yours?"

"Mary's fine. She has a job teaching art at a local school. My oldest, Lucia, will be graduating from university in a month and Rosarita will finish high school at the end of this year."

"You must be very proud of them."

"I am a lucky man."

"Well, despite your shortcomings, they've done alright for a husband and father."

"Ha! I hope you can see my finger."

Blake laughed. "There's another reason I called you."

"What?"

"I need your help."

"Sure, if I can, what is it?"

"I've got some evidence that links the Ramirez drug cartel to a Hong Kong triad run by a man named Simon Fung."

"Ramirez! He's my prime case right now."

"I picked up an encrypted message from Ramirez to Fung that refers to the partnership and a new drug . . ."

"How did you get this?" Mendoza interrupted.

"My brother Raymond stole it and I think he was murdered because of it."

"Murdered? I'm sorry, Blake, what happened?

"It's a long story; I'll tell you when I see you. Can you get some time free to help me?"

"Absolutely. It fits perfectly into our investigation here. I'll put a team together to work with you."

"I don't want it official yet. I haven't talked to the DEA either. There may be a mole or someone in The Company involved."

"Look, I know you like this Lone Ranger stuff, but we'll need help."

"I've got you."

Mendoza sighed. "Alright, although it's against my better judgment. I'll take some vacation time."

"Hey, just like old times, my friend. Meet me in Mexico City. My brother's wife, Sabrina will be with me. I'll call to confirm our arrival time."

"Alright, I'll see you then."

Blake hung up the telephone and threw on his jacket. Time to talk to Inspector Lai, he thought to himself.

22

Jack Cross stopped at the door and looked at the name plate: "Benjamin Cranston, Director of Covert Operations," and then knocked on the door.

"Come," Cranston voice called out from within.

Cross walked in. "What's up Ben?"

Cranston was sitting at his desk. "Sit down, Jack," he said, pointing to a chair in front of his desk. A worried look spread across Cranston's furrowed face. "The DEA's and Senate Intelligence Committee's inquiries into covert activities have hurt us. Even our strongest supporters are privately nervous."

"I've got it under control, Ben," Cross replied calmly, "we've jettisoned some our problematic assets in Central America and a few retirements will lead people to believe we've cleaned house."

"We can't afford any scandals while we're trying to get more Congressional support."

"How is that going?"

"No breakthroughs yet, but I'm working on Senator Connor. You said you were working on some creative solutions?"

"Still working on it . . . I'll be out of the country for a while, checking with our operations in Asia."

Cranston stared at Cross. "Whatever needs to be cleaned up, Jack, do it. I don't need to tell you this, but if they go after me, you'll go too."

Several moments of silence passed.

"Is there anything else, Ben?" Cross asked.

"As long as you understand me, Jack."

Cross got up and walked to the door. "Perfectly, Ben, perfectly." And then he closed the door behind him.

Inspector Peter Lai of the Hong Kong Police stood at his office window looking at the parking lot. A knock on the door broke the silence. A uniformed officer came in followed by Jack Cross.

"Sit down, Mr. Cross," Lai said, motioning to a chair in front of the desk. Lai sat in his chair facing Cross.

Cross smiled and slowly let his six-foot-four inch frame sink down into the simple upholstered chair. He glanced at the police academy pictures and framed certificates of commendation on the wall and the Hong Kong Cricket Club trophy on the bookcase. "Spartan has always been the British way, hasn't it?"

"Office furniture has never kept us from getting the job done," Lai replied.

Cross slapped his leg and laughed. "With notable exceptions, such as the group of renegade cops than ran their own little crime operation here and then took it to the Netherlands and Canada."

Lai gripped the seat of his chair tightly with one hand. "Every law enforcement organization has its bad apples, even the CIA."

Cross looked at Lai with a bemused look for several moments. "Something we can debate over a beer someday."

Lai nodded. "What is it you wanted to talk to me about?"

"The United States government believes that a number of undercover law enforcement and intelligence agents' identities may be compromised and that information passed on to the Peoples' Republic of China."

"How does that involve the Hong Kong Police, Mr. Cross?"

"We have a few possible suspects. One who works for the DEA, Blake Morgan. You know him?"

"We've talked. His father, Wang Chan and his brother, Raymond, were both murdered."

"Unlucky family . . . Morgan was recently suspended for insubordination. But what's more of concern to us are his public accusations of corruption against The Company. I think it's his way of diverting suspicion away from himself."

"Have charges been laid against Mr. Morgan?"

"At this stage, he's just under surveillance, which is what brings me here."

Lai looked at Cross expectantly.

"I want you to share all the information that you have on Morgan and his sister-in-law, Sabrina Chan."

"What kind of information?"

"Business, personal, his activities—everything."

"With all due respect, Mr. Cross, I don't have the resources to . . ."

"I've already cleared it with your boss," Cross interrupted, "he's promised me your cooperation. I want you to report to me regularly." Cross handed Lai a business card. "My private number is on there."

Lai stared at Cross. "Is there anything else, Mr. Cross?"

Cross stood up, stretching his long frame so it towered over the shorter Lai. "I understand that you have political ambitions. Your cooperation could mean a lot for your future, Inspector."

Lai walked to the door with Cross. "Yes, I'm sure a word from you in the right places could help a man—or hurt him."

Lai closed the door after Cross left and leaned against the door. His shoulders sagged. He stood still for several long moments, staring at the polished shoes. And then he opened the door and strode out of the office.

23

Simon Fung took a handful of fish food from the bag in his hand, threw it into the pond and sat back on the wooden bench in Hong Kong Park, a lush, twenty-five acre oasis of lakes, gardens and a large rainforest aviary, located at the intersection of Queensway and Garden Road in the heart of what is called Hong Kong Central. Fat koi fish swam to the surface and greedily snatched the food. Fung grinned. Twenty feet away, standing by one of the trees, one of Fung's bodyguards kept a vigil.

The bodyguard straightened up when Jack Cross approached. Fung waved his hand and the bodyguard relaxed. Cross sat down on the bench next to Fung.

"These fish are like sharks," Fung said.

Cross looked at the brightly colored fish. "A murderous instinct behind a pretty appearance. Like some people I've met."

Fung laughed. "I'll take that as a complement."

"Let's get down to business. I've come to tell you that I'll have to let the DEA prosecute your people in Seattle."

Fung stared at the fish. "If my memory serves me correctly, the deal was that you'd provide protection in exchange for your cut."

"I've protected you from prosecution, but I can't offer the same for your men in Seattle. Too much heat."

"What prompted this?"

"Some people in the DEA are nosing around, trying to make a connection between you and an unknown person in The Company. They've asked me for help and of course I volunteered to do an internal investigation."

"Which people?"

"A DEA agent named Blake Morgan, Special Prosecutor Angela Townsend and a man named David Quinn from the DEA's Internal Affairs. We won't have to worry about Quinn any more."

"Blake Morgan!"

"You know him?"

"We met recently. He's trying to find out who killed his father and brother. Another American hero."

"You involved?"

"Morgan's father, Wang Chan, used to launder drug money for me through his companies. He made the mistake of threatening me."

"And Morgan's brother?"

"He stole valuable financial information from me—drug shipments and public official bribes—that could put me at risk. Are you worried about Morgan?"

Cross shook his head. "He's just a cop. If he becomes bothersome, we'll have to take care of him." He looked at his watch and stood up. "By the way, make sure those payments go through at least two banks before they're deposited in my Cayman's account."

Fung took another handful of fish. "What are you going to do with all that money?"

"I told you . . ."

"Ah yes, fight America's enemies."

"At least I believe in something other than the almighty dollar," Cross snapped. "Just remember, this is a business arrangement. I have no desire to be your friend or impress you."

"Ha! Life has no subtleties for you Americans."

Cross turned and walked away.

The brass M on the elevator doors opened. Blake punched the top button. His haggard face stared back at him in the burnished brass control plate. A minute later, he stepped out into the restaurant/bar on the top floor of the Mandarin Oriental Hotel. Two large ceramic dragons guarded the entranceway to a large room enclosed by glass. Cherry wood and brass tables and chairs were enclosed by small hand-painted Chinese wooden screens and potted plants.

Blake walked over to the bar.

A husky Filipino bartender shook the martini mixer with rhythm. "Welcome sir. The bar or a table?"

Blake waved his hand. "Thanks, I'm going to look around first."

The bartender nodded and returned to his drinks. On the stools at the far end of the bar, two Japanese men in rumpled suits were haggling, their faces flushed and sweaty. At the circular tables to Blake's right, two middle-aged Caucasian couples slumped in their seats, flanked by a dozen shopping bags. To Blake's left, a young German couple were kissing and talking quietly. Blake's eye caught Inspector Lai waving at him from a table in the far corner. He walked over and sat down.

A cocktail waitress appeared. "May I offer you something to drink?"

Blake ordered Vodka on the rocks, Lai, a beer. The waitress returned, placed the drinks on the table and left.

Lai lifted his glass. "To good health."

Blake clinked his glass against Lai's.

"Would you like to order dinner? The chef here does a wonderful thing combining French with Chinese cuisine."

"No thanks Peter," Blake replied, "how's the investigation going?"

"Which one—Wang Chan's or your brother's?"

"Both."

"Still no suspects for Wang Chan. Again, only rumors about his business dealings with the triads."

"If we assume he was doing business with the triads, why would they kill him?"

"Betrayal. Greed. Any number of reasons."

"And what about Raymond?"

"We've been able to partially trace his movements. He left by high speed train from Hong Kong to Guangzhou. He stayed at the Guangdon International Hotel. He was seen meeting and leaving the hotel with men known to the Chinese police."

"The Hung Se Ying?"

"No. One of Fung's competitors. From the hotel, we don't know where your brother went. Except . . ."

"What?"

"The night before your brother was found dead in Tai Po, there was a gun battle at a restaurant on the river in Guangzhou, a place frequented by members of the Hung Se Ying triad."

"Gun battle?"

"Five men were killed in the street. Three were known members of the Hung Se Ying. One of them, the oldest, was a "bagman" for Fung. The other two men killed were members of a competing triad."

"So what's the connection to Raymond?"

"Some people in the restaurant that night saw a well-dressed, middle-aged man who fits Raymond's description."

"Anyone who saw him in the gun battle?"

"No witnesses. But there's a record of Raymond renting a car that evening. It was found in the border crossing parking lot, but neither the guards nor the police on both sides have a record of him crossing that night."

"So he probably went over the wire."

"It appears so. But why would he? He had proper travel documents and identification."

"Sounds like whoever he was running from, caught up with him. Can you guess who?"

"Could have been Fung's men or the competition. Maybe they weren't after your brother but something he had."

"Such as?"

"Drugs, information, money are the usual reasons. Maybe keeping him silent."

"I don't believe drugs and Raymond was filthy rich."

"So why do you think he went to Guangzhou?"

"To be honest, I think he hired someone to find Wang Chan's killer and something went wrong."

Lai looked at his drink for a moment. "I'm Chinese and I've never understood this saving the family honor thing. Not if your life is forfeited. Tell me Blake, are you now on a quest to revenge Raymond's death. To save family honor?"

"I want to see his killer brought to justice."

"And what happens to Raymond's fortune now?"

"I do believe you're sounding like I'm a suspect, Peter. If I didn't know better, I'd think you were desperate."

"If you were a suspect, we wouldn't be talking in such pleasant surroundings."

"To answer your question, Raymond's estate has been left to me, but I plan to share it with Sabrina Chan. Why would that be surprising?"

"It isn't. I'm just curious. Can't take the job out of the man, they say."

"One final thing before I leave. Are you planning any action against Simon Fung?"

Lai sighed. "He'd be on the top of my list. But we've only been able to arrest minor players in his organization for drug trafficking, prostitution and illegal gambling."

"Well, just to let you know, on my last assignment to Seattle, we busted a large heroin and illegal alien operation. Witnesses fingered Fung as the head of the whole operation."

"Then the DEA is going for extradition?"

"No. The case was taken over by The Company. For national security reasons, we were told."

Lai nodded thoughtfully.

"This leads me to my next question. Have you been contacted by The Company?"

"Why do you ask?"

Watching Lai's eyes, Blake knew he was hiding something.

"Well, unless there's something else, I've got to run." Blake stood up and shook hands with Lai.

"If you find out anything that could help our investigation, I'd appreciate a call."

Blake smiled. "Sure. I suspect you're keeping track of my movements anyway."

Blake walked away, having decided he couldn't trust Lai with the information about the microdots or his plans to go to Mexico. Deep in his heart, he believed Lai wasn't involved with Fung, but Lai wasn't being entirely forthcoming either. He looked at his watch. Ten p.m. It was time to pay a visit to Fung.

Tang pulled the car up to an old brick building with the sign "Nathan Tailors" on the front. "The second floor is an illegal *Pai Kow* gambling den," Tang said.

"Wait for me for an hour," Blake said, "if I'm not out by then, call Inspector Lai."

"You want me to go with you?" Tang asked.

"Thanks, but I need to handle this myself," Blake said, putting his hand on Tang's shoulder.

Blake got out of the car and looked in the dark windows. He knocked on the door. After a minute, it opened and a huge man filled the doorway. His hands, touching either side of the door frame, were broad at the base with strong fingers that tapered almost to points at the fingertips. Each finger was a swollen discolored knot of tissue and between the knots, the skin shone like tanned leather. The knuckles were obscene swellings of bone and gristle. A fighter's hands.

"Blake Morgan to see Simon Fung," Blake said.

The big man grunted. "Follow me."

Blake followed him through the tailor shop to the storage room and up a flight of wooden stairs. He opened the door and they entered a large room smothered in cigarette smoke. A hundred people, mostly men, were banging *Pai Kow* cards on the tables. Wads of money were quickly thrust down and scooped up from the table. Old men with trays moved among the tables, serving tea and brandy and emptying overflowing ashtrays. The big man and Blake wound their way among the tables to al old service elevator. The big man closed the gate and punched the button for the third floor. Blake looked carefully. A formidable opponent, Blake thought. But his weakness would be his lack of mobility. Hopefully, he wouldn't have to test his theory. In the meantime, he liked the feel of the Glock in the small of his back. It was a great equalizer.

The elevator door opened and Blake walked into a work room. Simon Fung stood as if he were attempting flight, his arms outstretched, and his legs apart. In front of him, a little old man, with skin like an old leather chamois, was measuring Fung's trouser legs.

"Same as always," the old man whispered to a young assistant holding a notebook.

Blake looked around. The walls were lined with shelves piled high with rolls of cloth. A large oak desk stood behind Fung. To his left was an ornate, carved, free-standing mirror. A bodyguard wearing a brown suit and with his hair cut in mainland "pudding basin" style on a chair.

"I'll have to ask my man to relieve you of your gun if you have one," Fung said, looking up at Blake.

Blake shook his head. "I'll keep it for now."

Fung motioned to his bodyguard.

The man in the brown suit moved forward, and swung his hand in a lateral arc at Blake, who swayed left, blocking the man's arm and drawing his weight past Blake on the right side. Blake thrust his palm into his sternum, blasting the air from the man's lungs and sending his attacker reeling backwards. The man came at Blake again, whirling his hands in the air. Blake accepted the double arm attack and turned it back at the last moment, trapping the man's arms and chopping his throat with the edge of both hands. Completing the circular movement, Blake hooked one arm about the man's neck and cranked his locked elbow high in the air. As his attacker began to fall, Blake brought his knee crashing upward to meet his shoulder. A loud crunch echoed in the room and the man screamed in pain, grabbing his shoulder.

"Enough," Fung yelled.

The bodyguard retreated and Blake straightened his clothes, but kept his weight on the balls of his feet, ready.

"Like I said," Blake said, "I'll hang onto my gun for now."

Fung waved the cowering tailor and his assistant out of the room. He walked over to the desk, his suit still hung together by pins and marked with chalk. "You have two minutes. What do you want?"

"I want to know who killed my brother," Blake replied. He picked up a chair and sat across from Fung.

Fung pulled up his trouser leg that had caught on his heel. "What's in it for me?"

"Something you've lost."

"What?"

"Information stolen from your men in Guangzhou."

Fung's eyes opened wide. "What information?"

"A record of drug shipments and bribes paid to public officials."

"You stole that from me?"

"Your competition did. Somehow my brother got involved and ended up with it."

"You have it here?"

Blake smiled. "Again, you underestimate me. It's safe and if I don't return, it'll end up in the hands of the police."

"So you've come to blackmail me."

"I want to find out who killed my brother. I'm proposing a trade. The information in return for my brother's killer."

A long silence followed. Blake's senses bristled. He heard the shouting voices in the casino below, the bleating horns of the cars on the street and his own slow measured breathing.

Fung's hand slid off the desk into his lap. Blake relaxed his body, ready to spring. Fung took out a cigarette, lit it and inhaled deeply. The smoke swirled around his head, back-lit by the light from the window. "Agreed."

"And I get to keep a copy as life insurance."

Fung hesitated a moment. "Agreed, but I give you a warning. If you decide to turn your copy in after our trade, I'll kill you and the Chan woman."

"Have we got a deal or not?"

"Agreed. But you must give me a week."

"Forty-eight hours. The exchange to be made at the Po Lin Monastery on Lantau Island. Both of us to arrive alone."

"That's impossible."

"Forty-eight hours or I take your information to the police."

Fung's looked intently at his cigarette. "Alright." He reached into his desk drawer and pulled out a bottle of brandy and two glasses. "I always drink to seal a bargain."

Fung poured brandy into the two glasses and placed them on the desk. Blake took one and waited for Fung.

Fung raised his glass. "As you English say, bottoms up."

Blake waited for Fung to drink and then took a sip of his brandy. Then he slammed the glass on the table, got up and walked back to the elevator. He looked back. Fung was standing in the front of the mirror again, looking at his suit.

Blake followed the big man back downstairs and outside to the car.

"Where to now?" Tang asked.

"Let's go home," Blake said.

Blake sank into the back seat, thinking about his bargain with Fung. A dangerous but calculated risk. "Get the boat ready, Sabrina and I will be going for a cruise tomorrow night."

25

A dark storm cloud crept toward Lantau Island, masking the light of the light of the full moon. Blake's light cotton shirt stuck to his body like a second skin. He tied the dingy to a wooden cleat and then jumped the boat to the dock. He waved his flashlight to Sabrina in a large power boat fifty yards away. She signaled back, powered up the boat and took it further out into deeper water. Blake walked down the dock toward the shore. An old man in ragged clothes sat on a wooden stool under a dim light, repairing a thin rope. A brown bird with a bright crimson beak sat calmly beside him, tilting its head as the old man talked to him. It blinked at Blake with double eyelids as he approached.

Blake knelt down beside the fisherman. "How can you fish in the dark?"

"The bird is my eyes and the fish cooperate," the old man said in a raspy voice.

Blake laughed. "Smart bird."

The old man shook his head. "Smart fisherman."

He smiled a toothless grin and then put his hand on Blake's arm. "Pull up the rope." He pointed to a rope lashed around a wooden cleat.

Blake grabbed the rope and strained against a heavy object. He pulled again, heaving a basket full of thrashing fish onto the planks. Blake stared at the ball of fish and then the old man in amazement.

"May Tin Hau always fill your baskets," Blake said, wiping his hands with his handkerchief.

The old fisherman bowed. "And may you tame all your dragons."

Blake stared at the old man. "Have we met before?"

"Never, and yet you've known me all your life."

"Why do you speak in such riddles?"

"Why do you ask questions to which you know the answers?"

The old fisherman threw the rope over his shoulder, motioned to the bird to follow and slowly dragged the basket full of fish along the dock toward a small boat.

Blake shook his head at this odd meeting, turned and resumed his walk to the beach. He stopped and looked back to catch a glimpse of the old fisherman, but he had vanished. Blake turned and walked to the beach and looked up. A giant bronze Buddha towered into the sky above the cliffs. After all these years, it still took his breath away. He climbed the switchback of a hundred stone stairs, lost in thought. He needed only to make the exchange with Fung. Then what? Take revenge? He took a deep cleansing breath when he reached the top of the stairs.

He looked at his watch. Twelve p.m. Blake stood in the shadows at the edge of the clearing beneath the giant Buddha and waited. He took the Glock from his waistband and checked the firing mechanism. Fifteen minutes later the sound of voices at the edge of the clearing made Blake crouch down, ready. Two men walked into the light. Blake recognized Fung's rooster-like strut. Despite the heat and humidity, he was wearing a white linen suit. The other man who walked beside Fung was in his late thirties, of medium build and smooth, black hair.

Fung looked side to side. "Morgan, you here?" He stopped in the circle of light below Buddha.

Blake waited for a few moments and then stepped out of the shadows. "Here." He walked toward Fung, his gun by his side.

"Have you got the microdots?" Fung asked.

Blake reached into his pocket and held out the plastic cylinder in his hand.

"Who's this?" Blake asked, "I told you to come alone."

"Daniel Lau, he's the man who killed your brother," Fung replied.

Lau looked down to the ground.

Blake stood in front of Lau. "Why did you kill my brother?"

Lau looked up. "His father, Wang Chan was involved in the murder of my father."

"Who was your father?" Blake asked.

"Yip Chen Lau. He was wrongly accused by Wang Chan of being an informer against one of the triads. I've waited thirty years for revenge," Lau replied.

"Did you kill Wang Chan?" Blake asked.

Lau shook his head vigorously. "Someone else did me that favor."

"Who?" Blake asked.

"I don't know," Lau replied.

"How did you kill my brother?" Blake asked.

"I've been following him for a long time. I saw him alone for the first time in Tai Po. I followed him to the warehouse and shot him," Lau answered.

"Did Fung order you to do this?" Blake asked, shooting a glance at Fung.

"I told you, this was personal," Lau snapped.

Blake paused. Lau's story was so bizarre, he didn't know what to think.

"Enough, you have your man," Fung said.

Blake held up his hand. "I'll tell you when I'm done." He turned to Lau. "Why did you turn yourself in?"

Lau glanced at Fung. "He promised to have my brother freed from prison in China. He's been a political prisoner for five years."

Blake shook his head. "Sorry, I don't buy bridges." He turned and started to walk away.

Fung drew a gun from inside his jacket and aimed it at Blake. "Take Lau or not, it doesn't matter to me. But you don't leave this island with the microdots."

Blake heard the hammer cock on Fung's gun and stopped, using the seconds to consider his options. Blake turned around and slowly walked back. He took the cylinder from his pocket and threw it high into the air toward Fung. Instinctively, Fung reached for the cylinder with both hands. In that second, Blake leveled his gun at Fung.

"Drop the gun," Blake called out.

Fung paused, looked at the cylinder. "If you've given me a fake, I'll hunt you down."

Blake stared at Fung. "You and me. I'd welcome that."

Fung dropped his gun, spun on his heel and walked out of the clearing back toward the beach.

Blake picked up Fung's gun and motioned to Lau. "Come with me."

Blake pushed Lau out of the clearing into the darkness of the bushes, and then he took his gun and held it beneath Lau's chin. Lau's facial muscles quivered and his eyes filled with terror. Blake pulled back the hammer of the trigger.

"You understand revenge, don't you?" Blake asked through clenched teeth.

Lau cowered.

"Down on your knees," Blake ordered.

Lau fell to his knees. Blake walked around behind Lau and put the gun to his head. Blake's eyes narrowed and his gun hand shook. After a few long moments, Blake's arm dropped by his side. He released the hammer on the trigger, the gun back into his waistband and dragged Lau to his feet.

"Come on, let's go," Blake said.

"Where are we going?" Lau asked.

"I'm turning you into the police," Blake replied.

Blake escorted Lau back to the dock and together they got into the dingy and rowed out into the water. Blake signaled with his flashlight and in a few minutes, Sabrina's boat appeared alongside. Blake tied up the dingy and with Lau they climbed on board Sabrina's boat.

"Sabrina?" Blake called out.

She emerged from the boat's cockpit. Her facial muscles were tight and her eyes narrowed. "Who's this?"

"Daniel Lau," Blake replied, "he says he killed Raymond. I don't know what to make of it. I'll let the police sort it out."

Suddenly a shower of blood and flesh exploded from Lau's head with the sound of a stick being hammered into sand, followed by the echo of a gunshot across the water. Lau fell on top of Sabrina. Blood and bits of flesh splattered over the front of her blouse and face.

Blake pushed Lau off of Sabrina and threw himself on top of her. "Stay down. When I tell you, crawl as fast as you can to the cabin and get us out of here. He took out his gun, slid over to the gunwale and fired blindly. "Now! Go! Go!"

Sabrina scrambled into the cabin, leaving a trail of Lau's blood on the deck. Blake peeked over the railing, gun ready and looked for signs of activity on the black water. Sabrina rammed the throttle into full speed. The boat sat up in the water and quickly reached top speed. After a few minutes she cut the engines and the boat stopped. She ran back to Blake.

"Is there a boat chasing us?" she asked.

"No, nothing," he replied.

She went inside the cabin with Blake, sat at the table and rocked back and forth, staring at the blood on her hands.

Blake knelt beside her and held her hands. "I'll help you clean up." He went to the sink and grabbed a wet sponge and clean cloth. He slowly scrubbed the blood off her hands and face. The wounded animal look in her eyes made Blake's throat constrict. Sabrina unbuttoned her blouse, tore off the blood-soaked garment and threw it into the corner.

"You'll feel better if you wash off in the shower," Blake said.

He stood up, led Sabrina to the shower stall and turned to go back the main cabin.

She grabbed him by the arm. "Please don't go."

He brushed her cheek gently with his hand. "I'll be here when you're finished."

Sabrina slipped out of her pants, turned around, undid the hook on her bra and tossed it aside, slid out of her panties, trailing one open hand back toward Blake. "I need you, Blake."

Blake stared at her naked body for a moment. "I told you that I can't." He turned around and walked back into the galley. "I'll make us both a drink."

Sabrina glared after him for a moment and then stepped into the shower and slammed the door.

Fifteen minutes later, Blake sat at the table in the dining area looking at a map, then went to the cabin to check the boat's positioning equipment. He returned just as Sabrina emerged from the sleeping quarters, wearing a pair of white shorts and a white sleeveless blouse. She had her dark auburn hair tied back into a pony tail.

"Do you think Lau was the killer?" she asked, her voice showing no signs of her earlier anger.

"If Fung's responsible, he covered himself by completing his end of the bargain. He delivered a self-confessed killer who can't talk."

Sabrina took Blake's hand and studied the strong fingers and bulging veins. "Did you think about killing Lau?"

Blake listened to the waves gently slapping the boat side to side. "Yes, for a few moments."

She kissed him gently on the cheek. "Let's spend the night on the boat. I'd feel safer." She glanced at the bedroom cabin.

"Right. We can anchor at the Aberdeen Marina. I'll drop Lau's body on the dock and leave an anonymous tip about Lau's body with Inspector Lai." He pushed the cushion. "I'll bunk out here. Tomorrow, we're off to see Dr. Bivar."

Sabrina suddenly stood up. "Fine," she snapped. And then she walked back to the sleeping cabin and slammed the door.

Blake studied his muscular hands. Sabrina's erratic behavior troubled him. Her incessant romantic overtures were probably the result of the extreme stress she was under, he thought. He had a duty to be close to her and protect her. He wanted to tell her openly about his feelings for Angela, but somehow he didn't want to say the words out loud. With a heavy heart, he climbed up into the cockpit, turned the boat around and headed it back toward Aberdeen Harbor.

26

Blake and Sabrina stood waiting at the boarding gate of Mexico City's international airport.

"You've known this Mendoza for a long time?" Sabrina asked.

"About ten years. We took DEA training together one summer," Blake replied.

"I thought you didn't want to tell the police?"

"I don't. Xtimal has taken vacation time and is helping me as a personal favor."

Blake pointed at a short, stocky, middle-aged man with course jet-black hair and smooth chocolate-colored skin, walking among the deplaning passengers. "There he is." He waved at Mendoza. "Xtimal, over here!"

Mendoza waved back and walked over to them.

"We almost missed you. Are you getting shorter in old age?" Blake quipped.

"At least my face is not shriveling up like a prune," Mendoza retorted.

Blake patted Mendoza's rock hard stomach. "Getting a little soft I see."

Mendoza faked a punch at Blake's stomach, making him flinch. "Ha. And you've slowed down, old man."

They both laughed and embraced each other.

"I hate to interrupt this locker room play," Sabrina said softly.

Blake stepped back. "I'm sorry. I'd like to introduce Sabrina Chan. Sabrina, this is Xtimal Mendoza."

Mendoza shook her hand. "I'm sorry to hear of your loss, Mrs. Chan."

"Thank you, and please call me Sabrina," she said, "I've heard a lot about you, Xtimal."

Mendoza looked at Blake. "All true. I know Blake wouldn't lie about me."

They laughed together again.

"Xtimal, that's an interesting name," Sabrina said, "it doesn't sound Spanish."

"My mother was Mayan, or more accurately, a native Indian of Mayan ancestry. My father was Mexican," Mendoza said.

"We've got a taxi waiting," Blake said, "we can go directly to Dr. Bivar's office."

They began walking through the terminal toward ground transportation.

"Do you know Dr. Bivar?" Mendoza asked.

"He's an old friend of Sabrina's," Blake replied.

"So get me up to date," Mendoza said.

Blake nodded. "Raymond was found murdered on the outskirts of Hong Kong. It looks like he was so frustrated by the lack of progress in his father's murder investigation that he made a deal with one or some of the triads: steal information from Simon Fung, their competitor, in return for helping Raymond find his father's killer."

"So I gather your brother never did find out," Mendoza said.

"Before he died, Raymond managed to get the information that he stole—in the form of microdots—to his uncle, who in turn passed them on to us," Blake said.

"What was on the microdots?" Mendoza asked.

"A record of Fung's drug shipments and bribes to public officials, a partnership offer by Ramirez to develop a new drug and a set of Mayan or Aztec symbols, supposedly giving some details of this drug," Blake replied.

Mendoza whistled softly. "Now there's a time-bomb."

"And it's ticking," Blake added. "I met with Fung to exchange the microdots for information about Raymond's killer."

"You believe in living dangerously," Mendoza said.

Blake smiled. "At the exchange, Fung produced this man, Daniel Lau, who admitted killing Raymond as revenge for Wang Chan's involvement in the death of Lau's father."

"So why would he turn himself in?" Mendoza asked.

"Sacrifice himself to save his brother. He said that Fung could get Lau's brother, a political prisoner in China, released from prison," Blake answered.

"Do you buy Lau's story?" Mendoza asked.

"Didn't matter. Sabrina and I were ready to take him into the police when Lau was shot and killed," Blake said.

"Fung?" Mendoza queried.

Blake nodded. "Who else? He got rid of any witness who could tie him to Raymond's death."

"Except us," Sabrina said.

Blake looked at Sabrina.

Mendoza reached into his pocket and took out a piece of paper. "We found this on Ramirez' men in that shootout in Tijuana."

Blake looked at the embossed red dragon on the paper. "It's the symbol for Fung's Hung Se Ying triad."

"Another piece of the puzzle," Mendoza said.

"Time is a pressure here now. Fung will be contacting Ramirez soon, or vice versa," Blake said.

They continued walking through the airport doors onto the sidewalk where hundreds of taxis and buses lined up.

"Ramirez is at war with the other drug cartels in Mexico. We suspect he ordered several executions," Mendoza said.

"If we could get the goods on Fung and Mendoza at the same time, it would be a bonus," Blake said.

"You said the coded message mentioned a new drug?" Mendoza asked.

"That's where Dr. Bivar comes in. Hopefully, he can decode the symbols and they'll tell us more," Blake replied.

Sabrina pointed at a black limousine at the curb. "Let's take this one. I hate those taxis."

The limousine driver opened the door and loaded their luggage into the truck. Blake, Sabrina and Mendoza climbed in.

"*Muséo Naçíonal de Antropología*, and hurry," Sabrina snapped, "and put the air conditioner on high." She wiped her forehead, cheeks and neck with a handkerchief.

The limousine driver nodded and punched a button on the console.

"Has Bivar got the authority and resources to gain access to any archeological site without interference?" Blake asked.

Sabrina nodded. "Absolutely. The academic community and the indigenous peoples revere him for his work preserving ancient cultures here."

Twenty minutes later, the limousine lurched to a stop in front of the Museum of Anthropology. Blake got out of the car with Mendoza first and helped Sabrina step out. He glanced to see the limousine driver looking appreciatively at Sabrina's buttocks and smiled.

"Follow me," Sabrina said, heading for the massive front doors.

They quickly found Professor Bivar's office. Sabrina knocked on the door and a voice called out, "*Entre.*"

They walked into Bivar's office which was lined with bookcases and shelving units overflowing with pieces of pottery, maps, carvings and statues. A large wooden desk was covered with papers and books. An intricate wooden carving of a figure—half man, half serpent—sat on the desk.

"Come in, come," a balding man in his late fifties, with a brownish-gray beard and bright brown eyes, said.

"*Hola*, Rodrigo, it's good to see you again," Sabrina said. She embraced him and kissed him on the cheek.

"Ah, Sabrina, it's been so long. You look wonderful," Bivar said, holding the embrace.

Sabrina gently pushed him away after a few moments. "Thank you so much for agreeing to help us."

Bivar held her hands in his. "I'm sorry about your husband."

"Thank you," she said. She turned to Blake and Mendoza. "I want to introduce you to Blake Morgan, Raymond's brother."

Blake shook Bivar's hand firmly. "A pleasure Professor."

"Please accept my condolences on your brother's death," Bivar said, "Sabrina has told me a lot about you."

"Thank you," Blake said, "and whatever Sabrina said about me, I deny."

Bivar and Sabrina laughed.

"And this," Sabrina said, motioning to Mendoza, "is Xtimal Mendoza, a friend of Blake's."

Mendoza shook Bivar's hand. "An honor, Professor, I've heard of your work."

Bivar waved his hand casually. "I've done what I can to preserve Mexico's ancient cultures." He pointed to a sofa and chairs beside his desk. "Please sit down." He gathered up books and papers strewn on the sofa and chairs and piled them on the floor.

Blake, Sabrina and Mendoza sat down and Bivar wheeled his chair around from the desk to sit close to them.

"I don't know if I mentioned it or not, Rodrigo, but Blake works for the Drug Enforcement Agency in the U.S. and Xtimal works for its equivalent here in Mexico," Sabrina said.

"That must be exciting work compare to mine," Bivar said.

"It can be," Blake and Mendoza said in unison.

"You said you wanted my help?" Bivar asked.

"We believe that the man who may be responsible for Raymond Chan's death, the head of a Hong Kong criminal organization, is forming a partnership with a prominent Mexican drug cartel run by a man named Ramirez," Blake said.

Bivar scratched his head. "What would that have to do with ancient cultures in Mexico?"

"We've intercepted a message from Ramirez that makes reference to the existence of an ancient drug but the contents of the message are in symbols that we think are Aztec or Mayan," Blake replied.

"Rodrigo, finding the person responsible for Raymond's death is a personal matter, as well," Sabrina said.

Blake took a piece of paper out of his pocket. "Tell us what these symbols mean." He handed the paper to Bivar.

Bivar looked carefully at the symbols. "First, I'll tell you that they're Mayan and a little about their language. It's far more sophisticated than ours. The symbols can spell single words with single signs called logographs that are phonetic signs representing syllables. They could also be written with a picture of a convoluted stone or personified as an animal. To avoid confusion, the Mayans attached syllable signs to the logographs to indicate how to pronounce them. The whole system was very complex and artistic."

"It sounds very sophisticated," Sabrina said.

Bivar smiled, got up and pulled out a large sheet of paper from under his desk and pinned it to the bookcase. He copied the symbols with a felt pen onto the paper, flipped open a large Bible-sized book entitled, *A Lexicon of Mayan Hieroglyphics* and then proceeded to decipher each of the symbols. The scratching of his pen filled the silence in the room for the next twenty minutes.

Bivar suddenly clapped his hands together. "This is amazing. But there must be more."

Blake and Sabrina exchanged glances.

"That's all there was," Sabrina said.

Bivar stroked his beard and searched his pockets for the glasses perched on his head. "These hieroglyphics describe the ball game ceremony that took place in many Mayan cities. The purpose of the ball game has been hotly debated for a century." He pointed to several symbols on the large sheet of paper. "Here. A priest with a feathered headdress is directing slaves to crush a plant, mix it with roots and then siphon off a liquid mixture."

"What plant?" Blake asked.

"Patience," Bivar said irritably. He pointed to several other symbols. "Here the symbols show a priest pouring the mixture into bowls and the ball game warriors drinking it. It must be a drug like *Ayahusasca,* called the vine of the soul by the Mayans."

"Does it say *Ayahuasca*?" Blake asked.

"No," Bivar replied.

"Is there any reference to the name of the plant or where it can be found?" Blake asked.

Bivar examined the symbols again. "No, but they mention where a more detailed history of the ball game can be found. It might be there."

"Where?" Sabrina asked.

Bivar walked over to the bookcase with several enlarged photographs of Mayan ruins. He stabbed his finger at a photograph of ruins with a towering four-sided pyramid. "Here. *Chich'en Itza* in the Yucatan."

"That's a fully explored site, Professor. Is it likely we'd find anything new there?" Mendoza asked.

Bivar sighed. "Consider the great pyramids of Egypt. Plundered and explored for centuries. Yet only recently they've discovered new chambers and tunnels." He rubbed his hands together excitedly. "I've got to tell you, this could be a major discovery."

"Well, how soon can we get going?" Mendoza asked.

Bivar put his hands on his hips. "This is not a downtown trip, Mr. Mendoza. We need money for supplies, transportation, and clearance from authorities."

Sabrina looked at Blake. "Blake and I will cover all the costs, Rodrigo, including a generous donation to your ongoing research."

Bivar smiled broadly. "That's wonderful."

"And I'll expedite all clearance to access the ruins and restrict public access for a few days," Mendoza said.

Bivar scratched his head. "Then we should leave immediately. I'll give my notice for a short vacation."

Sabrina stood up and embraced Bivar. "Thank you, Rodrigo."

Bivar held her embrace for a few long moments. "I would have volunteered for nothing to spend time with you."

Sabrina gently pushed herself away. "We all appreciate your help."

Blake and Mendoza shook Bivar's hand warmly.

"What are the travel arrangements?" Blake asked.

"We fly to *Merída*. From there we take a small plane to *Valladolid* and then a short jeep ride to *Chich'en Itza*," Bivar replied.

"Oh, and one final thing, Professor," Blake said.

"Yes?" Bivar replied.

"Please don't talk about our plans or destination with anyone," Blake said.

Bivar nodded. "I understand. Undercover operation and all that."

Blake looked at Mendoza and winked and then they, along with Sabrina left Bivar's office and headed back to their hotel.

"Please put up the privacy screen," Blake told the limousine driver.

The driver complied.

"Do you think Bivar is taking this seriously?" Blake asked.

"It must be the excitement of undercover police work that makes him appear a little immature," Blake said. He nudged Sabrina with his elbow. "Or the prospect of being with his former flame."

"Jealous, Blake?" Sabrina asked teasingly.

"No, but it's obvious he still has a thing for you," Blake replied.

Sabrina smoothed her skirt with here immaculately manicured fingers. "Rodrigo has a real interest in our expedition. The opportunity for a new discovery, publishing his findings and more money for research are great motivators. Don't underestimate him."

"Ouch! I think you stand corrected, Blake," Mendoza said.

Blake laughed. "It wouldn't be the first time . . . To change the subject, is there anything more you can tell us about Ramirez?"

Mendoza nodded. "A ruthless and very intelligent man. He worked his way out of the gutter to become a drug dealer, assassin and then ran the Vera Cruz operation for the Juarez cartel. He set up his own operation a few years ago and has been in constant war with the other cartels since. The other cartels have tried to kill him several times but he's managed to survive and that's made him hit back with a vengeance."

"Do you think this drug, *jfuri*, if such thing exists, can realistically cut into the cocaine market?" Blake asked.

"Good question. I don't know about Fung, but the problem that Ramirez faces is basically a supplier-territory problem. The other cartels have got a lock on the cocaine suppliers in South America, so even if he wanted to expand his operation dramatically, he couldn't get the product. So he's had to go to war against the other cartels and take their territory. With a new drug, like with many of the chemical drugs in the past, the market is wide open," Mendoza said.

The limousine stopped in front of the hotel and they got out.

Sabrina looked at her watch. "We've got a few hours before we leave. I want to pick up some appropriate clothing and freshen up."

"Right. We can meet later to see if we've got everything we need," Mendoza said, opening his jacket and flashing his handgun.

Together, they walked into the hotel.

Raoul Ramirez paced along the azure blue tiles of his swimming pool, chewing a cigar and holding the telephone with his other hand. "I've been waiting for your reply to my message."

"It seems that the message got delayed," Fung replied at the other end.

"What?"

"Nothing. You say that you've got reliable evidence of this new drug, *jfuri*?"

"Yes, at some old Mayan ruin in the Yucatan called *Chich'en Itza*."

"Why haven't I heard of this *jfuri* before?"

"It's an ancient drug used by the Mayans in some ceremony. Like many of their traditions, all record of it must have been destroyed by the Spanish—until now."

"Ah, yes, the destruction of culture in the name of your God."

"Let's get to the point. If this drug can be easily harvested from the plant that produces it, we could make a serious dent in the cocaine market."

"What kind of drug is this *jfuri*?"

"A combination of a hallucinogen with the qualities of cocaine, but with no violent side effects as with other hallucinogenic plants."

"So where does the plant grow that produces the drug?"

"First the partnership. Fifty-fifty. Agreed?"

"Agreed."

"I want to keep this to ourselves for now. Meet me in Mexico City and just the two of us will go to *Chich'en Itza*."

"I told you that I won't extend my risks without some additional protection."

"Meaning?"

"We'll have to give our associate in The Company his usual cut."

"Out of your share?"

"Nice try. Shared equally."

"Maybe we don't need him anymore."

"I don't understand what's in it for him."

"The prospect of money and power can tempt anyone."

"My father told me never to trust an honest man or a patriot. I hope he's neither of those."

"So are we agreed?"

"Alright, we share his cut."

"Good, then I'll pick you up at the airport in Mexico City. I'm bringing along an archeologist on my payroll who can decipher any more symbols we may find."

"Right. I'll see you then."

Ramirez put down the telephone. "Raphael!"

Raphael Salinez, Ramirez' number two man in the carte, emerged from the house. "Yes, boss?"

"Bring in the professor."

Salinez went into the house and re-emerged carrying a briefcase. Beside him walked an old man with wire rimmed glasses.

"Boss, this is Professor Gonzales," Salinez said, 'he's the expert on Mayan culture from Guatemala that I hired."

Gonzales shuffled up to Ramirez.

"Sit down, Professor," Ramirez said, "have a drink of bottled water." He poured a glass.

Gonzales sat down. "Thank you, *Senõr* Ramirez." He took a sip of the water.

"Congratulations on deciphering the symbols on the piece of bark," Ramirez said.

Gonzales nodded. "It was not difficult."

"Are you familiar with the ruins at *Chich'en Itza?*" Ramirez asked.

Gonzales took another sip of water and nodded. "Yes, I've studied the site in detail many times."

"Good! You'll be going there with me. I need to find details of what plant this drug *jfuri* comes from and where to find the plant," Ramirez said.

"Of course, I hope the information you seek is there," Gonzales replied.

Ramirez examined a piece of tobacco on his finger. "I believe Raphael said that you would be paid one hundred thousand dollars for your work." He nodded to Salinez.

Salinez opened the briefcase to reveal wads of paper currency. Gonzales's eyes opened wide.

"Fifty-thousand now, and fifty thousand when your work is complete," Ramirez said.

Gonzales wiped the sweat off his forehead. "Of course, of course."

"Good! Raphael, the professor and I leave immediately."

Salinez nodded, and walked with Gonzales back into the house.

Ramirez took his soggy cigar, squashed it in the ashtray, grabbed fresh one of box on the table and smelled it appreciatively before lighting it.

27

Blake's and Sabrina's shoes scraped the bricks in unison as they walked across the *Merída en Domingo* square. Above the square soared the pristine white cathedral, built by the Spanish in 1561 in *Merída*, a city of half a million people in the middle of the Yucatan peninsula.

"Oh, Blake, look," Sabrina called out. She pointed to several brightly painted wooden stalls around the perimeter of the square. She pulled Blake by the hand, snaking her way through the dozens of people in the square. Sabrina stopped by the flower stall and kneeled beside a little girl, bundling flowers together into bouquets.

"How much?" Sabrina asked.

The smooth-skinned girl with large, deep brown eyes held up three fingers. "Four *pesos*."

A young woman called out from behind the little girl. "Juanita!"

"Juanita, is that your name?" Sabrina asked.

"*Sí,*" she replied shyly.

"Juanita is a beautiful name," Sabrina said, gently stroking the little girls' hair.

"*Graçias.* How many flowers do you want? Three? Four?" the little girl asked.

Sabrina and Blake laughed.

Blake took thirty pesos from his pocket and paid for a bouquet. The young girl handed the flowers to Sabrina and fluttered her big brown eyes. "Thank you, and may God bless you."

Sabrina held the bouquet to her face, breathing in their perfume. Blake smiled at her expression of joy.

"Are you hungry? There's a great little café on *Callé Hermosa*, near the *Casa de Huspedes,*" she said.

Sabrina entwined her arm with Blake's and steered him to the café. A low peach-colored adobe wall with arbors of red and purple hanging bougainvillea welcomed them. On a huge entrance beam the name, Rosarita's, was hand-carved.

A portly woman in an embroidered dress greeted them at the entrance. "*Hola*, honeymooners."

"We're not, but thank you for your hospitality," Blake said.

Sabrina squeezed Blake's arm. "But we could be."

"Sabrina, we've talked about this," Blake replied in a hushed, frustrated tone.

"Oh, Blake, don't be so serious, I'm just having fun," Sabrina replied.

Rosarita led them to a table surrounded with flowers overlooking the square. A soft delicate breeze, carrying the perfume of the flowers and the smell of food in the kitchen drifted through the open café patio.

"*Dos cervazas, por favor*," Blake said.

"*Sí*, right away," Rosarita replied.

Sabrina took Blake's hands in hers. "Blake, let's forget the whole business."

Blake's eyes widened. "What about Raymond? And busting the drug syndicate?"

"I know, but in the beauty of this place, with you, it doesn't seem so important anymore."

Before Blake could reply, Professor Bivar and Xtimal Mendoza appeared at the café entrance.

"I've been looking all over the city for you two," Bivar called out.

Bivar and Mendoza joined Blake and Sabrina at their table.

The gregarious café owner, Rosarita, appeared and placed the beer on the table with a flourish. "*Hola, profesor*."

"*Más cervazas*, Rosarita," Bivar said, "and bring us some of your wonderful *Mukbidollo*." He turned to Blake. "A large tamale stuffed with chicken, pork and spice, wrapped in banana leaves and baked in the earth."

"It sounds delicious," Sabrina said.

Rosarita smiled. "Right away, *profesor*." They left and returned with more beer and her specialty food.

Bivar raised his glass in the air. "Here's to our new discoveries," he said, and briefly touching Sabrina's arm, "and to rediscoveries."

They raised their glasses and touched them in salute.

"I've made arrangements for our plane and a jeep with all the gear we'll need. We'll leave tomorrow," Bivar said excitedly.

"Until then, let's enjoy every moment here like it's our last," Sabrina said.

They ate and drank and laughed into the night. After thanking Rosarita for the wonderful meal, they arose and walked back to the hotel.

"I'm tired," Sabrina said, "I think I'll go back to my room to rest."

"My thoughts, exactly," Bivar said, "we have a big day tomorrow."

"I'm going to walk around for a while," Blake said.

"I'll join you," Mendoza said.

Bivar escorted Sabrina back to the hotel.

Blake and Mendoza walked along the cobblestone streets through an empty square and found a late night bar still open. They sat down at a table and ordered beer.

"You and Sabrina, you seem like a couple," Mendoza said.

Blake shook his head. "I'm involved with someone back in Los Angeles. Angela Townsend, a Special Prosecutor for the DEA."

"Forgive me, I misread the situation."

"*De nada.* Sabrina would like us to get together, but I think she's turned to me out of need."

Mendoza slapped Blake on the shoulder. "It's obvious she loves you. I never give advice about religion or love, but you should make sure she doesn't believe that your friendship and compassion are love. And if you're in love with this woman Angela, tell her and tell Sabrina."

Blake sighed. "I know, you're right." He looked at his watch. "It's getting late and I want to make a telephone call before I go to bed."

"Angela?"

Blake nodded.

They got up and walked back to the hotel. Back in his room, Blake picked up the telephone and dialed.

"Angela, it's Blake."

"I was hoping it might be you."

"I'm in *Merida* in the Yucatan with Sabrina and an old friend of hers, Dr. Rodrigo Bivar, an archeologist and my old buddy, Xtimal Mendoza."

"What have you found out?"

"Dr .Bivar was able to decipher the symbols on the microdot. They're Mayan and make reference to detailed information about this ancient drug called *jfuri*, which the Mayans used in their ball game ceremony."

"That sounds exotic."

"The symbols refer to the Mayan ruins at a place called *Chich'en Itza*."

"I've heard of it; it's supposed to be very old."

"We're heading there tomorrow and hopefully we'll get the rest of the story before Fung and Ramirez find out."

"This Dr. Bivar, you have faith in him?"

"He's one of the most renowned Mayan experts and he's got a crush on Sabrina. He wants to help."

"I'm still worried about you, Blake, but I'm glad Mendoza is with you."

"He's the best. I trust him with my life . . . Is there anything new at your end?"

"Nothing. I'm still putting together a brief from my notes but I can't locate the witnesses we had before. I've been trying unsuccessfully to get in touch with Jack Cross to find out how his internal investigation is going, but he hasn't got back to me yet."

"Hmm . . . I'm not optimistic about that."

"Let's give Jack the benefit of the doubt, Blake."

"I suppose . . . it's good to hear your voice again."

"I miss your arms around me."

"You have been in my thoughts often. You know, Xtimal said something to me that I need to do something about."

"What's that?"

"He said that I should declare my feelings for you and make that clear to Sabrina."

"Xtimal is a wise man, Blake."

"Well . . . uh . . . I've never felt so close to someone as I have to you."

"Does that mean that you love me?"

"I don't know . . . I guess . . . I suppose."

"Oh Blake, you're such a pain. You're going to have to practice a lot better than that."

"Hey, it's a start."

"Well, I look forward to the next installment. And don't forget about Sabrina. I don't want her thinking you're fair game."

"Yeah, you're right . . . I've got to run. I'll be in touch soon."

"Come back to me safely, darling."

"I will. Goodnight."

Blake hung up the telephone and went to bed feeling warmth spread throughout his body from his talk with Angela. It knew that he would tell her that he loved her when they were together again.

Angela Townsend ruffled her usually neatly arranged hair in frustration. She answered the intercom on her telephone. "Yes?"

"A Mr. Jack Cross to see you," the voice replied at the other end.

"Jack, here? I'll come out," Angela replied.

She walked out of her office into the reception area. Jack Cross, dressed in a dark blue suit sat quietly in a chair.

"Jack, this is an unexpected surprise," Angela said. She embraced him.

"I was close by on other business and I thought I'd drop by," Cross said warmly.

"Please come in," Angela said. She turned to her receptionist. "Please hold all my calls."

"Yes, Ms. Townsend," the young receptionist replied.

Angela walked back into her office with Cross.

"Can I get you coffee, water?" Angela asked, waving her hand for Cross to sit with her at the coffee table.

"No thanks," Cross replied. He looked around the office. "I'm so pleased that you decided for government service, Angela. Not enough young, talented people choose service to their country over self-gain."

"I like the young person part," Angela said, laughing.

Cross leaned back into his chair. "First, I want to tell you how sorry I am about David Quinn."

"Thanks, Jack. David was a good man."

"He didn't seem like the type who'd be tempted by money."

Angela shook her head. "Blake and I believe that he was framed."

"For what reason?"

"Quinn was going to meet a man called Pantages, an ex-police officer, who told Quinn he had incriminating evidence on someone in The Company who was involved in laundering drug money."

"So you're saying that someone in The Company may have something to do with Quinn's and Pantages' deaths?"

Angela looked at him quizzically. "I didn't mention Pantages was killed."

"We got a report from the DC police . . . did you get any statement or other evidence from Pantages?"

Angela shook her head. "All the files Quinn was carrying are gone. I tried to get copies when I came back from Washington but his computer files and filing cabinet has been cleaned out. Doesn't that tell you that someone in The Company knew we were on to something?"

Cross carefully straightened the crease in his pants. "Perhaps. Or someone in the DEA. Or maybe Quinn really was dirty."

Angela shook her head vigorously. "I can't believe that."

Cross leaned forward and looked intently into Angela's eyes. "Sometimes we know the people closest to us least of all."

Angela stared at Cross for a few moments. "Have you made any progress in your internal investigation?"

"That's one of the things I wanted to tell you. I followed up on the cases that Blake mentioned in Costa Rica and Seattle."

"What did you find out?"

"In Costa Rica, the man that Blake arrested, Richard Bull, is one of the best sources of information that our country has about the movements of terrorists and insurgents in Central America. We've used his services—and you understand this is off the record—as a go between to supply government paramilitary groups with arms to fight the rebel groups."

"Is his usefulness worth the immunity from prosecution for drug trafficking?"

Cross nodded. "Working with valuable information sources like Bull is a delicate matter, Angela. If Bull went to trial, his exposure would be a great loss to us and we wouldn't want any public examination of our activities in Central America."

"Why not, Jack?"

"Covert activities by definition can't occur within public scrutiny any more than Blake's undercover work can be reported on the six-o'clock news."

"What about the Seattle case?"

"A different kind of problem. The head of the triad that was responsible for the heroin and illegal alien smuggling

operation is also a potential powerful ally for us in The Peoples'
Republic of China. His organization was once part of an elite
Red Army division who are no longer loyal to their country. In
the event we ever need to move against China, inside insurgents
like him are absolutely necessary."

"But Jack, these men are criminals!"

Cross nodded. "I know, and the DEA will be able to
prosecute the men they arrested in Seattle. But our main man in
Hong Kong can't be touched."

"Do you realize how people would react to this if it
became public?"

"First of all, they wouldn't believe it. Second, people
understand that The Company is constantly at war with our
country's enemies. It's a war we can't talk about but just as
necessary as the military battles that your father fought. He'd
understand that."

Angela shook her head. "I'm not so sure about that."

"Did you father ask you or the American people for
approval of the targets that we hit in Viet Nam, knowing full-
well that some innocent people would be killed?"

"I don't think that's . . ."

"The overall objective was to free the people from the
yoke of Communism, to not let South Vietnam be the first of
many nations to fall into Communist hands. To achieve that
objective, we had to do what was necessary. And sometimes that
meant playing dirty."

Angela stood up and walked back to her desk. She
looked at the photograph of her father with Cross in military
uniforms. "There's a line that must be drawn, Jack. The ends
don't justify the means."

"Do you think your father or Blake believes that?"

"I believe that the law of our country and that of the
civilized world is based on that proposition."

"The real world doesn't always work that way." Cross
got up and held Angela by her shoulders. "Suffice it to say that
I've taken steps to rid The Company of some of its more risky

assets and I'm grateful to you and Blake for bringing the matter to my attention."

Angela looked intently into Cross' eyes.

"And," Cross continued, "in recognition of that I'm authorized to offer you a job with The Company as legal counsel. We need people like you to keep old war horses like me honest. What do you think?"

Angela's mouth dropped open. "Well, I'm flattered . . . I don't know."

Cross squeezed her arms gently. "You don't have to give me an answer now. Just think about it and we'll talk again. It would be great having you close in Washington, like being family."

Angela smiled. "Thanks, Jack, I will think about it seriously."

Cross stepped back. "Is Blake on another assignment?"

"Nothing official. But while investigating his brother's death in Hong Kong, he stumbled across a conspiracy between a Hong Kong triad and a Mexican drug cartel."'

"An odd partnership. Did he mention the name of the triad connection?"

"Simon Fung."

"And the Mexican end?"

"Ramirez."

"So what's Blake doing about it?"

"He and an old friend in the Mexican DEA are in the Yucatan at the Mayan ruins at *Chich'en Itza*, trying to track down this new drug the conspiracy plans to market."

"Interesting." Cross abruptly looked at his watch. "I've got to run. It's been great to see you. Please pass on my progress report to Blake, and think carefully about my offer." He embraced Angela and left the office.

Angela sat back in her chair and looked at the photograph on her bookcase of Cross and her father.

28

The twin-engine otter raced toward the end of the runway. Its engines howled and its body shook so much that the faces in the cockpit blurred. Blake reached over and gently patted Sabrina's hand. She smiled warmly. Closer and closer the trees rushed toward them. Suddenly, as if the plane had dropped an enormous weight, it rose sharply above the jungle and climbed into the sky.

The pilot, Ramon Valenzuela, pushed back a baseball cap on his tanned, leathery forehead and laughed. "See, plenty of room."

Blake winked at Sabrina. "Nice take-off, Ramon. How do the other planes manage?"

Valenzuela pointed to the long airstrip below. "They use the regular runway."

Blake and Sabrina burst into laughter, which was soon drowned out by Valenzuela's bar room bellow. Professor Bivar, oblivious to this, wrestled with a large diagram of the *Chich'en Itza* ruins in his lap. Mendoza held up one corner of the map trying to look useful.

"How far, Ramon?" Sabrina asked, waving her khaki hat to cool her face.

Valenzuela turned around, still grinning. "The landing strip at *Valladolid* is about thirty minutes. From there by jeep to the ruins is another thirty minutes."

He banked the plane over *La Cuidad Blanca*, the White City, as *Merida* is often called. The gleaming white tower of St. Mary's Cathedral soared up toward the plane.

Sabrina leaned across Blake to look out the window. Blake felt her breast press against his arm. He thought about the languid afternoons in the courtyard of their white Spanish-style hotel, their slow walks among *Merida's* alabaster walls and brightly painted houses and the Sunday music and dancing at the *Merida en Domingo* square. Except for the times when Sabrina talked of romance, their time there had been pleasant. But Blake couldn't help thinking what it would have been like having Angela with him.

Valenzuela landed the plane in *Valladolid*, a small town close to *Chich'en Itza*. They ate an afternoon meal and then collected their gear and threw it into the SUV that Bivar had obtained.

Bivar adjusted the driver's seat. "We can go the usual tourist route, or this nice back road that I know. It won't take much longer."

"Let's take the back road," Sabrina said excitedly.

Blake began to protest and then nodded agreement.

Bivar guided the SUV down a narrow dirt road toward the jungle. The tree canopy dimmed the afternoon light. Blake closed his eyes. The jeep's tires ran over a carpet of soft grass and dirt, while around them cool seas of feathery ferns ebbed and flowed. The jungle smelled ripe-sweet. Blake opened his eyes again. As the sun continued to sink, the jungle green muted to blues and purples. In the dusk, the heady perfume of nocturnal moon-blossoms caught in Blake's throat.

After a few miles, the SUV emerged into an open area with giant crumbling ruins. Bivar parked the SUV and they walked to the entrance. The ruins had just closed for the day to the public and the last remaining tourists were escorted to a waiting bus by a tall uniformed security guard.

Bivar waved. "*Hola,* Juan."

"*Hola, Profesor*, it's good to see you again," Juan replied.

Bivar motioned his companions. "These are my colleagues, Sabrina, Blake and Xtimal. And this," he said, slapping Juan on the shoulder, "is Juan Lopez, head of security."

Lopez saluted. "Welcome to *Chich'en Itza*," he replied in a jovial manner, "I was just about to do a perimeter sweep to make sure there are no tourists hanging around. I've put up signs indicating the site is closed for two days."

Bivar nodded. "That's good, Juan, thanks for your help."

"You can park your vehicle in front of The Temple of a Thousand Warriors." Lopez detached a key from his ring of keys. "Here's the supply shed key in case you need more equipment or supplies."

"Thank you, Juan, that's great," Bivar said.

Lopez shook hands with everyone. "I'll treat you to *cervazas* at the *Cantína Chich'en* when you're done."

"It's a date," Bivar said jovially, "and we'll see you in the morning."

Lopez walked away. Blake, Mendoza, Sabrina and Bivar got into the SUV and Bivar drove it to the open area in front of The Temple of a Thousand Warriors and parked it."

"Professor, could you give us a quick overview before it gets too dark?" Blake asked.

Bivar pointed up the stairs of the Temple of A Thousand Warriors. "We can get a better view if we climb up the platform at the top."

They climbed thirty-six stone steps, flanked on each side by two stone sculptures of feathered snakes. At the top of the steps was a giant statue of a man reclining as though he was doing sit-ups. A structure was decorated with scores of heart-eating eagles and jaguars and Mayan warriors.

"The flat basin on the statue's stomach was used for sacrifice or to hold offerings," Bivar said, "and below, you see hundreds of stone pillars in what's called the Plaza of The Thousand Columns. A roof once covered the columns and the huge space below must have been a meeting place or market."

Bivar pointed to a crumbling dome on a stone platform in the distance. "The *Caracol*, or celestial observatory, is much like our modern ones. We're still astounded by the Mayan's knowledge of astronomy."

"Is that what they call *El Castillo*?" Mendoza asked, pointing to a huge four-sided pyramid with steps on all sides and a platform on top.

Bivar nodded. "That's what the Spanish called it. The Mayan referred to as *Kukulcan's* pyramid. Each side has ninety-one steps which added together with the top platform equals three hundred and sixty-five. It's a celestial calendar, developed hundreds of years before the Western calendar.

Sabrina took out her handkerchief and wiped the perspiration from her face. "Was *Kukulcan* a god or a man?"

"The Toltec people, who came before the Mayans and the Aztecs, called their great leader or god, *Quetzacoatl*. The Mayan texts refer to *Quetzacoatl* as *Kukulcan*. They saw him both as a man and a god."

Bivar pointed to the pyramid. "You won't be able to see it at this time, but on the spring equinox, the setting sun creates a shadow of a serpent moving down the stairs from the platform on top. *Kukulcan* is always depicted as a feathered serpent. The moving shadow is a representation of him descending from his throne in heaven to earth for religious observation."

"Do you think *Kukulcan* is connected in anyway to what we're looking for?" Mendoza asked.

"I know that no one has ever solved the mystery of the whereabouts of his tomb," Bivar replied.

Sabrina opened another button on her blouse and blew down the front. "So where are we going?"

Bivar pointed back to the right, beyond the pyramid. "There, The Temple of the Jaguars next to The Great Ball Court."

They climbed back down the stairs, loaded their gear into packs and walked toward the Temple of the Jaguars. The approaching night brought out the sounds of nocturnal insects and animals as though the ruins had suddenly been invaded. They switched on their lights and soon faced an elevated temple flanked by two large serpentine columns opening to chambers within and a lower smaller enclosure with columns around the doorway. The columns and walls were marked with the images of jaguars, eagles and warriors.

Bivar pointed to the large enclosure below the temple lined by stone walls. "The *Juego de Pelota*, the ball court. Experts still argue over the purpose of the game. Some say human sacrifice, some say religious ceremony and others say gambling on sport."

Blake laughed. "The gambling on sport I understand."

Bivar waved them on. "We must go to one of the side walls of the lower temple."

In a few minutes, they were at the wall and they dropped their packs.

"Now, according to the symbols that I deciphered, an entrance panel to passage and chamber should be along here," Bivar said. He ran his hands along the large stones and then stopped. "This should be the one."

The stone was carved with pictographs of warriors with spears, jaguars and the image of a feathered serpent. The last rays of the sun sprayed the stone, illuminating the sunken relief a feathered serpent.

"Xtimal, help me get the pry bars in the supply shed," Bivar said.

They walked back to the shed. Blake and Sabrina sat down on the stone floor, their backs against cool stone.

Blake took a swig of water from his canteen and then offered it to Sabrina. She took a mouthful and splashed some down her blouse. The cloth stuck to her skin, making her nipples show through the fabric. Blake glanced at them unconsciously and then into Sabrina's eyes. She smiled.

"Blake, how can you deny that you feel something for me?" she asked.

"I don't deny that you are a beautiful and desirable woman," Blake replied.

"That's not what I asked."

Blake didn't reply.

Sabrina began humming a tune.

"Do you recognize that song?" she asked.

"It sounds familiar."

"Remember the Governor's Ball?"

"That was a lifetime ago."

"Let me paint the picture for you. It was the first time that you'd returned from the States after you'd gone to college there. The Governor's Ball was the highlight of the social season. Many of Hong Kong's elite and distinguished foreign guests were there. A hundred beautiful young women in silk and satin dresses with plunging necklines and scores of handsome young men in their uniforms and tuxedos."

"I remember."

"I saw you walking down the winding staircase, a glass of champagne in your hand. You were handsome, athletic, proud. Women were in heat at the sight of you."

"Oh come on, you're making this up."

"I was dancing with Raymond on the ballroom dance floor. He liked the sedate foxtrot. After every turn, I would look up to see if you saw me."

"You wore that backless velvet dress that caused more than a few men to walk into walls."

Sabrina laughed. "Except you. After our dance was over, I came over to you with Raymond and I asked you to show me your best moves."

Blake laughed. "And I said, let's dance first."

"I pulled out you out onto the dance floor for a waltz. You were a bit stumbly at first, but when you held me tighter, you gained confidence."

"Slow dances have never been my strength."

"I can still feel your strong hand on the bare skin of my back."

"I remember when the dance was over; the orchestra took up the tango, my kind of dance."

"It was like the music released some powerful animal in you. You moved me at will, your hands and legs surrounding me. I was dizzy when it was over."

Blake cleared his throat. "Yes . . . the tango is a more interesting dance."

"Oh, Blake, stop pussy-footing. I suppose you don't remember begging me to walk down to the gazebo in the gardens. And how we drank champagne out of the same glass and how our tongues entwining became a frantic race to tear off our clothes and make love there on the gazebo bench?"

"I . . . remember."

Sabrina closed her eyes. "I can smell the sweet odor of the tea roses even now. You slipped the strap of my dress down over my shoulder, your lips tracing the skin of my neck till you found my breasts."

Blake shook his head. "Sabrina, why are you doing this?"

"I'm just reminiscing to show you that we had something special together."

"That may be, but we can't go back."

Sabrina held Blake's face between her hands. "But we can, Blake, we can correct the mistakes of the past. I admit that I married for money and it's been a consuming thing for me since my father left me alone and penniless. But Raymond's death and having you close again has made me see the truth."

Blake wanted to run. He had been in love with Sabrina for years after he left Hong Kong, but eventually had accepted the fact they'd never be together. Now he saw the love for him in her eyes and it pulled at something in his chest. But not his love. That belonged to Angela.

"I know our crisis has brought us closer, but I am in love . . ."

Blake was interrupted by the sound of Bivar and Mendoza climbing up the steps. They were carrying large metal pry bars, wooden blocks and a wooden box. Blake pulled his hand away from Sabrina and stood up. Bivar's eyes glanced between Blake and Sabrina questioningly.

"What's in the box?" Blake asked.

"Some C4 explosives," Mendoza replied.

"Are we going to blow up the temple?" Blake asked.

"It can be used selectively in small amounts to make an opening if the tools don't work," Bivar said, "I've used it before."

They wedged the pry bars between the stones against the blocks of wood and together they began rocking the bar back and forth until it gradually worked its way deeper into the cracks between the blocks of stone. Two hours later, with the blackness of night around them, there was enough space between the stone in question and the one beside it to let a person pass through.

They collapsed against the wall, sweating profusely and breathing heavily. Sabrina took her handkerchief, soaked it in water and wiped the sweat off Blake's face and neck. Bivar looked at her expectantly, but Sabrina just passed him the water canteen.

After they'd rested for fifteen minutes, Bivar got up and took a nylon rope out of his pack. "Put on your packs and I'll tie this guide rope between us and the other end to that pillar," he said, pointing to the stone column by the entrance. After they'd been roped together and with Bivar in the lead, they squeezed themselves through the opening between the stone blocks.

After passing through the opening, Blake reached out for the wall with one hand to steady himself. His hand found a cool damp surface. They walked slowly for another fifty feet, their lights illuminating a higher and wider passage. The sound of their shoes scraping the stone floor like sandpaper on rock was sucked into the blackness.

Bivar stopped. "Did you notice the passageway is gradually sloping downwards?"

"And I thought I'd just got my second wind," Blake said.

Several minutes later, they stood facing a solid stone wall covered in moss and cobwebs, partially obscuring a mass of hieroglyphics and pictographs.

Bivar removed his pack and wiped clean a portion of the wall with a small brush. "I think this is it. Let's get all your lights focused here."

They pointed their lights at the wall and Bivar continued to brush the dust and cobwebs off of the symbols.

"!*A Mi Dios*! This is incredible," Bivar yelled, "I want to take photographs and charcoal rubbings."

Bivar took sheets of paper and charcoal from the packs and handed some to Blake and Mendoza. "Use the charcoal to make rubbings of each of the symbols." Bivar handed Sabrina a camera. "Take photographs of each of the symbols, from two different angles."

Bivar walked slowly in front of the wall, taking notes and translating the symbols. For the next two hours, all that could be heard was the scraping of pen and charcoal and the whirring mechanism of the camera shutter, their shadows illuminating freeze-frame on the ancient walls by the cameras' flash unit.

"Come here, everyone," Bivar shouted excitedly, his voice echoing in the passageway.

Sabrina was the first one to Bivar's side. "What is it, Rodrigo?"

Bivar pointed to the symbols in the right-hand corner of the wall. "These are a continuation of the symbols that were in the message you gave me. Here's a set showing peasants harvesting a plant from along a river in an area the Mayans called *Xicalanco*, which is now known as *Yaxchilan*."

"That's deep in the jungle along the *Usamacinta* River," Mendoza said.

Sabrina rubbed Bivar's shoulder. "What plant?"

"The Mayans call the plant *yage,* but I don't know what the modern name would be. The drug *jfuri* was extracted from it," Bivar said.

Bivar pointed the symbols again. "The plants seem to be growing along the sides of ponds or *cenotes*. You know there's a huge underground river system connecting these sunken wells throughout the Yucatan because of the limestone formations. Many of these *cenotes* and the connecting underground rivers are unexplored or covered by heavy vegetation."

Bivar pointed to some other symbols. "We've been told the ball game was a bloody contest, often played with prisoners of war, and that it ended in a blood sacrifice to please the gods."

"What kind of sacrifice?" Sabrina asked.

Bivar made a cutting motion across his throat with his hand. "Decapitation. Their bodies were thrown into the *cenotes,* the sacred wells."

"So tell me what it's like to play the ball game?" Blake asked.

Bivar smiled. "Imagine putting heavy leather and wooden pads on your waist, elbows and shins. Your job is to hit and bounce a large leather or rubber ball down the court and through the stone ring high on the wall. Of course, the opposing players try to stop you."

"A bit like English rugby," Blake said.

"Except that in the ball game you can't use your hands or feet," Bivar said, "but more importantly, the ball game was a spiritual and religious ceremony, a metaphor for life death. The ball game represented to the Mayans a crack in the carapace of the Great Cosmic Turtle."

"The what in the what?" Blake asked.

"Put simply, the ball court gave the ball players access to what they called the Otherworld. The Egyptians call it the Underworld, we call it the Afterlife," Bivar said.

"And the drug, *jfuri*?" Mendoza asked.

"It put the ball players into a hallucinogenic state to help them gain spiritual access to the Otherworld," Bivar replied.

Mendoza pursed his lips. "Now I understand. Although the ball game and the sacrifices were physical, the purpose of the whole thing was spiritual."

Sabrina hugged Bivar. "You did it. Blake and Mendoza can now locate the plants."

Bivar held her hands. "There's more!"

"What, Rodrigo?" Sabrina asked.

Bivar pointed to the symbols at the center of the wall. "There's a far greater treasure here. The symbols say that *Kukulcan's* crypt lies beyond this wall." Bivar pointed to the symbols. "Look. A sarcophagus with *Kukulcan's* characteristic markings, the feathered serpent."

His hands shaking, Bivar ran his hands over the adjacent symbols. "It says, 'Beyond this wall lies the mighty *Kukulcan*, the Father of all Rulers."

Bivar brushed away the dust from more symbols. "Do you notice that the figure of *Kukulcan* is not like the Mayan people we know?"

Blake looked at Mendoza's smooth round facial features, his hawk-like nose and hooded eyes. Then he looked at the pictograph of a tall *Kukulcan* with his large circular eyes, straight nose and a beard.

"The only two histories of the Mayan people that the Catholic Church didn't destroy describe *Kukulcan,* or his Aztec counterpart, *Quetzacoatl,* as tall, fair-skinned men with big eyes and long beards."

"What happened to *Kukulcan?*" Mendoza asked.

"The Mayan stories say that he vanished as suddenly as he appeared, back to the ocean. Here the pictographs show Kukulcan arrived in the Gulf of Mexico, just after the Great Flood."

"Arrived to do what?" Mendoza asked.

"It says here that *Kukulcan* and his companions were the Lords of Light and Learning, the Gods of Peace and Order. They were the givers of law, the architects of the Mayan cities, the makers of their calendars and systems of astronomy," Bivar said, excitedly, "then, mysteriously one day, *Kukulcan* and his companions went back to the ocean, vowing to return one day. And listen to this; it says that *Kukulcan* came from an ancient civilization that flourished thousands of years before the Mayans in the Atlantic Ocean."

"It sounds like you stumbled onto an enormous discovery, Professor," Blake said.

Bivar jumped up and danced around, his flashlight carving arcs on the stone ceiling. And then he spun Sabrina and Mendoza around in jubilation.

Sabrina embraced Bivar. "It looks like you'll be back to find out what's on the other side of that wall, and I'd like to provide financial backing for your return expedition." She looked at Blake.

"We both will," Blake said.

Bivar embraced Sabrina. "I don't know how to thank you. Could you stay and help me?"

Sabrina patted Bivar on the back. "At this point I'm thinking only of providing financial support."

Bivar looked at her sheepishly. "Yes, of course . . . I'm grateful to you, and of course to you too, Blake."

Blake nodded, restraining his impulse to laugh.

Mendoza folded all the charcoal rubbings into Bivar's pack. "Now we know where the *jfuri* comes from I can arrange for surveillance throughout the area one we've located the plants."

"How would you prevent others from finding out?" Sabrina asked.

"There are several options. We could destroy the symbols on that wall or defoliate all the plants," Blake said.

Bivar looked shocked. "You're not suggesting defacing the wall. I'm in the business of preserving history, Blake, not destroying it."

"It seems to me the issue is not the existence of *jfuri* or where to find it, but preventing people like Ramirez and Fung from making a criminal enterprise out of it," Xtimal said.

Blake nodded. "You're right, as always. I guess it's like thinking we can stop illegal drugs if we destroy all the cocoa plants."

"And the important thing is that you and Xtimal can prevent Fung and Ramirez from forming their new partnership based on the drug," Sabrina said.

Bivar slipped his pack onto his shoulders. "I'm anxious to get back and make arrangements for my return expedition."

"*Cervazas* are on us, Professor. You're going to be famous," Mendoza said jovially.

They packed up the remaining gear and retraced their footsteps down the passage to the entrance.

Blake saw the light shining through the opening ahead. "I can taste that cold beer."

The others squeezed through the opening first. Blake was blinded momentarily by the brightness of the rising run as he went through the opening.

" *Mio Dios*!" Bivar called out.

Three silhouetted figures, their backs to the sun, stood before Blake. Like a camera slowly adjusting its lens, his eyes focused on Simon Fung, Raoul Ramirez and an old skinny man. Fung and Ramirez had guns in their hands pointed at Blake and his companions.

"*Buenos días*," Fung said with a smile. Sweat stains spread across his neatly pressed khaki shirt like large patches of blood.

"Drop your packs!" Ramirez barked. His Glock was aimed at Blake's heart.

Blake reached back to feel for the gun in his waistband and then he remembered that he and Mendoza had put their guns in their packs while they worked on the hieroglyphics inside the temple.

"I said, drop your packs," Ramirez snapped.

Blake, Bivar, Sabrina and Mendoza removed their packs and dropped them on the stone floor. Blake opened the pocket in his pack which contained his gun as he placed it on the ground.

"Our paths keep crossing, Mr. Morgan, but I think for the last time," Fung said.

"Who are these people?" Ramirez asked, spitting a piece of his cigar on the ground.

Fung pointed at Blake. "Blake Morgan, DEA agent." He waved his gun at Sabrina. "And the beautiful Sabrina Chan, Morgan's sister-in-law." He looked at Bivar and Mendoza. "Who are you?"

"Dr. Rodrigo Bivar, Professor of Anthropology at the *Muséo Naçional de Antropología* in Mexico City," Bivar said. He looked over at the skinny old man beside Ramirez. "Gonzales, what are you doing with these men?"

"Shut up," Ramirez said, "we'll ask the questions here." He pointed his gun at Mendoza. "Who are you?"

"Xtimal Mendoza, Ministry of Public Safety," Mendoza said, "and you're Raoul Ramirez."

Ramirez stepped over to Mendoza and hit him across the face with the barrel of his gun. "Pig! You killed my men."

Mendoza staggered back, blood oozing from his cheek.

"Enough of this, let's get on with it," Fung said.

Ramirez motioned toward the opening in the wall. "What did you find inside?" he asked, looking at Bivar.

"A new discovery, Gonzales," Bivar said, ignoring Ramirez, "*Kukulcan's* tomb."

Gonzales mouth dropped open. "His tomb?"

"What else did you find?" Fung asked.

Bivar looked at Blake and Mendoza.

"Gonzales, go look for yourself," Ramirez ordered.

Gonzales walked over to Bivar's pack and took out the charcoal rubbings and Bivar's notes and looked over them. "Yes, yes. The tomb, and yes, here the description of the *jfuri* and where to find the plant, *Yage*. It's all here."

"Bring it over here," Ramirez ordered.

Gonzales put the material back into Bivar's pack and carried it over to Ramirez.

"Now we don't have to crawl around in that filthy place," Fung said.

Ramirez pushed the box of C4 explosives forward with his foot. "Let's finish it."

"What are you going to do?" Sabrina asked nervously.

"You said that there's a dead man in the tomb in there. You're all going to join him," Fung said.

Ramirez stuck his gun in his waistband and used two hands to pry open the box.

"No, you can't destroy the temple, inside is the greatest discovery ever," Bivar yelled, his face flushed.

"*Senõr* Ramirez, is there some way that we could take what you need and leave the ruins intact?" Gonzales asked.

"You're paid to decipher symbols, Professor, nothing more," Mendoza said.

"Morgan, you and Mendoza pick up the box and go back inside. Bivar and the lady, follow them. We'll be right behind you," Fung ordered.

"You'll never get away with killing all of us," Mendoza said.

"Why not? You entered an old fragile ruin with explosives. Accidents happen. Besides, do you see any witnesses here?" Ramirez said.

"Now move it," Fung snapped.

"Listen, you can get what you want without killing us," Blake said. His mind was racing to buy time.

"Again, you underestimate me, just like Wang Chan and your brother," Fung replied.

"You killed Wang Chan?" Blake asked.

"He betrayed me and like your brother who tried to steal from me, people who betray me, pay the price," Fung replied.

"And Daniel Lau?" Blake asked.

"His story was the truth. But I couldn't have you taking him to the police and making a connection with me. I misjudged you, Morgan. I thought you'd take out your revenge and kill Lau yourself. You obviously didn't have the balls," Fung replied.

"I should have killed you when I had the chance," Blake said through clenched teeth.

"That's the difference between us. Mercy is a weakness," Fung said, smiling.

"If you've finished this nice chat, I'd like to get on with this," Ramirez snapped.

"No! You can't!" Bivar yelled, running at Fung and Ramirez.

It was the moment that Blake was waiting for. Simultaneously, he and Mendoza launched themselves into action, retrieving their guns from their packs and rolling on the ground to get a clear shot of Ramirez and Fung.

Bivar had taken two steps when Fung began firing his gun at him, hitting his chest and stomach. Bivar yelled out in shock, spinning around like a rag doll to the stone floor. Fung fired his gun at Mendoza. One of the bullets struck him in the shoulder, knocking the gun out of his hand. Fung then turned his gun on Blake.

"Lookout, Blake!" Sabrina yelled, stepping between Fung and Blake as Fung fired again. Two of Fung's bullets hit Sabrina in the stomach. Her cheeks puffed outwards. She screamed out in pain as she was slammed against the wall by the force of the bullets. One of Fung's bullets creased the side of Blake's head. Blood poured out of the cut onto his face. Blake fired at Fung, hitting him in the neck and head, jerking him backwards.

Ramirez had withdrawn his gun from his waistband and started firing at Mendoza and Blake, but missed. Continuing to roll on the ground, Blake fired another burst of three bullets, hitting Ramirez squarely in the chest. Ramirez dropped to his knees, his mouth open, firing wildly. One of the bullets struck Gonzales in the temple, exiting with a clump of blood and brain matter from the other side of his head. Gonzales collapsed in heap.

The firing stopped and except for Sabrina's moaning, a sudden silence descended.

Blake scrambled on his knees over to Fung and Ramirez, taking their guns from them and checking their vital signs. They were both dead. He glanced over to Mendoza.

"I'm okay," Mendoza said, his hand holding his bloody shoulder. "I'll check on Bivar."

Blake went over to Sabrina, who was slumped against the wall, a smear of blood growing into a pool on the stones beneath her. He propped her up in his arms and looked at her stomach wound. He took her hand, put his hand over it and pressed hard on the stomach wound. The blood from Blake's head wound dripped onto Sabrina's chest and mingled with her blood.

Sabrina lay there, her auburn hair, sprayed down over Blake's thighs and onto the stones, the color slowly ebbing from her face.

"I'll get help," Blake said softly, "you'll be alright."

Sabrina reached up with a bloody hand and softly stroked his Blake's cheek. "So cold." Her eyelids fluttered.

Blake shook her. "Stay awake."

She opened her eyelids wide. "Please don't leave me," she pleaded in a childlike voice.

Blake held her tightly. "I won't. I'm here."

"I've made mistakes," she groaned.

"No more than me," Blake said.

"I must tell you . . . I love you . . . we should have been together all along," she said.

Blake kissed her forehead.

"I'm sorry that . . . I chose money over . . . love . . ."

"I know," Blake said.

"Tell me . . ." She cried out in pain. "Tell me . . . that you love me . . . that we could have been . . ." she whispered.

Blake looked at the life ebbing from her eyes. "I love you Sabrina. I know in my heart we could have been happy together."

"Kiss . . . me . . ." she moaned.

Blake bent down and kissed Sabrina on her lips and she kissed him back with passion and then her lips relaxed and her body sank back into his arms. Blake rocked her back and forth gently in his arms for several long moments, tears forming in his eyes. "Maybe now, you'll find peace."

He gently lay Sabrina down on the stones, took off his shirt and covered her head. After a few long moments, he looked over at Mendoza who was examining Bivar. Blake wiped the tears from his cheeks and crawled over to Mendoza. "Are you alright?"

"Just a flesh wound. The bullet went right through. Bivar's dead, though. Sabrina?"

Blake looked down.

"I'm so sorry, my friend," Mendoza said.

Blake embraced him for several long moments. "All my family is gone now."

Mendoza held him, patting Blake on the back.

The sound of a voice calling out below broke the silence of the next minute.

"Professor, Mr. Mendoza, I heard shots," Juan Lopez, the head of security called out as he mounted the steps. *"!Santa Maria*! What happened?" he exclaimed when he saw the carnage on the temple floor.

"No time to tell you now, call for help, Juan, quickly," Mendoza said.

"*Sí, Senõr* Mendoza, right away,' Lopez replied. He ran back to the security hut.

Blake's eyes went out of focus and he fell unconscious.

29

Blake took a deep cleansing breath of hospital ammonia laced with the smell of bougainvillea, which hung from the wall trellis outside the window and opened his eyes. White gossamer curtains beside the open terrace doors billowed like a ship's sails. His head ached like a truck had run over it. He touched the bandage on his head and then looked at the blood on his fingers with a sense of satisfaction of a warrior in battle. Yet the real pain he felt was in his heart. He could still see Sabrina's lifeless body lying there on the stones at the Temple of the Jaguars.

Blake pushed himself to the edge of the bed. A middle-aged nurse with a warm smile entered his room, and rushed over to hold Blake's arm. "Easy does it, you might still be a bit woozy. Let me help you into the wheelchair."

Blake used her steady arm to lower himself into the wheelchair. "Where's Mendoza?"

"He's in the next room. He'll be fine."

Blake nodded and wheeled his chair out of the room into Mendoza's room.

Mendoza was lying on his bed, with his eyes closed.

Blake rolled the wheelchair close to the bed and watched Mendoza for a few minutes. Mendoza opened his eyes, sensing someone's presence.

"*Amigo*, you look good in that wheelchair. Suits your age," Mendoza said.

"Hey, who's still whimping out in bed?" Blake retorted.

They both laughed raucously.

"How's the shoulder?" Blake asked.

"It'll be good as new in a few weeks." Mendoza got off the bed and sat a chair beside Blake. "How's the head?"

Blake touched the bandage on his head. "I was lucky, the bullet just grazed me. Got a hell of a headache, though."

Several moments of silence fell between them.

"Still thinking about Sabrina?" Mendoza asked.

Blake swallowed hard. "She took bullets meant for me."

"She really loved you."

"She finally figured out what's important in life and then she's not given a chance to live with her choice."

"What are you going to do now?"

"I'll take her body back to Hong Kong."

Mendoza nodded.

"In a way, I feel sorry for Professor Bivar. He never got a chance to be with Sabrina nor to revel in his great discovery," Blake said.

"Only you and I know that."

"How's that?"

"I had Juan Lopez seal up the entrance to the Temple again. No one but us knows what we found."

"What about Bivar's great archeological discovery?"

"It's been there for centuries. It won't hurt to leave it there a while longer until we figure out what to do with it."

Blake nodded. "At least we stopped the Fung-Ramirez conspiracy."

"I've still got a lot of mop up to do with the Ramirez cartel and as you know, when one bad guy goes down another seems to easily take his place."

"It's crazy isn't it, this war on drugs?"

"We both know it's a war we can't win regardless of how many guys like Ramirez and Fung we bring down. Until our governments are prepared to clean up the corruption within and go after the banks that launder the money and take sanctions against the drug producing countries, we're fighting a losing battle."

"Then what's the point in our job?"

"There's still a right and wrong. And for now society has decided selling certain drugs is wrong. Maybe that'll change in the future, but that's not for you or me to decide."

"Yah, I know, our job is to stop the criminals. It's just getting harder and harder to recognize the criminals from the good guys."

"You've got your big inheritance. Why don't you retire?"

"There's still some unfinished business back home. You remember that Angela and I are trying to put together a case against someone in The Company who's either involved in drug trafficking or interfering with DEA investigations."

"Any progress?"

"Other than my testimony about The Company's interference in two cases in Costa Rica and Seattle, no. The other money laundering witnesses and files have gone missing."

"Sounds like someone was cleaning house."

"Yah, and I think that someone is in The Company."

"Who?"

"The only other people who knew about our case were Jack Cross, Deputy Director of Covert Operations and Senator Bryce Connor, head of the Senate Intelligence Committee. My bet is on Cross."

"Why would he purposefully obstruct DEA investigations or worse, work with drug traffickers?"

"Certainly not for the money. I'm told he's filthy rich. I just have a hunch Cross is dirty despite Angela's defense of him."

Mendoza reached over and picked up a business card from the bedside table. "Well, this may be of some help. My men found several telephone numbers in Fung's wallet. They put a trace on them and found was Wang Chan's private number and another was a surprise."

"Who?"

"The private line number for Jack Cross."

Blake slapped his thigh. "I knew my gut hadn't betrayed me."

"A telephone number doesn't mean he was in with Fung."

"Why else would he have his number?"

"Maybe you can figure out a way to flush him out, incriminate himself."

"Hmm, good thought . . . listen, I've got to call Angela. I'll be back in a few minutes."

Blake wheeled his chair out the room down the hallway to the nurse's station. "*Téléfono?*"

The nurse looked up from looking at a chart and pointed to a booth in the corner.

"*Graçias,*" Blake said. He wheeled himself to the telephone and dialed Angela's number.

"Angela, it's Blake."

"Oh, Blake. I've been so worried about not hearing from you since you left Merida," Angela replied at the other end of the telephone.

"I don't know where to begin. We found what we were looking for regarding the drug *jfuri* and its plant origins from inside a temple at *Chich'en Itza*. We got there before Fung and Ramirez."

"Congratulations, Blake. Are they behind bars now?"

"They're dead."

"What happened?"

"When we came out of the temple, they were waiting for us. They were going to blow up the temple with us inside to destroy all the evidence."

"Oh my God!"

"Professor Bivar distracted them long enough for Xtimal and me to get our guns."

"And?"

"Bivar, Fung, Ramirez and an archeologist working for Ramirez named Gonzales were all killed."

"But you, Xtimal and Sabrina are alright?"

Blake didn't answer for a moment.

"Blake?"

"Sabrina saved my life by stepping between me and Fung . . . she's . . . dead."

"Oh no, Blake, I'm so sorry."

"She had a traumatic and unhappy life. She thought getting back with me would bring her happiness, but I told her about my feelings for you . . . maybe now she's finally found peace."

"I know what she meant to you."

"She looked so much like the child I remember when she died."

"Oh sweetheart, I wish I could be there to hold you."

"I wish that too."

"Are you and Xtimal alright?"

"I got a little cut on my head. Xtimal took a bullet in the shoulder. He's playing it for all the sympathy he can get, but he's alright . . . and there is something else you should know."

"What's that?"

"Mendoza found Jack Cross' private residential telephone number in Fung's wallet."

There was a long moment of silence.

"Blake, I don't know how to tell you this."

"What?"

"I'm ashamed to say that I might be responsible for Fung and Ramirez knowing that you'd be at *Chich'en Itza*."

"What do you mean?"

"Jack Cross came to visit me just before you left *Merída*. He gave what seemed to be a reasonable explanation for those incidents in Costa Rica and Seattle. He said that Richard Bull was a crucial source of information for insurgent activity in Central America and that Fung had a potential invaluable network of insurgents inside China. He promised to prosecute Fung's people in Seattle."

"Did he?"

"I checked it out. Two of Bull's associates and the men you arrested in Seattle are now facing charges."

"What about Bull?"

"Cross said both Fung and Bull would continue to have immunity."

"Figures."

"I'm so sorry, Blake, for betraying your trust. Jack seemed so sincere. I feel like such a fool."

"It's alright, it wasn't your fault. Fung and Ramirez had the original message and their archeologist to point them in the right direction."

"Still, at the time, I didn't know that. How can I make it up to you?"

"Hmm . . . there may be a way, something Xtimal said. I'll talk to you later about it."

"What are you going to do now?"

"I'll take Sabrina's body back to Hong Kong first."

"I want to be there."

"I'd like that too. Meet me at the Chan home."

"Alright, Blake. I can't wait to hold you in my arms."

"That's the best offer that I've had for a while. I'll see you soon."

Blake hung up the telephone and wheeled himself back to Mendoza's room.

"I just talked to Angela. She said that Cross' internal investigation has cleaned house of some foreign assets, but the primary culprits, Richard Bull and Fung were still being protected."

"Sounds like Cross is your man."

"If Cross actually was involved with Fung and Ramirez, not just covering up shoddy intelligence work, then he's got to be stopped. Like you said, I've got to think of a way of having him incriminate himself."

"Make him think he's got to negotiate a new deal now that Fung and Ramirez are dead?"

"Exactly what I was thinking."

30

Blake got off the plane in Hong Kong and looked through the throng of people in the terminal for Tang, then saw the old Chan family servant waving at him in the crowd. He walked over to Tang and embraced him.

"It's good to see you again, sir," Tang said. He bowed deeply. "I'm so sorry about Mrs. Chan."

Blake saw the look of pain and sadness in Tang's usually expressionless eyes. "I'm sorry for you, too, I know she was close to you."

"She was always very kind."

They walked in silence to the car. Blake got in and Tang drove out of the airport.

"I'll make arrangements for a burial service in a few days," Blake said. "Has Angela Townsend arrived?"

"Yes, last night," Tang replied.

"Good! Angela is a Special Prosecutor for the DEA that I'm working with on a case."

"She's very kind and beautiful. She reminds me of Mrs. Chan in some ways."

"Yes, my old friend, I can see that."

"Will she be staying long?"

"I'm not sure. I'm not even sure how long I'll be staying."

"The Chan home is yours now."

"I don't know if I'll make Hong Kong my home. But don't worry; I'll make sure you don't have to work for the rest of your life."

"It's never been the money that has kept me in the Chan home, sir."

"I just wanted you to know that I'm appreciative of your service to the Chan family."

"Thank you, sir. And I would be honored to continue to serve you as well."

"You won't have to serve anyone anymore."

"I forgot to mention, sir that Inspector Lai contacted me to inquire as to your return. He said that he wanted to speak to you."

"Did he say what it was about?"

"No sir."

"Okay, let's head to his office before we go home."

Tang nodded and turned the car onto the road to Wan Chai.

During the rest of the drive, Blake sat quietly thinking. Tang's comment about the Chan home being his, along with the entire Chan estate and Chan Enterprises, finally sunk in. Should he stay in Hong Kong and take over the business? Could he leave behind all the painful memories? Or did his future lie back in Los Angeles with Angela?

Twenty minutes later, Tang parked the car in the lot at police headquarters. Blake found Inspector Lai in his office.

Lai shook Blake's hand warmly. "Good to see you Blake."

"You wanted to see me?"

Lai walked over to the window and looked out. "I wanted to tell you that I'd been asked to do something that didn't sit well with me."

"What?"

"Someone in The Company requested that I put you and Mrs. Chan under surveillance and in essence find some personal dirt on you, using the pretense that you had given secret information to the Chinese."

"Who?"

"Jack Cross, Deputy Director of Covert Operations."

"Did you do what he asked?

Lai looked a bit sheepishly at Blake. "At first. I had orders to cooperate. But my gut told me something didn't ring true. We had Fung under surveillance. The same day Cross paid me a visit, he was seen meeting with Fung. Being naturally suspicious, I called Cross' boss, Benjamin Cranston. He knew nothing about Cross' request to put you and Sabrina under surveillance, nor the reasons for Cross' meeting with Fung."

"What did Cranston do?"

"He wouldn't say. You understand that I had no choice in investigating you and Mrs. Chan?"

Blake waved his hand. "You were following orders and sometimes orders don't make sense. I'm just glad your nose told you something didn't smell right."

"I've made a report to the Hong Kong government and they're taking the matter up with the U.S. Embassy here."

"That'll go nowhere. Did you get an incriminating evidence on Cross in connection with Fung's activities?"

"Nothing. Just their meeting . . . can you give me a snapshot of the big picture as you see it?"

"Fung killed Wang Chan because he wanted to dissolve their business arrangement of Wang Chan laundering Fung's drug money."

"So my suspicions about Wang Chan were right."

"Yes . . . Frustrated by your lack of progress in finding Wang Chan's killer, Raymond impulsively enlisted the help of the other triads. They snookered him into stealing incriminating evidence regarding Fung's drug dealing and bribes of public officials, promising to help him find Wang Chan's killer. Raymond hooked up with Fung's opposition in Guangzhou and they stole the information which is on microdots. The other men were killed and Raymond escaped, convinced he's being pursued by the Chinese police. He crossed the border illegally and just as he got to his uncle's warehouse, he was shot and killed by Daniel Lau who had been pursuing Raymond. But Raymond managed to get the microdots to his uncle before he died and his uncle passed the microdots onto Sabrina."

Lai's eyes opened wider.

"We deciphered the microdots which contain detailed information about Fung's activities and a message from the Ramirez drug cartel in Mexico, proposing a partnership and a series of Mayan symbols which describe an ancient drug called *jfuri*. Fung and Ramirez were going set up a new syndicate to market this drug."

"I need that information to go after Fung's organization, Blake."

"All in good time, Peter, all in good time."

"Good! Go on."

"I met with Fung, proposing a trade: the microdots for Raymond's killer. We met on Lantau Island, and he produced Daniel Lau, who confessed that he had followed Raymond and killed him in revenge for his father's death years before, which he claimed Wang Chan was party to."

"The same Daniel Lau that we recovered in Aberdeen Harbor?"

"Yes. But Lau didn't tell the whole truth. Fung put him up to it promising to arrange for the release of his brother in a Chinese prison. Fung was betting that I would kill Lau out of revenge. When he saw I was going to turn Lau into the police, he killed him."

"You made the anonymous tip about Lau's body?"

"I didn't have time to explain. I had decided to follow the trail of these Mayan symbols to prevent Fung and Ramirez from developing this drug *jfuri*. With the help of an old friend in the Mexican DEA, Xtimal Mendoza, we went to Mexico and found the details of the drug and the plant it comes from in an ancient Mayan ruin called *Chich'en Itza*."

"So Mendoza was already chasing Ramirez?"

"Yes. When we came out of the ruins, Fung and Ramirez were waiting for us. They decided to blow up the temple with us in it to get rid of the evidence. Professor Bivar made a run at them, distracting them long enough for Mendoza and me to get our guns. In the battle that ensued, Bivar, Fung, Ramirez and Sabrina were killed."

Lai pointed to the bandage on Blake's head. "That's where you got that?"

"I should be dead, but Sabrina stepped in front of two bullets from Fung meant for me."

"I'm so sorry, Blake. She must have loved you to sacrifice her life like that."

A hard lump formed in Blake's throat. "We were family."

A few moments of silence followed.

"So what about this drug *jfuri*?" Lai asked.

"Mendoza is now going after the rest of Ramirez' cartel. It might be a good idea to contact him."

Lai whistled a long appreciative whistle. "So that ties up all the loose ends."

"Except for someone in The Company."

"What do you mean?"

"Although the evidence is circumstantial, Mendoza, Angela Townsend, a DEA Special Prosecutor and I believe that Jack Cross is Fung's silent partner and has interfered with DEA operations."

Lai eyes opened wide.

"To make any charges stick against Cross, we've got to incriminate him."

"How?"

"Will you help?"

"Nothing would give me greater pleasure than to see his arrogant face behind bars if he's guilty of working with Fung and Ramirez."

"Good! I haven't worked out yet what I'll do, but I'll take your offer to help and contact you soon."

Lai stood up and shook Blake's hand. "I'm glad I can help . . . and Blake?"

"Yes?"

"I'm sorry for having doubted you."

Blake smiled. "Forget it. You were under a lot of stress."

They shook hands again and Blake left Lai's office feeling better about his motives and grateful for his offer to help.

Twenty-five minutes later, Blake arrived at the Chan home. It felt like coming home in a strange way, Blake thought.

His throat tightened. Except that Raymond and Sabrina would not be there.

The front door of the house opened and Angela Townsend stood there, dressed in a royal blue dress that highlighted her bright blue eyes. As soon as she saw Blake, she flew into his arms, embraced him and kissed him passionately on the mouth. Blake returned her kiss with equal fervor. They stood there wrapped in each others' arms for several long minutes.

Angela touched the bandage on Blake's head. "You're hurt." She gently kissed his head.

"I'll be alright. Thick head." He stepped back and looked appreciatively at her. "I've missed you, Angela."

She pinched his arm. "Good. You should have."

They walked, arm in arm into the house together.

Tang cleared his throat. "Shall I take your bags up to Mrs. Townsend's bedroom?"

Blake looked at Angela. "No, the guest bedroom will be alright."

Angela shook her head. "Take them to my bedroom, Ho."

Blake laughed. "Go ahead."

Tang took the bags and walked upstairs.

Angela took Blake's face between her hands and looked deeply into his eyes. "I am so sorry about Sabrina."

"She . . . was like a sister and more." He looked away trying to keep his composure.

"It's alright. You're safe with me."

Blake suddenly embraced Angela and a sob deep within his soul erupted from his chest. Tears flowed down his cheeks and his body was gripped in spasms. He held Angela tighter and tighter.

"They're all gone now," Blake said.

Angela stroked his hair and whispered into his ear. "You'll never be alone again."

She took his hand and led him up the stairs into the bedroom.

Blake awoke the next morning to the sound of silverware clunking. He looked up to see Angela carrying in a bed service table. "Room service, sir."

She was wearing a fuscia-colored robe and her hair was piled up on her head with a few strands casually hanging down.

Blake stared at her, believing he had never seen such a beautiful woman and knowing that he was totally in love with her. He sat up and shifted in bed to make room for her. He looked at the food on the tray. "My favorite, poached eggs, dry toast and coffee."

Angela smiled. "I know you better that you think."

Blake touched her cheek gently with the back of his hand. "Better than anyone ever has."

She cut off the top of one of the eggs, dipped the corner of one piece of toast, put it in Blake's mouth and laughed. "Let's feed each other, Blake."

"Fight! Fight!" he said jokingly. He took a spoonful of egg and delicately placed it in her mouth.

She bit a piece of egg and grasped the spoon with her lips, running her tongue over it while she watched Blake's eyes.

He pushed the food tray away, grabbed her and kissed her passionately, parting her robe and finding her breasts with his mouth. She moaned, threw off the bed sheet from him and sat astride his hips. They moved together slowly and tenderly until they both screamed each other's names over and over.

After, Angela lay back in Blake's arms. "I love you, Blake. I can't imagine going through life without you."

Blake caressed the smooth skin of her shoulder. "That's something that you won't have to worry about . . . I'm in love with you Angela."

"You are? I mean you love me?"

She kissed him several times on his mouth and cheeks.

They laughed together and then got up, showered and went down to the terrace. Tang had a flesh pot of coffee and sticky buns waiting. They sat together overlooking the South

China Sea, a light breeze blowing in the faint scent of bauhanias from the garden.

"We need to talk about Jack Cross," Blake said.

"I still feel like a fool. I looked up to him," Angela said.

"Here's another piece of the picture for you. I met with Inspector Lai before I got here. He told me that Cross had coerced him into putting Sabrina and I under surveillance. Lai also told me that while his men had Fung under surveillance, they saw him meeting with Cross."

Angela's eyes looked sad. "What do you think happened?"

"It's obvious now. Cross was involved with Fung and Ramirez in drug operations either as a partner, laundering money or providing protection and taking a cut. He was behind the interference in DEA operations in Costa Rica and Seattle. And I think he followed Quinn and had he and Pantages killed, and took all the evidence."

Angela paced back and forth on the terrace. "What I can't understand is the reason. It can't be for the money."

"Maybe, like Quinn said, Cross is part of a bigger problem with our intelligence agencies believing that it's okay to deal with criminals to protect our country's interests."

"I think you're right."

"We need to find out if Cross is really dirty. Smoke him out, let him incriminate himself."

Angela let out a big sigh. "How?"

"If Cross was involved with Fung, he's going to know that Fung and Ramirez are dead and will want to renegotiate with their successors. So we invite him to a meeting to work out a new arrangement."

"How will we do that?"

"Inspector Lai says he'll help. He'll call Cross to give a report about the surveillance that Lai had us under; telling Cross that he found out that Sabrina was a silent partner with Wang Chan and Fung. Then Sabrina will call Cross and invite him to renegotiate. If Cross is guilty, he'll come."

"But Sabrina is dead."

Blake looked intently at Angela. "That's where you can help. You're going to be Sabrina."

"Oh no, Blake, I can't . . ."

"Look, Cross has never heard Sabrina's voice. He thinks you're in Los Angeles. Just disguise your voice a little."

"I don't know . . ."

Blake put his arms around Angela. "You want to find out if Cross is really guilty, don't you?"

"Yes, but . . ."

"We've got nothing to lose. If Cross is innocent, he won't come."

Angela sighed. "Alright, I'll do it. I owe it to you."

"Good! I'll call Inspector Lai."

Blake walked over to the telephone, and dialed Lai's number.

"Hello, Peter, it's Blake. I'm going to take you up on your offer to help."

"What do you have in mind?" Lai said at the other end of the telephone.

"If Cross was doing business with Fung, he'd want to make sure his arrangement would continue with Fung's successor. I want you to contact Cross and tell him that you found out that Sabrina was Fung's silent partner and had worked with Wang Chan all along."

"'But Sabrina is dead."

"He won't know that. Mendoza kept that information secret. So we have to move fast. Angela Townsend, the Special Prosecutor for the DEA has been working on the case with me back in the States and is here with me. She'll call Cross and pretend she's Sabrina after you've called him. She'll invite him to Hong Kong to renegotiate his business arrangement."

"Do you think he'd be fooled that easily?"

"If he was in business with Fung, he'll want to protect his arrangement as soon as possible. Besides, we don't have many options at this point. And what you say about Sabrina is not going to harm her. In fact, I think she'd feel good about being able to help in this way."

"I've always liked a good bluff."

"Make sure you rehearse, Peter. This is your chance to show your acting skills."

"It'll be the performance of a lifetime."

"Good. Call me when you're done."

Blake hung up the telephone and looked at Angela. "You heard?"

"Yes. I just hope he's convincing."

Blake walked over and stroked her hair. "I know you both will be."

31

A medium-height man in a dark blue suit with slicked-back hair and a moustache knocked on the door of Benjamin Cranston, Director of Covert Operations for the Central Intelligence Agency.

"Come in, Biggs," Cranston called out.

Biggs walked in and sat in the chair in front of Cranston's desk. A deep furrow ran across Cranston's forehead.

"What have you found out?" Cranston asked.

Biggs opened the file that he was carrying. "Mr. Cross had telephone conversations several times with Simon Fung, the head of a Hong Kong triad called the Hung Se Ying."

"Any record of Jack meeting with Fung?"

"No sir."

"Anything else?"

"Yes sir. Mr. Cross intervened in DEA investigations in Costa Rica and Seattle. He declared drug traffickers as Company assets and gave them immunity from prosecution."

"Do you know why?"

"He told the DEA in Costa Rica that the drug trafficker in question, an American named Richard Bull, was a crucial source of information regarding terrorist and insurgent activities in Central America."

"Is that true?"

Biggs leafed through the file. "Yes sir."

Cranston rubbed the furrow in his forehead with his fingers. "And Seattle?"

"The DEA busted a heroin and illegal alien smuggling operation run by Simon Fung. Mr. Cross told the DEA that Fung and his men were valuable sources of information regarding China's political activities and were resources we could turn to if we initiated any covert activities."

"Is that correct?"

"Fung and his key men were former Red Army elite forces that have extensive networks in China."

"Is that all?"

"No sir. We've been able to determine that Mr. Cross has an offshore bank account and has made large deposits in recent months."

"How large."

"Millions of dollars, but . . ."

"Yes?"

"As far as we can tell, all the money is being used to fund covert operations."

"Is the bank listed as one of our proprietary companies?"

"No sir."

"Were you able to determine where the money came from?"

"No sir. The bank has been only partially cooperative."

"That's it?"

"Yes sir."

"Alright. Thanks for your report."

"Is there anything else you want me to do?"

"Not right now. And the information you've uncovered and our conversation is to remain only between us. Is that understood?"

Biggs nodded. "Yes sir." He got up, left the file on Cranston's desk and left the room.

Cranston smashed his fist on his desk. "Damn! What the hell are you doing, Jack?" He leaned forward and picked up the telephone. "Get Jack Cross in here."

Fifteen minutes later, Cross walked into Cranston's office.

"Sit down, Jack," Cranston said.

Cross sat down in the chair across from Cranston. "You look worried, Ben. What is it?"

"How's your internal investigation going regarding the DEA's allegations?"

"Nothing has checked out so far. You know the DEA has always been a bit paranoid."

Cranston clenched his jaw muscles. "Did you declare drug traffickers in Seattle and Costa Rica Company assets and give them immunity?"

Cross narrowed his eyes. "What is this, Ben? You've never questioned day-to-day operations before."

"Just answer my question!"

Cross smoothed the crease on his pant leg slowly. "The man in Costa Rica, Richard Bull, has been providing the best intelligence we've got regarding terrorist and insurgent groups in Guatemala and El Salvador. His information has allowed us to thwart several attempts to overthrow the friendly governments there."

"But according to the DEA, he's a drug trafficker."

"Ben, you know the best sources of inside information won't come from nuns and schoolteachers. This guy is well connected. Besides, he promised to discontinue his drug activities if we pay him more money."

Cranston twisted his pen even harder. "And Seattle?"

"The Hung Se Ying was established by former Red Army soldiers like its leader, Simon Fung. They still have an incredible network inside China, but they're no longer loyal to the government. To expose Fung and his organization would jeopardize valuable sources of information that could affect our national security."

Cranston threw his pen on the desk. "Have you taken any money from these traffickers?"

Cross stared at Cranston.

"How do you explain your mysterious offshore bank account that you're using to fund covert activities?"

Cross stood up, stretching his six-foot-four frame and looking down on Cranston. "Ben, if you're accusing me of something, come out with it. This innuendo is pissing me off."

Cranston held up his hand. "I'm trying to protect the integrity of The Company."

"I was doing that long before you arrived. Do you remember we sat in my den discussing the need for more money to finance covert operations? You told me to come up with some creative options."

"Jack, this is beyond . . ."

"Don't be so naïve," Cross interrupted, "The Company has always had relationships with borderline characters where the difference between a government friendly to our country and a Communist-leaning government can be determined by a few well-placed people. Sometimes these people are also criminals."

Cranston stared at Cross in shock.

"So, in return for some immunity and protection, we get an absolutely essential source of information and, if necessary, people prepared to take action in our best interests. Taking a cut of their enormous profits seemed to be a logical extension of a business arrangement already in place."

Cranston's face flushed. "Do you think I'm going to allow you to . . ."

Cross leaned across the desk, his jaw muscles rippling. "If you expose me, Ben, I'll take you down with me. I'll tell everyone it was your idea. I have our conversation in my study on tape."

Cranston's mouth opened agape.

"Not only could I withstand the financial costs of a legal defense better than you, I think a good many people in government and the public in general would see that The Company needs to do whatever it takes to protect our country. And turning a blind eye to a few drug traffickers is a small price to pay."

Cranston closed his mouth.

Cross pointed his finger at Cranston. "So think about that. Can you personally afford the scandal? Do you want The Company under attack, which would only further weaken our country's defense?"

Cross turned on his heel and walked out, slamming the door. Cranston slumped into his chair, his chin sagging to his chest.

32

Inspector Peter Lai of the Hong Kong Police picked up the telephone dialed and waited. "Mr. Cross, this is Inspector Peter Lai. You told me to inform you of any significant activities by Blake Morgan and Sabrina Chan."

"So what have you got to report?" Cross said at the other end of the telephone.

"Apparently, Blake Morgan and Sabrina Chan found out about a criminal conspiracy to market a new drug between Simon Fung, the head of a Hong Kong triad and a Mexican drug cartel run by a man named Ramirez. They were able to thwart their plans, but Fung, Ramirez and Blake Morgan were killed in a shootout in Mexico." "

"Really? That's very interesting, Inspector . . . Is there anything else?"

"Yes, before he left for Mexico, we had Simon Fung, the head of the Hung Se Ying triad, under surveillance for suspicion of murder and drug trafficking. Our surveillance team saw Sabrina Chan meet several times with Fung. We decided to place a wire tap. We overheard conversations that clearly establish Sabrina Chan as a silent partner with Fung. Apparently, Wang Chan had been laundering Fung's money for years and Fung killed him when Wang Chan wanted out. Sabrina Chan was the old man's right hand man, so to speak. Now, she's in a powerful position, having inherited Chan Enterprises and become the heir apparent to Fung."

"You're saying that this woman was partner with Fung?"

"That's what it looks like. We're trying to produce more hard evidence to lay charges against her."

"Is there anything else?"

"No."

"Thank you for the progress report, Inspector. Good work."

"Very good, Mr. Cross, goodbye."

Lai hung up the telephone and double-pumped his fist in the air.

Blake sat on the sofa next to the telephone in the Chan home study. "You ready?"

Angela Townsend at a desk a few feet away, her hand on another telephone. "What if Jack recognizes my voice?"

Blake shook his head. "I couldn't during your practice runs. Besides, he wouldn't be expecting to hear your voice."

Angela wrung her hands together. "I've never been so nervous. Trying criminals in court is easy compared to this."

Blake winked. "You'll be fine."

"Well, here goes." Angela picked up the telephone and dialed.

Blake picked up the extension telephone at the same time.

"Is this Jack Cross?" Angela said a few moments later.

"Who is this?" Cross answered at the other end of the telephone.

"Sabrina Chan."

"How the hell did you get this number?"

"That doesn't matter. You'll want to hear what I have to say, and I know this is a secure line."

"I don't know a Sabrina Chan and I'm not interested in what you have to say."

"Then why did you have the Hong Kong Police investigate me?"

Several moments of silence passed.

"I'm listening," Cross said.

"Fung, Ramirez and Blake Morgan are dead."

"Is this an obituary report?"

"The alternative to you paying attention to what I've got to say is me taking all the evidence I have about your business arrangement with Fung to the American media."

"Go on."

"I'm now a major player in Fung's organization and I plan to market the new drug that Fung and Ramirez found in Mexico."

Cross didn't reply.

"Whatever arrangement that you had with Fung now has to be renegotiated with me," Angela said.

"I don't know what you're talking about."

Angela stood up and started to pace back and forth in front of the desk. Blake motioned her to calm down.

"That's fine. I gave you a chance. I hope you read the morning newspapers," Angela said.

"Wait! What do you propose?"

"Don't make the mistake of not taking me seriously again. Meet me and we'll discuss this personally."

"Where and when?"

"Chan Enterprises' warehouses at the North Point pier in Hong Kong. Ten p.m., the day after tomorrow."

"Alright."

"And one other thing."

"What?"

"Come alone."

"I'll think about it."

"If you're not here alone, I go to the media."

Blake made a cutting motion across his throat. Angela hung up the telephone.

He walked over to her, embraced her, spinning her around. "An Academy Award performance."

Angela was shaking. "I don't know, Blake, he was very suspicious."

"That's his nature. You told him enough of the truth for him to show up. Now let's get ready to meet Cross."

Jack Cross turned the car onto Chai Road a mile and a half south of the North Point Ferry Terminal, parked close to the chain link fence, fifty feet from the gate. The light from the overhead pole cast a strobe-like flicker on his face.

He sat back in his seat, his black raincoat melding with the black leather upholstery. He took his Glock from his holster, opened the slide on the gun, checked the chamber, took out the magazine and checked it and then pressed the slide release. The gun clicked loudly. He pressed the trigger and the hammer fell. He loaded the magazine with hollow-point bullets, put one bullet back in the chamber and screwed on the silencer. He pushed the gun back into its holster. And then he pulled up his pant leg, removed a small caliber handgun from its holster around his ankle and repeated the same routine.

Cross got out of the car and crept among the containers and crates along the pier. He moved slowly in widening semicircles toward the Chan warehouse. A single dim light lit up the entrance door.

He opened the door to darkness. He flicked the light switch by the door up and down several times without success. He walked into the warehouse a few steps along the wall and took the Glock out of his holster.

"Sabrina Chan, are you there?"

"I'm here," Angela's muffled voice called out from behind the crates.

Blake stood beside her, wearing night vision goggles. He rubbed her arm in reassurance.

"What's with the lights?" Cross asked.

"Safer for me. You've probably got a gun," Angela replied.

Cross looked down at his gun and squinted into the darkness. "I don't like walking into dark rooms."

"I don't like guns," Angela replied. "Now, let's get down to business."

Cross moved quietly toward the sound of her voice. "Why don't we sit down and talk with the lights on."

"Don't come any closer," Angela snapped.

"You can't see . . . oh, night vision, smart," Cross said. He retreated around the corner of one of the crates.

"The previous arrangement with Fung gave you ten percent of any operation that you protected for Fung. I'm offering you a partnership. Eighty-twenty. I get the eighty, of course," Angela said.

Cross laughed loudly. "That wasn't the deal. You'll have to do better than that."

Silence followed for a few moments.

"I'm prepared to go seventy-thirty. Without my protection you'll never see an once of that drug jfuri on the market. Besides, all I have to do is make a phone call and you're in jail, or worse," Cross replied.

"You give me your word that you'll keep the DEA off my back?"

"Easy. I did it for Fung."

"Then I think you've got more than you've bargained for, Jack," Angela said, her voice normal now.

"You're under arrest for conspiracy to traffic drugs," Blake called out. "Put your gun on the floor and kick it toward the crate directly in front of you."

Cross turned from side to side, trying to pinpoint the origin of the voice. "Who the hell are you?"

"Blake Morgan. I can see you, Jack and I have my gun trained on you," Blake said.

"So you're not dead," Cross replied.

"Jack, this is Angela Townsend, not Sabrina Chan. Do as Blake says. We have our conversation on tape."

"Angela? Not you! Where's Sabrina Chan?" Cross queried.

"Dead. Now how about it, Jack?" Blake asked.

"So you are in this together. How cozy," Cross said. He looked around. "I'm surprised you don't have the police with you."

"Please, Jack, put down your gun. It's over," Angela pleaded.

Cross stepped out from behind the crate, put his gun on the floor and kicked it forward.

"Now lie down on the floor and put your hands behind your head," Blake ordered.

Cross slowly lay down on the floor.

Angela walked over to the circuit breaker and pushed a switch. The lights came on. Blake walked toward Cross, his gun pointed at him. Angela emerged holding a tape recorder and directional microphone in her hands.

Cross looked up and smiled. "You think you can make your allegations stick against the Deputy Director of The Central Intelligence Agency? Just think about your record of success so far."

A look of uncertainty passed over Angela's face.

Blake took a set of handcuffs out of his pocket. "Hands behind your back, Jack, and don't make any sudden movements."

Cross didn't move. "Look, we can work this out. You can have more money than you've ever dreamed of."

"Enough to buy back my brother's life? Or Sabrina's?" Blake asked.

"We can go after the triads and Mexican cartels together," Cross said with hint of desperation in his voice.

Cross looked at Angela. "The money is not for me. It's so The Company's covert activities can operate independently. So we can defend our country against its enemies and not have to beg politicians for money. Don't you see?"

"Put your hands behind your back!" Blake ordered.

Just at that moment, the warehouse door opened and Inspector Peter Lai walked in.

"I got your message . . ." Lai said and then froze in mid-sentence when he saw Cross.

Blake and Angela turned to see Lai. In that moment Cross quickly reached down to his ankle, pulled out the small hand gun, rolled over and fired at Blake and Sabrina, hitting Blake in the shoulder. Blake was knocked backward onto the floor. Cross rolled up to his knees. As soon as Blake hit the floor he instantly recoiled, leveled his gun at Cross and fired a burst of three bullets at Cross. One of the bullets struck Cross in the neck, passing through and a second hit him in the chest. Cross grunted as the bullets slammed him to the floor and he lay there, not moving. Lai took out his gun and scrambled over to Cross, keeping his gun pointed at him.

With his other hand, Lai took out his radio. "This is Lai. Get a couple of ambulances down to the Chan warehouse fast."

Angela looked over at Blake, who'd fallen back on the floor. "Oh no, Blake," she screamed. She ran over to him and held him in her arms.

Blake's eyes fluttered. "I'm alright," he grunted. "Cross?"

Lai was bending over him using his fingers to push pressure on the gushing blood from his neck wound. "Looks bad."

Blake and Angela scrambled over to Cross. In the distance, the sound of ambulance sirens approaching could be heard.

"Lie still, help is coming," Lai said.

"Why, Jack, why?" Angela cried.

Cross looked at her and then at Blake. "Must protect . . . our country . . . from its enemies . . . every means possible," he moaned.

"But to work with criminals!" Angela said.

"A true patriot . . . not afraid to dirty hands . . . cause is just," Cross whispered.

"The cause has never justified what you did, Jack," Blake said.

With one bloody hand, Cross grabbed Blake's wrist and held it tightly. "You bloody hypocrite!"

"Don't . . . drag The Company into the mud, Cross whispered. His voice trailed off and then his eyes glazed over.

Lai checked his pulse and shook his head.

Angela covered her face with her hands, sobbing. "Oh, Jack."

The ambulances pulled up outside the warehouse, their lights flashing, casting eerie shadows in the warehouse.

Angela looked at Cross sadly. "If only you could have known him when he served with my father. He was once a true patriot."

Lai and Angela helped Blake walk to the door and out to the waiting ambulances. "Have you got your evidence?"

Blake nodded.

"As of this moment, my report will read that you shot Cross in self-defense," Lai said.

Blake took an envelope from his pocket and handed it to Lai. "Here's the information about Fung's drug shipments and public official bribes from the microdots. I'm sure you'll know what to do with it."

Lai took the envelope. "You can bet on it."

Angela helped Blake onto the ambulance gurney. "Let's get him to the hospital."

33

Blake walked along the rows of gravestones, some over a century old, until he reached the Chan family plot. Angela handed him the bauhanias and he knelt down and placed them on two gravestones.

"Raymond would have been happy knowing you'd placed him here beside his father and his wife," Angela said, rubbing Blake's arm.

"I'm the last one left in my family now," Blake said.

He and Angela bowed their heads in silence for a minute and then Blake sighed deeply. "There's nothing left for me here any longer."

Arm in arm, they walked slowly back to the car, stopping at the gate to the cemetery.

"What do you want to do about Jack Cross?" Angela asked.

Blake gently rubbed his wounded shoulder. "I know that he was a hero and patriot. I know that The Company has protected our country from our enemies but . . ."

"But what?"

"Cross took the same oath as you and I did to serve our country with honor and for truth. If he and others like him who have so much power can violate the peoples' trust, then our oath is worth nothing."

"I'm with you, Blake. We must expose Cross' actions, go after others that may have worked with him and bring public attention to the abuses of The Company."

Blake put his good arm around Angela. "I promised Xtimal that I'd find the right time to say this."

"What's that?"

"I want to spend the rest of my life with you."

Angela looked deeply into his eyes. "You said back there that you were the last one in your family. I'd like to remedy that." She reached up and kissed him passionately.

After a few minutes of embrace, Angela looked at Blake. "So where do we go after we finish our work?"

Blake looked out into the shining South China Sea. "It doesn't matter. Wherever you are, is home."

They walked back toward the car. Blake stopped near the gate and walked over to the stone grave marker in the shape of a dragon, painted red. He put his foot on the marker and pushed hard. It toppled over and smashed into pieces. And then he took his gun out of his jacket and threw it and his DEA badge on the broken fragments.

"Now both the dragons are tamed," he said.

He took Angela's hand and they walked out of the graveyard.

THE END

Quick Order Form

Fax completed order form to: (250) 383-6814

Telephone orders: Toll-free (888) 232-4444

Or mail to: Trafford Publishing, Suite 6E, 2333 Government St., Victoria, B.C. Canada V8T 4P4

Website: www.trafford.com

Shipping & handling charges will apply.
Please select regular (surface mail) ___ or expedited (UPS 2-day) ___

Name:_____

Street Address:_____

City:_____

State/Province: _____**Country** _____

Zip Code/ Postal Code: _____

Credit card: __Visa __ Master Card __Amex

> **Card Number** _____
> **Name on Card**_____
> **Expiry Date** _____

ISBN 155395276-6